W9-ATC-636

"You haven't g— ... here, have you?"

Dori shook her head. "There was no reason. Somehow coming in here seemed disrespectful."

"It's not, you know. You can't live in this house and completely ignore Tyler and Marisa's room," Chase said, realizing that as executor of the will, it was his job to go through his brother and sister-in-law's possessions.

She gazed up at him, her eyes full of doubt. "I suppose."

Not giving her a chance to change her mind, he took her hand and led her into the closet. She didn't resist. With her slender hand in his, a powerful, protective feeling emerged toward her. If only he could make sure nothing would hurt her.

"Now, that wasn't so hard," Chase said.

"None of this is easy." She stared at him, her arms folded across her midsection.

Her stance told him she was closing him out again. For just a moment, he had broken through that barrier, but she had resurrected it in a second.

Could he ever tear down the wall of her distrust?

Books by Merrillee Whren

Love Inspired

The Heart's Homecoming #314
An Unexpected Blessing #352

MERRILLEE WHREN

is the winner of the 2003 Golden Heart Award for Best Inspirational Romance manuscript, presented by Romance Writers of America. In 2004, she made her first sale to Steeple Hill. She is married to her own personal hero, her husband of twenty-nine years, and has two grown daughters. She has lived in Atlanta, Boston, Dallas and Chicago but now makes her home on one of God's most beautiful creations, an island off the east coast of Florida. When she's not writing or working for her husband's recruiting firm, she spends her free time playing tennis or walking the beach, where she does the plotting for her novels.

Merrillee loves to hear from readers. You can contact her through her Web site at www.merrilleewhren.com.

AN
UNEXPECTED
BLESSING

MERRILLEE
WHREN

Steeple
Hill®

Published by Steeple Hill Books™

If you purchased this book without a cover you should be aware
that this book is stolen property. It was reported as "unsold and
destroyed" to the publisher, and neither the author nor the
publisher has received any payment for this "stripped book."

STEEPLE HILL BOOKS

Steeple
Hill®

ISBN 0-373-87374-3

AN UNEXPECTED BLESSING

Copyright © 2006 by Merrillee Whren

All rights reserved. Except for use in any review, the reproduction
or utilization of this work in whole or in part in any form by any
electronic, mechanical or other means, now known or hereafter
invented, including xerography, photocopying and recording, or in
any information storage or retrieval system, is forbidden without
the written permission of the editorial office, Steeple Hill Books,
233 Broadway, New York, NY 10279 U.S.A.

All characters in this book have no existence outside the imagination of
the author and have no relation whatsoever to anyone bearing the same
name or names. They are not even distantly inspired by any individual
known or unknown to the author, and all incidents are pure invention.

This edition published by arrangement with Steeple Hill Books.

® and TM are trademarks of Steeple Hill Books, used under license.
Trademarks indicated with ® are registered in the United States Patent
and Trademark Office, the Canadian Trade Marks Office and in other
countries.

www.SteepleHill.com

Printed in U.S.A.

Be merciful, just as your Father is merciful.
Do not judge, and you will not be judged.
Do not condemn, and you will not be condemned.
Forgive, and you will be forgiven.
—*Luke* 6:36–37

To my editor, Diane Dietz, who helps make
my stories better.

To my Texas nephews, Garrett and Chase,
who lent me their names for the hero of this book.

To Martin Hearne, Pam Hillman and Stephanie
Gillenberg, whose advice helped with this project.

And, as always, to my hero of heroes—
my husband, Bob.

Chapter One

"**W**hy is Warren Davis coming here today? He didn't even come to his own son's funeral." Dori Morales gazed out the twelfth-story window at the Dallas skyline. The glass and steel structures in the distance reflected the late morning sun. Turning from the window, she glanced at Brady Houston who sat at a monstrous mahogany desk. She struggled to tamp down the fury roiling through her mind. "Is that horrible man going to disown his grandson just as he did Tyler and Marisa?"

Getting up, Brady joined her near the window and laid a hand on her shoulder. "I don't know what Warren Davis wants as far as his grandson is concerned. He's coming today because he's mentioned in the will. So maybe we'll learn his intentions." Brady turned back to the desk and brought out two folders.

With a heavy sigh, Dori stared at them. The words printed across the top screamed at her. The Last Will and Testament of Tyler W. Davis. The Last Will and Testament of Marisa M. Davis. When her sister Marisa and brother-in-law Tyler had written a new will and asked Dori to be their child's guardian, she never imagined that a month later they would be dead.

Dead. Dori still didn't want to believe it.

Now her sister's baby was Dori's responsibility. Her child.

Brady adjusted his glasses as he rearranged the file folders on the desk. "Sorry we have to wait, but the others should be here shortly."

"I don't care if they ever get here," Dori replied, thinking about baby Jacob, who was in her mother's competent care. Being away from the tiny infant made Dori realize how much her nephew meant to her. She loved him and wanted to keep him safe from someone like Warren Davis. Blinking back the threatening tears, she shook her head. "I'm not sure I can be civil to Warren Davis."

"He is a difficult man to deal with, but you don't have to say a thing." Brady rubbed his hand across his balding head as he again sat behind his desk. "I'll do the talking. Don't let him rile you. There's no sense in letting him know he's upset you. Your anger will only incite him."

Anger was the only thing that kept Dori from crying when she thought of the awful car accident that had taken the lives of her sister and brother-in-law. Anger at Warren Davis and anger at God. How could God allow loving people like Marisa and Tyler to die when hateful people like Warren Davis lived and prospered?

"I don't understand why Tyler left him anything. Do you think Mr. Davis will contest the will?"

"Legally, I can't think of any grounds he has to contest it."

"I don't trust that man."

"Don't fret over it. Have a seat. Try to relax until they get here."

Fighting back tears, she sat in a blue leather wingback chair. She crossed and uncrossed her legs. She picked at a piece of lint on her navy-blue skirt and brushed the sleeve of her navy-and-white plaid jacket. As she fought against the misery that welled up inside her, she surveyed the shelves of law books lining three walls of the mahogany paneled room, then glanced at her watch.

The intercom on the desk suddenly crackled and Brady's secretary said, "Mr. Garrett is here."

Going to the desk, Brady punched the button. "Send him in."

"Who's Mr. Garrett?" Dori's heart jumped into her throat.

"Tyler's brother," Brady answered as his eyebrows knit in a puzzled frown. "I thought you knew Tyler had a half brother."

"Yes, but they've been estranged for years. Why is he here?"

Before Brady could answer, the door opened. Not daring to look, she huddled in the big chair. What did this man want now that his brother was dead? Was he after part of Tyler's estate?

"Good morning, Chase." Brady's greeting was congenial. "Is your father on his way?"

"I don't know. I haven't talked to him."

"While we're waiting for your father, let me introduce you to Marisa's sister, Dorinda Morales."

As the man came into view, Dori's stomach lurched and her palms grew moist. His gray, pinstriped suit emphasized his broad shoulders and his height, which had to be over six feet. He strode toward her with a look of confidence. She willed herself to be calm as she smoothed her hair that was drawn back in a loose knot at her nape.

He smiled, and a dimple appeared in his right cheek. Despite his friendly demeanor, she didn't want to like him. It wasn't the Christian thing to do, but he had never associated with Marisa and Tyler when they were alive. Now that they were dead, he suddenly appeared. She wanted to pray that God would help her treat Tyler's brother as she should, but God had sometimes seemed far away in the past few weeks.

Surreptitiously wiping her hands on her skirt, she stood and extended her hand. "Hello, Mr. Garrett."

"Please call me Chase. May I call you Dori? That's what Tyler called you." His large hand closed around hers.

"Sure," she said, unable to deny his request even though she didn't want to like him. His infectious smile immediately disarmed her while little shivers ran up her spine. Surely they came from her desire not to like him, but she wasn't certain of anything.

When had Tyler ever mentioned her to Chase Garrett? Why was he having this effect on her? There was nothing to like about a man who hadn't bothered to be part of his brother's life for ten years. Like Warren Davis, this man hadn't attended Tyler's funeral. She withdrew her hand and returned to her chair. She should know by now she wasn't a very good judge of men, and her reaction was nothing more than her propensity to fall for the wrong type.

Dori observed Chase as he settled in the chair next to hers. The only clue to his thoughts was the rigid set of his shoulders. His eyes, a kaleidoscope of blues, greens and browns orbiting the sunburst around his pupils, held no hints to what he was thinking. His handsome features remained unreadable.

The secretary's voice came over the intercom, but before she finished speaking, Warren Davis barged into the room. His finely tailored charcoal-gray suit, flamboyant tie and Italian leather shoes subtly reminded Dori that he was a very rich and powerful man. His black hair, except for the touch of gray at the temples, and his blue eyes were just like Tyler's. Except Tyler's eyes had been like a warm summer sky while Warren's made her cold, like the dead of winter. Chase, with his tobacco-brown hair and multi-colored eyes, didn't look like either one of them.

Casting her a derisive look, Warren took a seat on the other side of Chase.

"Hello, Mr. Davis," Brady said with a nod. "Now that we're all here, we can get started."

"Good," Warren said, leaning forward in his seat. "Let's get right to the point. I'm not going to sit here and let my son's estate fall into the wrong hands. The Morales family has been after Tyler's money ever since he married their daughter. They aren't going to have it now."

Rage boiled inside Dori. She clenched her fists in her lap. Heat suffused her cheeks as she glared at Warren. He glared back. She wanted to lash out at him and tell him to keep his false accusations to himself, but she looked at Brady and ignored the two other men. No matter what they thought, she had the truth on her side.

"Mr. Davis," Brady said calmly, but forcefully, "I'm in charge of this meeting. Please be quiet and listen."

Brady got up from the desk and handed each of them a folder. "In the folder you'll find a copy of Tyler's will and a copy of Marisa's will. You can see they are mirror images of each other. Since they are both deceased, we go on to the next of kin being the minor child, Jacob Tyler Davis.

He inherits the bulk of the estate, which is held in trust for him until he reaches the age of twenty-five. Dorinda Morales is named as guardian for the minor child. Chase Garrett is the executor and trustee of the estate. One hundred thousand dollars goes to Warren Davis."

Taking in Brady's last statement with disbelief, Dori looked at Chase and found him staring at her. She returned his gaze. How could Tyler have named his estranged half brother as executor of his will? Why had Marisa agreed to it? What had they been thinking? And why had Tyler left money to the father who had disowned him? Dropping her gaze to her lap, Dori's mind buzzed with the questions. She jumped when Warren surged to his feet.

"I've heard enough." He strode to the door. "Are you coming, Chase?"

Standing, Chase looked across the desk at Brady, then at his father. "No, I'm staying. No matter who inherits this estate, I'm still executor."

"Suit yourself," Warren said, exiting the room.

Dori watched Chase, who took a deep breath and released it slowly as he returned to his seat. He appeared genuinely troubled by his father's behavior. But was this their version of a "good cop, bad cop" routine? She had no reason to trust either of them.

Finally, Chase looked at Brady. "What's going on here?"

"Didn't your father explain?" Brady asked.

"No, he's failed to tell me a lot of things." Chase looked puzzled. "Why is my father so upset about this will?"

Brady adjusted his glasses. "Your father seems to think the baby might not be Tyler's."

"What?" Chase asked, shaking his head. "That's crazy."

"Not to your father. He knew that Tyler and Marisa had been going to a fertility specialist for a number of years before they conceived Jacob. And he wants to make sure the child is really Tyler's."

Chase frowned. "Whether the child is Tyler's biological child or not doesn't make any difference, does it? The child is still his legal heir."

Brady nodded. "That's correct, but I believe your father thinks there's some way around that."

"You heard him." Dori stared at Chase. "He thinks my family is after Tyler's money. He thought that was the reason Marisa married Tyler."

"Tyler never said anything like that to me."

"When did you talk to him?"

Chase narrowed his gaze, as he appeared to contemplate his response. "A few weeks before he died."

Frowning, Dori shook her head. "I had no idea. I thought you never spoke to each other."

"We didn't for many years, and I regret that deeply."

"Ahem. Could we get on with this?" Brady interrupted.

"Excuse us. We'll settle this later." Gripping the arms of the chair, Chase eased himself back.

Brady proceeded to explain the rest of the will and the duties assigned to each of them. The hurt and pain surrounding the loss of her beloved sister and brother-in-law became more acute with every word. And she couldn't help wondering why Tyler and Marisa had never mentioned speaking with Chase.

Tyler's relationship with Chase became a convoluted puzzle in her mind. If they had the same father, why didn't Chase and Tyler share the same last name? Tyler had never talked much about his family. Whenever the subject came up, his unease had been obvious. He had readily adopted the Morales clan as his own, and they had taken him into their hearts. How did Chase fit into this enigma?

She glanced over at him while he listened intently to Brady's explanations. The more she learned the more evident it became with her as Jacob's guardian and Chase as the executor and trustee, she would have to work with him frequently. She could only pray that God would help her get over her bitter feelings toward a man who had been at odds with Tyler and Marisa for years.

When they were done, Dori stood. "Thanks, Mr. Houston, for your help. I'll be waiting to hear from you on the court dates."

"My secretary will call and let you know. If you have any questions, feel free to call me any time." Brady stood and walked around the desk to shake her hand.

"I will. I'd like to discuss some personal matters."

"Fine. See my secretary on your way out. She'll set up an appointment for you."

"Thanks again." She left the room without glancing back.

Chase wanted to run after her and make her understand he was grieving as much as she was, but he forced himself to remain seated. He couldn't shake the image of her chocolate-brown eyes filled with grief and distrust. After the door closed behind her, he wondered how he could ever work with a woman who obviously didn't think much of him. "Am I going to be trapped between two warring factions again?"

Brady sat behind his desk. "You mean Dori and your father?"

Chase nodded. "I want what's best for my nephew, but

if she can't work with me, maybe someone else should be executor."

"Even if there is friction between Dori and your father, don't let that stop you from carrying out Tyler's wishes. I hope you'll take my advice. Tyler did when I explained the importance of making a new will after the baby was born. He told me how competent you would be as executor."

"How well do you know Dori? Will she give me a chance?" Chase asked. Not that he cared about her, but as his nephew's guardian her approval mattered. Besides, Chase wanted to know what kind of woman was caring for Jacob.

"I know Dori only from my dealings with your brother. Right now it's obvious she is hurting, and it may take her a while to work through all this," Brady replied. "Tyler would want you to work it out. Go after her."

"You're right," Chase said, remembering her puzzled and hurt expression. "If she's not here, where can I find her?"

"She's been living at Tyler's. You know where that is?"

"Yes. He gave me the address when we talked." Chase headed for the door. "Thanks."

When he didn't see Dori in the outer office, he raced into the hall and toward the elevators. He managed to get there as the doors started to close. When he shouldered his way between them, they sprang apart. Dori stood at the back of the elevator. She grimaced and crossed her arms when he stepped in beside her. After giving him a cursory glance, she focused her gaze on the numbers above the door. Even though she wore heels, the top of her head barely reached his shoulder. Her dark brown hair gleamed in the overhead lighting.

Dori's response to his presence in the elevator reminded

him of the last time he had seen Tyler. Chase had been on his way to the accounting office in the W.T.D. Enterprises building when Tyler had stepped back into Chase's life after ten years of silence. His reaction to Tyler had mirrored Dori's reaction now.

"I'd like to talk with you." Stony silence met Chase's attempt to open the conversation. "Don't shut me out. We need to talk."

"I really don't think we have much to say." She didn't look at him.

"I'm not like my father."

Chase's statement caused her to glance his way. "And why should I believe that when you both refused to have anything to do with Marisa and Tyler?"

"Tyler didn't give me a choice."

"You had a choice. Maybe you made the wrong one."

Chase read the censure in Dori's eyes. Her last words echoed through his mind. *Wrong one. Wrong one.* Grief and agony over his brother's death plagued him. Sometimes it all seemed like a bad dream. Chase wanted to wake up and find his brother still alive, especially now that he had a son.

Dori knew him as a man who hadn't spoken to his brother in years, but she obviously didn't know the whole story. Most of all, she didn't know she made Chase's pulse race. Tyler had been right. She was beautiful. Changing her opinion wouldn't come easy, but less hostility from her meant an easier job taking care of Jacob's inheritance.

He had to make her understand. "When can we talk?"

The elevator stopped and the doors opened. Dori made a hasty exit. He strode after her as her heels tapped on the marble floor. She pushed open the glass door, and he followed her out into the noonday heat radiating off the high-rise buildings and concrete sidewalks.

Chase matched her hurried pace. The heat made his shirt stick to his back underneath the suit coat. "Dori, we need to talk. Let me take you to lunch."

Stopping, she turned, seemingly unaffected by the warm temperature. "I don't have time for lunch. I have to get home and take care of Jacob."

"Let me go with you. I'd like to see him."

She stood for a moment in obvious thought as she released a heavy sigh. "I'm sorry. This was a difficult meeting for me. I just don't feel like talking now."

"How about later today?"

She shrugged as her wary brown eyes searched his face. "I don't understand why you are so eager to see your nephew. You didn't bother to see Marisa and Tyler when they were still alive."

What would make her understand? Tyler's untimely death had ripped away their plans to get together after Chase's return from his business trip. He was grieving, too. Everything about this situation tore at his heart. "Why do you suppose he named me executor?"

"I have no clue." She turned on her heel and marched down the sidewalk.

Chase caught up to her. "I can explain. We have to work together whether we like it or not."

"Can you explain all the years of alienation with Tyler?"

"Give me a chance."

When she reached her car, she stopped to unlock it, then looked at him. "Okay," she said with a nod. "Come over tonight around seven. Do you know where Tyler lived?"

"Yes. Surprised?"

She shook her head. "Not anymore. After today, nothing would surprise me."

"Let me bring something to eat." He reached around her and opened the car door. Being near Dori made him remember Tyler's promise to introduce him to her. Now they had met, and he wanted her to like him and trust him. Doing the best thing for his nephew depended on it.

"That won't be necessary." Her eyes held no welcome, only duty. She got into the car and shut the door, closing him out.

Chase turned his silver Lexus on to the quiet street and looked for the house number written on the sticky note on the dash. The tall brick houses with the perfectly manicured lawns all looked the same, as though they had been cut from a giant cookie cutter and placed along the street against the backdrop of a bright blue Texas sky. His stomach churned and his heart thudded as he rang the bell. A shadowy figure appeared behind the leaded glass in the front door. Would Dori receive him with guarded acceptance or outright hostility?

The door opened, revealing a two-story foyer. Dori stood on an Oriental rug lying on a golden wood floor. The pink shorts and matching print top she wore made her look young, a sharp contrast to the sophisticated woman he had seen this morning. Tyler had told Chase she was twenty-nine years old, just four years younger than he. Now she looked barely out of her teens. With her dark brown hair falling around her shoulders, she appeared approachable, even friendly, but distrust still showed in her eyes.

"Come in," she said, moving aside.

After he stepped across the threshold, she closed the door behind him. On the right the formal dining room contained a beautifully crafted mahogany table, chairs and china cabinet. Straight ahead a curved staircase with a railing of ornate wrought iron led to the second floor. Glancing around the room, he regretted he had never set foot in this house when his brother was alive. Chase wondered what lay beyond these formal rooms. Would he find a part of Tyler there?

Dori went down two steps into the sunken living room. She motioned for him to sit. He settled on the edge of the off-white couch.

Sitting ramrod-straight in the nearby chair, she held her hands in her lap. "What do you want to talk about?"

"Where's Jacob?" he asked, fearing she might throw him out before he had a chance to see his nephew.

"He's sleeping."

"I'd like to see him. I promise not to wake him."

Her dark brown eyes studied him, making him feel as though she could see into his soul and gauge the sincerity of his statement. With a sigh she replied, "Okay."

"Thanks." If nothing else positive came of this meeting, at least he would see his nephew.

Dori walked toward a hallway on the left. "Follow me."

She stopped in front of a door, slowly opened it and peeked inside. In anticipation, Chase hovered behind her. She gradually opened the door to its full width. The room smelled of baby powder and Dori's perfume. A light oak crib, decorated with sheets and a mobile depicting bears with balloons in primary colors, sat against one wall.

Dori tiptoed across the room, and Chase followed. The tiny infant with a thatch of dark hair lay peacefully sleeping. Chase remembered the moment when he had seen the baby's picture and the proud smile on Tyler's face. If only Chase could see that smile again. Maybe he could catch a glimpse of Tyler in his son.

Chase looked closer at the tiny boy. The shape of the baby's nose and chin resembled Tyler's. A tight pressure swelled in his chest as his heart overflowed with emotions he couldn't define. Grief? Regret? Love? Life could be so cruel, snatching away his chance to make things right with Tyler. Maybe he could have a second chance with Tyler's son. Sharing in this child's life took precedence over everything else. Chase wanted the kind of family he never had. The kind of family who loved and cared for each other.

The urge to touch the baby played on his mind. He wanted to pick up Jacob and cradle him, feel this tiny life and cling to the fact that part of his brother lived on in this child. He tamped down the urge. There would be another time for that. He glanced up to find Dori staring at him. Her features softened, and a sad little smile graced her lips. Chase's heart raced. She was beautiful when she smiled. He forced himself to look away. This was no time to get entangled in the alluring look of a pretty woman. He made a promise. *Don't let tender feelings for this kid make you think you could care about his aunt.* Women were only trouble.

She put her hand on his arm and whispered, "Let's go."

Her touch radiated a warmth that forced him to realize keeping that promise was going to be difficult. He had to remember she was only being polite. She didn't think much of him.

They walked in silence to the living room. Standing near the couch, Chase waited for Dori to sit. An uneasy tension encompassed the room. He shifted his weight from one foot to the other and shoved a hand in the pocket of his khaki pants.

"Could I get you something to drink?" she asked.

"No," he said, then realized how sharp his reply had sounded. "I just ate," he added, trying to soften his response.

Finally she sat, and he took a seat on the couch. She looked a little more relaxed as she leaned back in the chair, but her words painted a different picture. "Now that you've seen the baby, what did you want to tell me?"

What could he say when there were so many answers to her question? He gazed at her while all the reasons for being there raced through his mind. "We have to understand each other and work together to do what's best for that little boy in there."

"I don't see any problem with that." Her conciliatory words didn't match the clipped tone of her voice or the set of her jaw.

Chase leaned forward. "You're saying what I want to hear, but I want you to mean it."

"I do mean it. I can work with you."

"But you don't like me, right?"

Her gaze dropped to the floor. Her silence gave him the answer. He got up and walked over to the fireplace. At least he didn't have to guess about her feelings. Studying the mantel clock, he told himself it didn't matter. He had worked out plenty of financial deals with people who didn't like him, but this was different. Her antagonism would eventually drive a wedge between him and his nephew. He couldn't let that happen, not as it had with Tyler.

Walking back across the room, he sat on the couch nearest her chair. "Why don't you like me?"

She gripped the arms of the chair and blinked. "I... you...you judged my sister, the sweetest person I've ever known, without meeting her. You didn't think she was good enough for your brother. You refused to associate with them. Now that they're dead you want to insinuate yourself into your nephew's life."

"You're judging me by my father's actions, not mine."

"As far as I can see, they're the same."

"No, they're not."

"And now you're going to tell me how they're different, especially since there's no one here to refute what you say." Her chin jutted out as a flush rose in her smooth olive complexion.

"You can choose not to believe me if you want to." Chase shrugged, feeling helpless to convince her. He had to remain calm and change her mind because having a good relationship with his nephew depended on it. This child was the only bright spot in his life. "Three weeks before he died, Tyler and I talked. He told me he'd just had a son and that he and Marisa were making new wills. They wanted me to be executor and trustee if both of them should die. He wanted me to see his newborn son."

Dori slumped back in her chair. "Why would he do that? You hadn't spoken in years."

"Tyler wanted to change that. He told me he had become a Christian and couldn't be right with God without being right with me. Do you share those beliefs?"

Dori stared at him for a moment. She appeared to be struggling for an answer. "Do you?"

"Tyler's death has made me aware I could be on better

terms with God myself. But you didn't tell me whether you shared Tyler's beliefs."

She turned away from him, then replied in a voice barely above a whisper, "I should, but it's not always easy to do the right thing."

"And what is the right thing?"

"To forgive you for judging my sister. To forgive my enemies." Dori turned her gaze on him again.

"I didn't know your sister. The split between Tyler and me had nothing to do with her. It was between him and me only." Pausing, he studied her. Why was she intent on making him the bad guy in all of this? "Do you consider me your enemy?"

"You always seemed like Tyler's enemy."

"Tyler and I were never enemies. We were just two brothers who had chosen different paths where our father was concerned."

She shook her head. "Tyler never mentioned talking to you."

"He tried to reach me for weeks at work because I have an unlisted number at home. Warren learned about it while I was out of town and made sure I didn't get the messages." Chase glanced at the floor, then back at Dori. "Tyler wanted to make amends."

"Tyler wanted to make amends?" A frown wrinkled Dori's brow. "What did he have to make amends for? You're the one who disowned him."

"That's not true."

"But you didn't even come to the funeral."

"I didn't know about it. When the accident happened, I was in China on business."

"Surely your father called you."

Sighing, Chase leaned his elbow against the mantel and put his head in his hand. He suppressed the rage that surfaced every time he thought about what Warren had done. The man had no heart. He hadn't cared about hurting his wife or how he'd driven a wedge between his sons. "No, he didn't. I got back two days ago. We hadn't talked until today in Brady's office."

Narrowing her gaze, she stared at him. "I never heard any of this."

"You never heard about the new wills?"

"I heard about the wills, but Marisa and Tyler never said anything about you being executor."

"Why are you so surprised I was named executor?"

Her expression wide-eyed, she said, "Because you hadn't seen each other in ten years. I don't understand anything."

He refused to let her goad him into saying something he would regret. "What don't you understand?"

"Why do you have a different last name than Tyler if he was your brother and Warren Davis is your father?"

Taking a deep breath, Chase walked over to the window and looked out. Why had he insisted on explaining everything to her? He had unlocked a door he didn't want to walk through. Now just the thought of revealing the past brought up old wounds he didn't want to share with this woman he barely knew. He hadn't bargained on making his life an open book. In the process of building a protective wall around his heart, he had buried a lot of hurt and pain he didn't want to unearth. Not now. Not ever.

He felt comfortable with the life he had etched for himself. When he'd come back from college and realized he'd walked into an emotional minefield, he had tried to make the best of a bad situation. In retrospect, Dori may have been right. He'd made the wrong choice.

He turned. She sat forward in her chair and stared at him with those wary, chocolate-brown eyes. He steeled himself against her reaction. "Warren Davis is my father, but he never married my mother or made an attempt to give me his name."

Chapter Two

Dori watched the muscle work in Chase's jaw as he stared at her. What could she say? She wished she could take the question back. If Warren had sent Chase away, why had he chosen to side with his father rather than Tyler? "I'm sorry. I didn't know."

Releasing a long, slow breath, Chase looked at the vaulted ceiling in the living room. "Don't be sorry. I survived."

Dori couldn't relate to a family like his. Her family had always stuck by her and helped her when she was in trouble, especially during the time she had suffered from depression. She couldn't imagine their turning away. Tyler's family had always seemed an anomaly. Now their feud had found its way into her life.

Her guardianship meant dealing with Chase, whether she liked it or not, so she should try to understand him. To her, he had always been the "bad brother." The brother who had sided with Warren in disowning Tyler. She had never considered that Tyler might have shared the blame. She had always seen him through her sister's eyes as the kind, considerate man who had given up the chance to run a financial empire for love. Was she ready to learn something different? "What caused the rift between you and Tyler?"

Chase lowered his gaze until he looked directly at her, sorrow radiating from his eyes. "Our father and stubborn pride."

"Please explain what happened."

Shoving his hands in his pants' pockets, he looked out the window again. "Why?"

"Because I want to understand."

"You said you wouldn't believe me anyway."

"I'll try. I'll listen."

"Can you listen with an open mind?"

She nodded. "So what happened?"

He turned his gaze on her. "After I finished my MBA, I came back to Dallas to work in my father's company. When I got here, I discovered Tyler and Warren were at odds over Tyler's elopement. He had left the company and gone out on his own."

"Did Warren say you couldn't associate with Tyler?"

"No, as far as he was concerned, that was my decision."

"So you did turn your back on Tyler."

"Not exactly."

"What do you mean? Either you did or you didn't."

"I called him, and we talked. He gave me an ultimatum. Either him or Warren." Chase looked at her as though he expected her to refute his statement.

She emitted an incredulous laugh. "And you chose Warren Davis, the man with no heart. This is supposed to change my opinion?"

"Don't decide before you hear all of it." Chase paced

back and forth in front of the fireplace. "Do you think it was right for Tyler to force me to choose between them?"

"As far as I'm concerned, there was no choice. Warren Davis deserves no one's loyalty."

"Maybe not, but at the time I didn't appreciate being told I had to choose one or the other. And I wasn't going to side with the person who forced that decision on me." Chase rammed his hands farther into his pockets. "I had spent nine years away from the only place I could call home. My stepmother had died, and I saw a chance to get to know my father. Tyler was telling me I had to throw it all away. I don't like people controlling my life or telling me what I should or shouldn't do." Chase stopped pacing and stared at her.

Dori stared back while her heart pounded. Could she believe him? What he was telling her didn't correspond with the Tyler she knew.

"Well?" He sat on the end of the couch nearest her chair.

"I don't know what to say."

"Say you won't hold my decision against me."

Could she do that? She could try, but it wouldn't be easy. Everything he said was in complete opposition to the picture she had formed in her mind over the years. But Jacob's future depended on working with this man. She should put aside her animosity for Jacob's sake. "I'll try." Eager to be rid of his unsettling presence, she scurried to the door and opened it. "I guess you'll be going now."

Chase followed. "But we haven't settled anything."

"What's to settle? You're the executor and trustee. You're in charge of the money. I'm the guardian, and I'm in charge of Jacob."

"He's *my* nephew, too." Chase took her hand off the knob and closed the door. "I'm not leaving until I get your input."

Attempting to ignore the tingling sensations that shot up her arm when he'd touched her, she took a step back. Staring at him, she tried to convince herself anger had ignited the sparks, but she couldn't forget how he made her heart trip when he'd smiled. "He's more to me than my nephew. He's my child, my responsibility now. Or did you forget?"

"No, I didn't forget." His kaleidoscope eyes gazed at her. "We have to discuss this."

"What's there to discuss?"

"I need information to do my job." He touched her arm. "Let's go back into the living room and sit down."

"What kind of information?" Wanting to get away from his disturbing touch, she darted into the living room. She sat on the chair. Maybe distancing herself from him would put her uneasy thoughts in order.

He followed and sat on the love seat which was perpendicular to the couch. "I have to pay all the debts to the estate. It's my duty to see that you have enough money to care for the baby. What do you need?"

She stared at him. Her mind buzzed. What did she know? Her mother had been helping her every day. She'd never taken care of a baby by herself. She had been using the things already in the house and hadn't thought beyond that. Suddenly overcome with the responsibility of Jacob and the loss of his parents, she bent her head and covered her face with her hands. Misery and uncertainty welled up inside her along with a sea of tears. She shouldn't cry in front of this man, but the tears came anyway. Sobbing, she felt the weight of this awesome duty.

Sensing Chase's presence beside her, she raised her head just as he put his hand on her arm. His touch unsettled her more than the worry over taking care of Jacob. She longed for a comforting touch, but not from Chase. She couldn't seek solace in the arms of a man who saw her only as a liability on the balance sheet. She wasn't supposed to like him. His past relationship with Tyler made her think he had no family loyalty. Despite Chase's story, how could she trust a man like that? She had misplaced her trust too many times in the past. She wouldn't do it again. Wiping her hands across her wet cheeks, she wanted to think about something other than the way he made her feel things she didn't want to feel.

Through a blur of tears, she saw his eyebrows knit together in a frown. "Are you all right?"

Slowly, she nodded. "I'm sorry. I'm not usually like this." She blinked and more tears trickled down her face. She quickly wiped them away. "I want to do my best for Jacob, but I never expected to have sole responsibility for my sister's child."

Chase wanted to ease her fears, but he sensed her reluctance to accept a comforting embrace. Knowing she wouldn't appreciate his attempts to soothe her worries, he withdrew his hand and reached into his pocket. He pulled out a handkerchief and handed it to her. "I'm here to help. Are there bills that need to be paid? That's part of my responsibility."

"Thanks." She took the handkerchief and wiped her face, then smiled. "There are bills from the cleaning lady, yard and pool services. Probably some utility bills, too. Maybe a credit card. I'll have to look."

"Good. Gather them together and give them to me, so

I can pay them. Do you want me to hire a nurse to help you?"

She shook her head. "No, my mom's been helping. Next week my younger sister will be home from college. She's going to stay with me until she starts her summer job."

"Are you sure that'll be enough?"

"Yes." She nodded. "What will happen to Tyler's company?"

"I can't be sure until I look at the books. Do you know where Tyler kept his personal records?"

Getting up from the chair, Dori pushed her hair behind her ears. "They should be on his computer. Business records, too."

"That's great. Did he use a password?"

Dori nodded. "Yes, but I know what it is. I'll show you the office."

"Do you mind if I do some work here tonight?" he asked, hoping she wouldn't deny his request.

She stared at him, then looked past him toward the hallway leading to the nursery. Sadness still etched lines across her pretty face. "I suppose. You have to start sometime."

"If you'd rather I waited until tomorrow, I can."

"No, no," she said, walking across the room, "you might as well work since you're here."

"Thank you." He followed her into the small hallway and stood beside her as she put her hand on the door handle.

Hesitating, she glanced up at him. "Tyler's study is off their bedroom. I haven't been able to go in here since they died."

"Do you want me to go in by myself?"

"No, I have to do this sometime." Pushing the handle down, she let the door swing open. She looked into the room, then back at him with a weak smile. "You're the last person I expected to be doing this with."

"I can imagine." He sensed a slight thaw in her attitude. Maybe this was going to work out after all.

While he waited for her to go in, he stared through the doorway toward the wall of windows looking out on the pool and backyard. The setting sun shone through the windows and glinted off the brass, king-size bed. The room's warm and inviting appearance revealed a lot about Tyler. When Chase had been thrust upon the Davis family, Tyler welcomed Chase, treated him like a brother. But in the end Tyler had turned away, too, just as everyone else had.

Chase took in the rest of the room, a room full of beautiful things, with no one to enjoy them. An archway trimmed with elegant moldings at the right side of the bedroom led to an alcove. A large cherry desk occupied the center of the area. A computer sat on a smaller desk at the back of the room. Was this what was left of his brother?

Chase's gaze returned to Dori. With a determined set of her shoulders, she let out a harsh breath and strode across the room. As he followed her toward the study alcove, he noticed the photograph of Tyler and Marisa posed in a traditional wedding picture. Stopping, Chase picked it up and studied it. They stood facing each other. The' expression on their faces told him these people loved each other deeply.

Chase's heart twisted in sadness as he swallowed a lump in his throat. A powerful regret enveloped his soul. As a young man he had adored and worshipped his older brother, but when Tyler had given Chase that ultimatum, he let his dislike of being told what to do get in the way. If only he could go back and do it all over again, but there was no going back. He had to move forward and make up for those mistakes by doing the right things for his nephew.

Chase looked at the picture further. What would it be like to share life with a loving woman? Deep in his heart, buried under all the scars, he wanted that as much as he wanted anything. But all the women he'd dated, he eventually learned, were more interested in his bank account than in him.

"They were a beautiful couple, weren't they?" Dori's question shook him from his thoughts.

Still holding the photo, he glanced up at her as she stood in the archway. "Yes, but I thought they eloped."

"They did. But even in Las Vegas you can get married in a gown and tuxedo." Dori motioned for him to join her in the study. "See this photo? It was taken a year later when they were married in the church. Mom always wanted that. You know how mothers can be."

"No, I don't." Chase went to the desk and turned on the computer. He wouldn't think about how his mother hadn't cared whether he lived or died. Women were all fickle. They cared about you until you got in the way of what they wanted. He had to remember that when he looked into Dori's eyes and started wanting more than a business relationship with her. If he knew what was good for both of them, he'd keep his distance.

She continued to gaze at him. "I don't suppose you'd care to elaborate on that statement."

"You're right. I don't." He looked up from the computer. She was fiddling with the paper clips in a container on the desk. Her uneasy expression told him she hadn't expected his reply. She had no idea what it was like to grow up having no one to care whether you came home, much less whether you got married in a church. Even Tyler, the legitimate son, had been given things rather than love. Warren Davis had been too occupied with his business, and Sally Davis had been absorbed with charity functions and social gatherings. Maybe Tyler had not only been entranced with Marisa but her family as well.

Not wanting to face more of Dori's scrutiny, Chase focused his attention on the computer screen. He typed the password, clicked the mouse and brought up the program that contained Tyler's financial dealings. Bank accounts, mutual funds, stocks, bonds, company records. "This should keep me busy for a while. I'll print some of this out and take it with me. Is there paper in the printer?"

"I don't know. We'll have to check it." She reached for the paper tray.

"Okay." He grabbed for it at the same time. When his hand accidentally touched hers, she jerked her hand away. Their gazes met and held for only a moment, but he was sure, judging from her startled wide-eyed look, she had felt something. It wasn't just his heart that was beating a little faster. She'd had that effect on him from the moment he had first seen her.

"Sorry. You check the tray. I'll find more paper in the storage closet in case you need it." She rushed across the room and rummaged through the shelves until she turned around holding a package of paper. Meeting his gaze, she held it out to him. "Here. There's more in there if you need it."

Taking the paper and laying it on the desk, he managed to break eye contact. "Thanks."

"You're welcome. There's a file cabinet in the closet. You might want to check that, too."

"Sure." He kept his eyes trained on the computer because looking at her only served to muddle his brain. The determined set of her chin told him she was ready to tackle the challenges set before her. There was no doubt she cared about her nephew. Knowing these things about her made him want to toss aside his reluctance to get close to people. How was he going to deal with her and keep his mind on these finances? "I'll work here for now."

"If I can get you anything, just let me know."

Before he could answer, a loud squall sounded from the speaker on the wall. "What's that?"

"The intercom. Jacob's awake. I've got to check on him." She headed for the door.

"I want to see him." Chase got up and followed.

She turned as he walked behind her. "You might as well keep working. I'll have to change him and feed him. When I'm finished, I'll bring him in."

Chase wanted to see the baby now, but he could tell by Dori's expression she would feel more comfortable if he did what she said. "Okay, but if you need help—"

"I'll be fine," she called over her shoulder.

He watched her walk away. Seeing her on a regular basis might make him care too much, but he had to take that chance. Being part of his nephew's life could help make up for the loss of his brother and help take away the sorrow. Still, he had to guard against getting personally involved in Dori's life. Their relationship needed to remain strictly business. Over the years, he'd built a protective barrier around his heart, and he'd be asking for trouble if he allowed her any chance to tear that barrier down.

Chase went back to the desk and started printing out the records from Tyler's bank accounts. While the printer slowly spit out the information, Chase went to the closet and looked in the four-drawer file cabinet. This wasn't going to be an easy job. The enormity of the task before him hit him hard as he stared at all the folders.

When he left the closet, he heard Dori's voice over the intercom. She was singing to the baby in Spanish. Her throaty contralto wove its way through his brain and into his heart. When she finished singing the words, she continued to hum the tune. Then there was quiet.

Just as the printer stopped, her voice came loud and clear over the intercom. "When we get done here, Jacob, I have to take you to see your big, bad uncle. He's here to take care of all your daddy's stuff."

Plopping in the chair, Chase released a long, slow breath. Had she said that forgetting he could hear her over the intercom, or had she done it on purpose to let him know how she really felt? Even after he'd told her the reasons for the break with Tyler, she didn't see him in a better light. He couldn't let her paint him as the bad guy with Jacob.

When Dori returned, she came alone.

"I thought you were bringing the baby with you," he said, looking up from his paperwork.

Staring at him, she tucked her hair behind her right ear. "He fell asleep again after I fed him."

"You could've called me after you were finished." Standing, he placed his hands palms down on the desk and glared at her. "I'm not going to let you shut me out of his life."

"I'm not trying to do that." She took a step backwards.

"I heard what you called me. 'Big, bad uncle.'"

"How did you hear that?" Her brows knit together in a puzzled frown.

"The intercom."

"Oh. I forgot." Even her olive complexion didn't hide the color rising in her cheeks as she looked at the speaker on the wall.

Resolved to make her understand she couldn't get away with poisoning his nephew's mind against him, Chase stepped around the desk. "I know you don't like me, but let Jacob form his own opinions."

"He's only six weeks old. He doesn't understand a thing I'm saying."

"He will some day." Crossing his arms, Chase leaned back against the desk until he sat on it. She probably thought he was crazy. He did feel a little foolish. "I'll be in Jacob's life for a long time. I don't want him hating me."

"I really didn't mean anything by it," she said with a sigh. "I was just—"

"Just expressing your feelings."

"Maybe." A pensive glimmer rose in her eyes as she again tucked her hair behind her ear. "I know we have to try and get along."

Studying her, he wondered whether tucking her hair behind her ear was a nervous habit. Did he make her nervous? He didn't want to.

"You're right. We do, but I want to make one thing clear. I won't let you or anyone else shut me out of my nephew's life." Chase walked behind the desk without giving her a backward glance. He went to work, busying himself with the papers the printer had spewed forth during their talk.

* * *

Dori's pulse throbbed in her head while she watched him. As he bent over the desk, the overhead light sent highlights through his wavy, brown hair. He shuffled through a pile of papers. He obviously didn't care about a response from her about his pronouncement.

Turning away, she left the room. After peeking in on the baby, who was still asleep, she went to the family room that opened into the kitchen. Sitting on the couch, she flipped on the TV with the remote control and went through all the channels. When nothing caught her interest, she shut it off and reached for a book. She tried to read, but she couldn't concentrate. Without Marisa and Tyler's love and laughter, the house was too quiet, too big and too empty.

Dori laid her head on the back of the couch and closed her eyes. Visions of Chase filled her mind. No matter what she tried to concentrate on, her thoughts kept coming back to him. His declaration about being a part of his nephew's life echoed through her brain. The deep timbre of his voice played across her mind. His speech was an odd mixture of the unfamiliar sounds of a New England accent shaded with only the slightest hint of a Texas drawl on certain words. Every once in a while, he'd say something that sounded just like Tyler. If she closed her eyes, she could imagine him standing there, saying the same thing in the same way. But when she opened her eyes, there was Chase, the other brother, the one she wasn't sure she could trust.

He seemed sincere, but part of her didn't want to trust him. He said he wasn't like his father, but did she dare believe him? Would he gain her confidence, then turn against her? And there was the other reason she feared him. Just looking at him made her pulse race and her heart do flip-flops. His touch sent out signals that short-circuited her ability to think clearly.

A sad weariness took over her mind and body as she relaxed for the first time since Chase had shown up. She felt as though she'd been running on a treadmill with no way to turn it off. Her emotions worked overtime, making her vulnerable to Chase's insistence that he share in Jacob's life. Although she hated to admit it, he had that right. Tired, she wished she hadn't said Chase could work tonight. Now she had to wait until he left to go to bed. While her mind spun with the complications, she slowly drifted off to sleep.

Soft crying penetrated the fog of sleep surrounding her brain. Why didn't it stop? How could she sleep with the constant noise? Like a pesky fly, it buzzed in her ears. Then with a sudden awareness, she jerked her head up from the couch. Jacob.

She jumped up and raced toward the nursery. Before she got there, the crying stopped. When she reached the door, she realized why. With his back turned toward the door, Chase picked up the tiny infant and awkwardly cradled him against his chest. She stood in the hallway and watched.

"We'd better find your aunt before you start squalling again, little guy." Chase patted Jacob's back. "She doesn't like me very much. I know that's hard to believe 'cause I'm such a good guy. You're going to have to help me out and put in a good word for me. Tell her I'm not so bad. You can even tell her I said she's pretty."

Dori slunk back into the hallway. She didn't want to get caught spying. Had he said all that to get on her good side? She didn't want to be suspicious, but the last time she had trusted a man, he had taken her heart and torn it apart. Saying all the things she had wanted to hear, he had used her to get what he wanted. She had to guard against misplacing her trust again.

The next morning when the doorbell rang, Dori picked up Jacob and hurried to the front door. Although the leaded glass distorted the image of the person on the other side, she recognized her mother. It wasn't Chase. A little pinprick of disappointment skipped through her mind. Why was she thinking of him? She didn't trust him. She didn't even like him.

Dori swung the door open wide, taking in the loving smile on her mother's youthful-looking face. The only hint that she could possibly be a grandmother was a sprinkling of gray amongst her dark brown locks, coiffed in a neat short style. Her coffee-colored eyes beamed when she saw the baby.

"Hi, Mom. I'm so glad you're here."

Teresa Morales reached for her grandson. "You look tired. Did this little man keep you awake last night?"

"Yes, he still has his days and nights mixed up. He just finished eating, so you might want this." Dori handed her mother a burp cloth, then the baby.

Teresa took the infant, nestled him against her bosom and patted his back. "How's my grandson? Have you been staying up all night? That's a bad habit to get into, young man. Your aunt can't get her beauty rest if you do that."

Gazing at her mother, Dori thought about her sleepless night. Jacob had awakened her in the night, but even when she'd had the chance to sleep, her mind was cluttered with thoughts of the baby's future and how she was going to deal with Chase.

Hearing her mother refer to her as an aunt somehow didn't feel right. She wasn't just Jacob's aunt. She was his guardian. His future rested in her hands. She vowed to preserve Marisa's memory for Jacob, but her absence made Dori feel like his mother. In the past couple of weeks a bonding had taken place. A bonding she had never anticipated. She loved him more intensely than she could have ever dreamed.

"Mom, you want me to take him?"

"No, honey, I'll take care of him." Teresa walked toward the family room. "We'll just go in here and sit for a while. Maybe if I keep him awake, he'll sleep longer at night. Why don't you lie down and get some rest?"

"I will, but first I want to discuss something with you." Dori joined her mother on the family room couch.

"What's that, dear?"

"I want to adopt Jacob."

Teresa stopped patting the baby and stared. "Are you sure? That's a big undertaking."

"What difference does it make since I'm already his guardian? I still have responsibility for him." Dori gripped the arm of the couch.

Her mother laid her free hand over Dori's. "This doesn't have to be a permanent arrangement. Your father and I would be glad to take on the guardianship."

"But I agreed to do it. And I want to do it."

"Don't feel guilty if you change your mind. When you agreed to be guardian, you had no idea you'd ever have to do this, much less that it would begin almost the day he was born." Teresa resumed patting the baby on the back.

"But I've been thinking about it ever since I met with the lawyer."

"One day's not a lot of time to assess something that will affect the rest of your life."

"I know. I've made an appointment to talk with Mr. Houston about it."

"That's good," her mother said, nodding. "Find out what's involved before you make any final decisions."

"I've made up my mind. Just hearing you call me Jacob's aunt didn't seem right. I'm more than his aunt. I can't explain the feeling." Dori rubbed her index finger along the baby's cheek. "I want to be his mother. For real."

"You think that now, but raising a child is a big responsibility, especially as a single mother. I know you said you were planning to go back to work."

"Yes. I've been looking at jobs where I can work from home."

"Do you have any prospects?"

Dori nodded. "A few."

"Have you prayed about it?"

"I've prayed about everything, and I'm not going to change my mind. Besides, going before the court to transfer the guardianship might give Warren Davis the idea that we don't want the responsibility for Jacob. He might try to seek custody."

Teresa frowned. "I thought the man didn't want anything to do with the baby."

"He doesn't right now because he doesn't believe Jacob is his grandson." Clenching her fists, Dori released a long, slow breath. "But when he realizes the truth, I have no doubt he'll try to take the baby."

"Do you really think so?"

"Yes, I believe he would. And besides that, Tyler's brother is the executor and trustee, and he exercises a lot of control over what happens to Jacob. He's coming over again today to work on Tyler's records. I don't know what to think of him." Pausing, Dori stared at the floor. How could she explain to her mother the fears connected with cooperating with Chase? She felt as though she was associating with the enemy. Glancing up, she asked, "How can we trust him when he turned away from Tyler?"

"Let him earn your trust. That's all you can do."

"I don't know if I can. I trusted Scott and look what happened." Closing her eyes, Dori thought about her failure in judging men. She had been engaged twice. First Ramon, then Scott. Both times the man she thought loved her had walked away. But Scott's betrayal went beyond her feelings. It had affected Marisa and Tyler as well. Scott had said he loved her, but all he really wanted was access to Tyler's company. Even six years later, it brought pain to her heart and a reminder of the darkest time in her life. Most of the time it seemed far in the past, forgotten, until someone such as Chase came along and reminded her how quickly relationships could fall apart. He made her remember how she had misplaced her trust, not once, but twice. She would never do that again.

Dori felt the touch of her mother's hand and opened her eyes. "Are you all right?"

"Yes, I'm fine," Dori replied, hoping her mother wouldn't press further.

"I didn't know you even thought about Scott anymore."

"I don't very often."

"Good. There's no sense in dwelling on the past." Teresa glanced down at the baby. "This little guy doesn't want to stay awake, does he?"

Dori shook her head. "No. He's a night owl."

"Since he's not going to cooperate with us, why don't you lie down and get some rest." Her mother patted her arm again. "Dori, adopting Jacob is a wonderful thought, but think it through. Pray about it."

"I have, and something in here tells me it's right." Dori placed her hand over her heart.

"Don't rush into this decision. Give it some time. Get settled with the baby. See how motherhood suits you. In a month or two you may feel tied down."

Dori shook her head. "My feelings aren't going to change. He's my son."

Chapter Three

Chase stopped his car behind the gray sedan parked in front of Tyler's house. Walking to the front door, he figured the car must belong to Dori's mother. Would she give him the same icy reception that Dori had? He hoped not. Taking care of Tyler's estate and seeing to the best interests of his son was all Chase wanted to do. He didn't need resistance from Dori or her mother.

Taking a deep breath, he rang the doorbell. He waited what seemed like an eternity, and still no one answered the door. He rang the bell again. Was Dori refusing to answer?

He strained to see any movement behind the leaded glass. Just as he was about to reach for the doorbell again, someone approached. He steeled himself for Dori's less than enthusiastic greeting. The door opened, and a woman stood there holding Jacob. Her remarkable resemblance to Dori momentarily scrambled his thoughts. "Aah…I'm Chase Garrett."

"Oh, yes. Come in, come in." Stepping aside so he could enter, she extended her hand and smiled. "I'm Teresa

Morales, Dori's mother. Dori has told me all about you. I'm glad to meet you."

"I'm glad to meet you, too." Chase shook her hand and wondered what Dori had told her mother. The woman's greeting seemed friendly enough. Maybe Dori hadn't said anything disparaging about him, or maybe her mother didn't express her disapproval as easily as Dori did.

"Sorry I took so long to answer. I didn't want to leave him alone." She looked down at her grandson, then back at Chase. "My condolences on the loss of your brother."

"Thank you." He closed the door as her nonjudgmental greeting allayed his fears. Maybe this wasn't going to be so bad after all. He looked at the baby nestled in his grandmother's arms. "My condolences on the loss of your daughter."

Teresa nodded. "Thank you for your kind words."

"I'm here to work on the estate. I hope Dori told you I was coming. Is she gone?" he asked, wondering whether she had decided to leave so she wouldn't be here when he came.

"No, she's resting. And she did tell me you were coming over. You can make yourself right at home and do whatever it is you need to do." She shifted the baby in her arms as she started to walk toward the kitchen and family room at the back of the house. "Would you like a cup of coffee before you start to work?"

"Sure." Following her into the kitchen, he hoped for a chance to hold his nephew. He'd never been particularly interested in children before, but this child had captured his heart. "Could I hold Jacob for a minute?"

"Certainly. Then I can get the coffee." She offered the baby to him.

Awkwardly, he took the child in his arms, fearful that he might drop the small bundle. He had held the baby last night, but then he'd been alone. He didn't want to do something stupid in front of the baby's grandmother. The baby's soft sleeper made him feel even more fragile. Chase moved toward the family room couch. "I'll sit over here."

"Fine. I'll be there in a few minutes," Teresa called from the kitchen.

The smell of brewing coffee mingled with the scent of baby powder as Chase held Jacob. The baby yawned and opened his dark eyes. They reminded Chase of Dori. While the baby's little fists waved in the air, Chase marveled at the tiny life.

Carrying two mugs of coffee, Teresa came into the room. She set the mugs on the coffee table, then joined Chase on the couch. "You can put Jacob in his carrier while we drink our coffee."

"Do you have other grandchildren?" Chase asked as he carefully placed the infant in the carrier sitting on the floor near his feet.

"Yes, nine others." Teresa reached for a photo sitting on the end table. "You do know what happens when you ask a grandmother about her grandchildren, don't you?"

Chase chuckled as he looked at the picture of a large group of people. "I guess I'm going to find out."

"Here's the whole family." Teresa ran her hand across the glass-covered photo. "This is our oldest son, Javier, and his wife Patti, and their children, Savannah, Isabel, Jamie and Emilio."

"And Tyler and Marisa." Chase pointed to the photo.

"Yes, and next to them are Timo and Linda and their kids, Elena, Cristian and Rafael. Then Dori and our youngest daughter, Natalia. And our youngest son, Carlos, his wife, Angela, and their two little ones, Laura and Andres."

Chase again pointed to the picture. "Is this your husband?"

"Yes, that's Luis." Nodding, Teresa looked up, her eyes bright with unshed tears. "We are so glad we had this photo taken last year because Marisa and Tyler are in it. The only one missing is our Jacob. He's our special grandchild. Marisa and Tyler waited and prayed a long time for this baby." Teresa leaned over and stroked the infant's head.

"You have quite a family." Chase settled back in his seat and took a sip of his coffee. What would it be like to have a family like that? He couldn't imagine. What should he say now? He wasn't very good with small talk, especially with someone he didn't know. Maybe this wasn't such a good idea. But he had wanted acceptance, and Teresa Morales had offered him that in her invitation to have coffee.

"What will you do as executor?" she asked.

Relieved for something else to talk about, Chase smiled. "First, I have to gather all the information about Tyler and Marisa's assets. When I get that done, I can formulate a plan."

"What will happen with Davis Import and Export, Tyler's company?"

"I hope to keep it running for the time being. I may have to sell it. Maybe I'll have some answers in a few days."

"How does Dori's guardianship fit into all of this?"

"Well, as executor, it'll be my job to see that she has the finances to raise Jacob. You don't need to worry. I intend to do my best for my nephew."

"I wasn't worried." Teresa set her coffee mug on the table. "Dori is."

"Did Dori tell you that?"

"Not exactly, but she gave me that impression." Chase released a long sigh. "She didn't tell you what a black knight I am?"

Teresa laughed and shook her head. "No, but she did admit she's not sure how to deal with you."

"That's been obvious from the beginning. She thinks I'm the enemy because of my father."

"Well, yes, that's true, but she knows you're not all bad." Teresa winked. "Give her some time. She'll come around."

"I'm not sure she will." Chase took another swallow of his coffee. "Why don't you have the same opinion of me as she does?"

"I like to form my own opinions."

"That's good."

Teresa picked up her coffee mug and took a sip, then looked at him over the top of the mug. "I meant what I said about Dori. She'll work with you."

"I'm sure she will."

"I meant she'll eventually be on your side."

"That'll be a switch." He laughed half-heartedly. "What makes you think so?"

"Dori's on an emotional roller-coaster right now. She was devastated by Marisa and Tyler's sudden death. This tragic situation has been hard on the whole family. If it weren't for our faith in God, it would've been even more difficult."

"Yeah, Tyler's death has made me realize I need to re-examine my relationship with God."

"It makes us all feel that way. We see how short life can be and how we need to make the most of every minute."

"That's true. Tyler mentioned to me when we met that he had become a Christian, and that's why he wanted to make amends. But I was worried that he'd start preaching at me," Chase said, surprised by how easy it was to talk with Teresa. Too bad he didn't feel the same with Dori.

"Do you come from the same agnostic point of view that Tyler held before he became a Christian?"

Chase shook his head. "No, I always believed in God, but it was never anything like what Tyler told me about when we talked. I knew it was something special because he had been completely disillusioned with any kind of religion after he saw the hypocrisy of our father's religion."

Nodding, Teresa smiled. "I know, but Tyler saw a different kind of faith in Marisa. Her life led him to his faith. Then after he made his decision to become a Christian, Marisa urged him to make things right with you. But it took a while for him to get up the courage to confront you. After the baby was born, he realized it was the right time."

"Then why was Dori so surprised that Tyler and I had talked?"

"Because he never told any of us."

"I wonder why? Marisa was there, too."

Teresa shook her head. "I can't explain it."

Chase puzzled over this information. What had prompted Tyler to say nothing about their meeting? Brady Houston had known. If Tyler had lived, when would he have told Marisa's family about their meeting? The answer came to Chase like a flash flood across the Texas prairie. "I think I know the reason. Tyler wanted to wait until I got back from my trip and our reconciliation was on firm footing. I'll have to admit I was somewhat reluctant to accept his apology in the beginning. He probably sensed my hesitation even though I agreed to be executor."

"I suppose that makes sense. You two had been estranged for many years."

"I wish it had been different. We were very close at one time."

"Probably like Dori and Marisa. They were more than sisters. They were best friends," Teresa said and smiled wryly. "You should have seen them together. No one was happier for Marisa than Dori when this baby was born. Dori lived here to help Marisa during her pregnancy. Her doctor had ordered complete bed rest so she could carry this little guy to term."

"So Marisa had a difficult pregnancy?"

"Always. She had four miscarriages before Jacob was born. We prayed every day that Marisa could carry Jacob to term."

"No wonder they were so happy."

"And that's why Dori is so protective. She knows what Marisa went through to have this child." Teresa gazed at him. "Dori wants desperately to do what's best for Marisa's baby. I just wanted you to know what it's like for Dori. Now this baby that was supposed to be someone else's is hers. Do you understand what I'm trying to tell you?"

Nodding slowly, Chase was beginning to realize what was going through Dori's mind. "That I should be gentle with her?"

Teresa's soft laughter faded into a smile. "Maybe I should tell her to be gentle with you. She can be a tiger. She has a tendency to see everything in black and white. There's no in-between. She likes to be in control, doing things her way. She's not very good at accepting help, but she has a loving and giving heart."

"I've seen that in the way she takes care of Jacob."

"I'm glad. There was an exceptional bond between Dori and Marisa. When your father rejected Marisa, Dori took it personally. Family is very important to her." Teresa looked down at the sleeping baby, then rubbed his tiny hand. "Especially this little guy. She'll work with you because she knows his future depends on it."

Chase stared at Jacob. Teresa's statement made him realize more than ever the importance of the job he had accepted, never dreaming he would actually have to do it. He had to have a part in this child's life that involved more than the finances, but would Dori allow that when she saw him as the "bad guy"? Tackling this job was going to test his endurance. He should get busy and not waste more time drinking coffee. But Teresa's kindhearted greeting was something he had needed after Dori's less than enthusiastic acceptance of his role as executor. Chase looked up into Teresa's warm, brown eyes, so much like Dori's, but he saw no censure in these eyes. What would it be like to have a mother, an advocate, like Teresa Morales on his side? "Thanks for the coffee. I'd better get to work."

"Okay," she said, taking his coffee mug. "If you need anything just call me. I'll be here all day."

Chase went back through the house toward the study where he had worked last night. As he passed by the baby's room, he noticed the door was shut. Was Dori in there? He had seen a twin bed in the room in addition to the crib. Thinking about what her mother had said, he wanted to assure Dori that she could trust him. Maybe the best way was to make everything in Tyler's estate a viable asset that his nephew would one day inherit.

He thought about his own life. Assets didn't mean a thing unless there was someone to share them with. He wanted to be in Jacob's life for school plays, awards and graduation. This little boy needed a man to teach him how to play catch, ride a bike and shoot hoops. Chase wanted to be that man. Tyler had been that person for a little while in Chase's life. Now he could do that for Tyler's son. Would Dori let him, or would she fight him?

Shaking away the frustrating thoughts, Chase set his mind to the task at hand. He took a deep breath and turned on the computer, bringing up Tyler's financial program. He had gone over all the papers he had printed out last night. What he had seen looked in order. Tyler had done well for himself in the years since he had split from their father. He had taken his W.T.D. Enterprises stock and used it as collateral when he started his own business. His entrepreneurial spirit had served him well. His import/export business was thriving. Chase didn't want to mess that up.

While going over the records, he had learned that Dori was an integral part of the operation. She was the company representative in dealings with several firms in Mexico and Central America. Did she plan to return to work now that she had responsibility for her sister's child? What did that mean for Jacob?

Chase rubbed his hand down his face. He'd done enough woolgathering. He had to get back to work. Sorting through the papers on the desk, he put them in order of importance as to what he should deal with first. He made lists of things he had to do and gathered addresses and phone numbers of people and places he had to contact. Using the computer, he made spreadsheets. As he printed out one of them, he heard a knock on the door. Looking up, he saw Teresa poking her head around the corner.

"Dori and I are having lunch. We wondered whether you'd like to join us," she said, stepping into the room. "If you want to keep working, I can bring your lunch in here."

Chase pushed back the chair from the desk and stood up. Stretching and rolling his shoulders, he walked around the desk. "I'll join you. I could use a break."

Chase followed Teresa through the house as she headed toward the kitchen. He kept telling himself the reason he agreed to join them for lunch came from his desire to see Jacob, but he couldn't forget Dori would be there, too. How would she greet him today?

When Dori heard footsteps, she looked up from the sink where she was slicing cantaloupe. Chase walked into the family room and immediately went to retrieve Jacob from his carrier.

Holding the infant in his large hands, he held the child out in front of him. "Hey, I see you're finally awake. It's your uncle Chase again. Have you enjoyed your visit with your grandma?"

The baby waved his fists in the air as if responding to Chase's question. Then Chase cradled the child against his chest. Dori couldn't deny the effect this scene had on her. Half of her had wanted him to stay in the office so she wouldn't have to deal with her conflicting emotions about him. The other half wanted to look into his intriguing eyes and take in his virile good looks. What cruel trick of nature made her physically attracted to a man she didn't want to like?

While Dori stared at Chase and the baby, her mother

came into the kitchen. "Here let me finish that. Go sit down. You're supposed to be taking it easy. I'm here to pamper you all day."

"Okay, if you say so." Dori put the knife on the counter, then went to the kitchen table. As she took a seat, Chase walked over, still holding the baby.

"Did you get some rest?" He sat in the chair next to her.

Dori nodded, unable to speak for the moment. She self-consciously smoothed the striped camp shirt over her jean shorts. Angry with herself for letting this man make her heart race, she wanted to scream. Emotional. That's the only way she could describe herself. Ever since the death of her beloved sister, her emotions had run rampant on so many levels. And Chase's presence continued to remind her of the past she had put firmly behind her. God had pulled her through those difficult times, and He would do it again. She just had to keep that in mind. Finally, she gathered her thoughts. "Yes, I'm feeling much more rested."

"Good," he said with his gaze still focused on Jacob, whom he now held on his lap.

"Did you get a lot of work done this morning?" she asked, trying to think of something other than the way his attention to the baby melted her heart.

Chase looked up at her. "Yeah, I did, but there's a lot more to do. The more I search, the more I find. It'll take a while to get a handle on everything."

"How long will it take?" she asked, wondering whether he'd be here indefinitely, upsetting her equilibrium.

"I'll do as much as I can this weekend. Brady's going to put me in touch with one of the tax attorneys in his firm. I could use one of the guys at our office, but I figured why do anything to irritate Warren."

Dori studied Chase. Was he once again saying what she wanted to hear to get on her good side because he knew she didn't like Warren? She should just take his statement at face value instead of trying to put some motive behind it. Her mother's advice rattled around in her mind. *Let him earn your trust.*

Teresa interrupted Dori's thoughts as she brought plates to the table. "Mom, let me help you."

"No, Dori." Chase got up while he held the baby against his shoulder. "I'll help. You can take Jacob."

Chase gently laid the baby in Dori's arms. When his hands brushed against her, their gazes met, and a sinking sensation hit her stomach. Immediately, she broke eye contact with Chase. When was he going to stop making her feel this way? When was she going to stop letting him?

After helping Teresa bring the food and drinks to the table, Chase sat down in the chair he had occupied earlier. Dori put Jacob in his carrier and set it in between her and Chase. The baby acted as a buffer against Chase's proximity.

After Teresa offered a prayer of thanks for the food, Chase and her mother talked while they ate. Dori merely listened, trying to get her emotional state in order. What would happen as she dealt with Chase for the rest of Jacob's life? In Chase's role as executor and trustee of the estate, he would be there until Jacob was twenty-five. Life would be simpler if she buried old wounds. She prayed that God would give her the strength to give Chase a clean slate. Whatever his offenses had been, the past was gone. She needed to keep emotions, old or new, out of the equation. Her dealings with him would be business, and that's the way it would remain. She needed to learn to forgive.

Her mind wandered to her plans to adopt Jacob. He

deserved to have a mom, not just a guardian. He needed that sense of belonging. But would that wipe out the memory of his real mother? No, if Dori did everything in her power to preserve Marisa and Tyler's memory for Jacob, that wouldn't happen.

Still thinking of her resolution to manage this situation, she reached for her iced tea. In the next instant, the glass tipped toward Chase's seat and tea flowed into his lap. He jumped up. Letting out a yelp, Dori grabbed the baby's carrier and moved it out of the way. Teresa blotted at the offending liquid with the napkins that had been sitting on the table. Jacob began to cry.

Dori picked him up and cradled him. Patting the baby's back, she looked apologetically at Chase who had a large wet spot on the front of his khaki pants. "I'm so sorry. Clumsy me."

Holding his arms out from his sides, he looked down at the mess, then back at her with a wry smile. "That's okay. It could've been worse. It could've been hot tea."

"I suppose," she said, feeling completely embarrassed. His smile dazzled her, making her catch her breath.

His smile made the attractive man absolutely gorgeous. His perfect white teeth were a testimony to great genes or excellent orthodontia. When he smiled, dimples appeared in both cheeks. She hadn't seen him smile since they had met in the lawyer's office. Was that any surprise? She'd never given him anything to smile about since that meeting. Now that smile was just one more thing she had to contend with on this emotional roller-coaster ride. She hugged the baby to herself like a shield against the on-slaught of Chase's devastating good looks.

"Dori, show Chase Tyler's closet so he can find something to change into. Then I can wash and dry his clothes," Teresa said as she finished mopping up the mess. "I'll take the baby."

Dori relinquished the baby to her mother's open arms. The idea of going into Tyler's private things didn't sit right, but it had to be done sometime. Marisa's things, too. She had to learn to deal with Chase as well.

Chase followed Dori as she led the way back to Marisa and Tyler's bedroom. Dori hesitated at the door. What was going through her mind?

She turned to look at him as they entered the master bath. "I'm really sorry."

"I know you are. Accidents happen. At least we were done eating."

"Well, this is it." Releasing a harsh breath, she opened the mirrored sliding door and motioned for him to go in. She looked as though she wished she were someplace else.

"You haven't gone in here, have you?"

Dori shook her head. "There was no reason. Somehow coming in here seemed disrespectful."

"It's not, you know. You can't live in this house and completely ignore this room," he said, realizing it was his responsibility as executor to go through these personal possessions as well as the financial aspects of Tyler and Marisa's lives. What would he find in the drawers and closets? What revelations about his brother would his belongings reveal? Unlike Dori, he wanted to find out.

She tucked her hair behind her ear. She gazed up at him, her eyes full of doubt. "I suppose."

He wanted an excuse to touch her, and this was as good an excuse as any. Not giving her a chance to change her mind, he took her hand and led her into the closet. She didn't resist. With her slender hand in his, a powerful, protective feeling emerged toward her. If only he could make sure nothing would hurt her. But the emotional trauma of dealing with the death of loved ones was something he could do nothing about. He just hoped he could make it easier because he was dealing with it himself. Guilt and all.

"Now that wasn't so hard." He dropped her hand even though he didn't want to, but he couldn't press his luck. He wanted to be her friend, not her enemy.

"None of this is easy." She stared at him, her arms folded across her midsection.

Her stance told him she was closing him out again. For just a moment, he had penetrated that barrier, but she had resurrected it in a second. She wasn't about to let him gain access again. Could he ever tear down the wall of her distrust?

"It's not easy, but it's part of saying goodbye," he said, resisting the urge to put his arm around her shoulders.

"You ought to know. You're pretty good at that part."

Chase felt the sting of her words as if she had slapped him across the face. "Ouch. I didn't deserve that."

She sank against the wall and put her hand to her forehead. "No, you didn't." Slowly she looked up at him. "I'm sorry. I'm not handling this well. I'll get out of here, and you can get some clothes."

When she turned to go, he reached out and gently grabbed her arm. Turning her around, he saw the tears welling in her eyes. He gathered her into his arms and held her close. The top of her head barely reached his chin. He caught the familiar scent of her perfume as she sobbed into his chest. A powerful ache surrounded his own heart, but he held back his own feelings. Men didn't cry.

When her crying subsided, she pushed herself away. Gazing up into his eyes, she smiled faintly. "Thank you. Truce?"

His heart felt lighter as he returned her smile. Maybe he had finally made some headway. "Truce."

"You change, and I'll take the clothes to my mom," she said, stepping out of the closet.

He poked his head out the door. "I'll be done in a minute."

After closing the door, he quickly perused the wall of neatly arranged pants and shirts. He put on a navy-and-tan Polo shirt and a pair of khaki pants. He looked down at his legs. The pants were too short. He had forgotten how much shorter Tyler had been. Surveying the closet again, he found some khaki shorts. He put them on and grabbed the other clothes to give to Dori.

When he emerged from the closet, Dori was sitting on the edge of the bed with a jewelry box in her lap and tears welling in her eyes again. He let the clothes fall on the bed. "Are you okay?"

Nodding, she smiled up at him through her tears. With a sigh, she replied, "Yeah, I was just looking at some of Marisa's things. Don't they say the first stage of grief is denial? I think I just got past that stage. It's finally sinking in that she's gone."

"Is that a good sign?" He sat on the bed next to her.

"Sure." Hopping up, she grabbed his clothes and headed out the door.

"Wait," he called after her.

She stopped and turned around. "Did I forget something?"

"Not exactly. I just wanted to be sure you were planning to come back."

"Why?"

"You have to help me go through this stuff. It's something that's got to be done. We might as well do it today."

"Today?"

"Yes. Tell your mother. She can help if she wants."

Turning, Dori left without a word. Did that mean she wasn't coming back? He'd give her a few minutes, and in the meantime, he'd start looking through the closet. Going over to the tie rack, he pressed a button and the rack slowly moved in a circle. While he watched the ties go around, he understood Dori's feelings about going through someone else's belongings. He shook those negative thoughts aside. He had this responsibility, and he would carry it out. No matter what happened.

Chapter Four

When Chase heard voices coming from the bedroom, he stepped out of the closet. Dori walked across the room with Jacob in his carrier. She placed him in the middle of the king-size bed, then glanced up at Chase. "We're here at your command."

"Good." Had he commanded her? Something told him no matter what he did she was going to take it wrong. He might as well not worry about it.

Teresa followed with a couple of large laundry baskets and several plastic bags. "Dori tells me you want to go through the closets. I think that's an excellent idea. What do you plan to do with everything?"

"I'm not sure. How about giving it to charity?" Chase asked.

"Are you going to get rid of Marisa and Tyler's things without a second thought?" Dori frowned. "You want to get rid of everything?"

"Not everything." Chase hoped this wasn't going to be a battle of wills. He gazed at Dori. It seemed that progress in making her trust him was one step forward, two steps back. Could he ever convince her that his intentions were honorable? "That's why I asked you to help me go through these things."

"But you can't just give this stuff away. It's not yours."

"That's true. It belongs to Jacob, but as executor and trustee, I have the responsibility of dealing with all his assets. That includes all these personal items. He'll never have use for most of this. We'll box up what you deem keepsakes for him, and the rest we'll give to charity."

Teresa stepped between Chase and Dori. Teresa put her arm around Dori's shoulders. "You can't make this place some sort of shrine. You have to let go, Dori."

"You're right, but it's not easy." She stepped away and sat on the edge of the bed.

"Let's get to work," Teresa said, patting Dori's arm. "Then maybe it won't seem so hard.

"I suppose," Dori said.

"Good. Let's get started." Teresa turned to Chase. "I think your plan to give most of this to charity is an wonderful idea. Our church has a clothing and food pantry for the needy. I hope you'll consider giving it to the church."

"That sounds good to me," Chase agreed. "I appreciate your mentioning it. Thanks for coming to help."

"I'm glad to do it. Anything for my newest grandchild." Teresa stepped to the bed and gently rubbed the baby's head. "What do you want us to do?"

Chase glanced around the room. "Dori, you can start with that jewelry box you were looking at. Does it have anything of value?"

"No." Dori shook her head. "Marisa kept all her good stuff in the floor safe. Do you know about that?"

"No, where is it?" he asked.

"In the closet, but I don't know the combination." Dori stood and looked at her mother. "Do you?"

"No." Teresa shook her head. "We can worry about that later. Dori, you show Chase where the safe is while you go through everything in there. I'll go through the drawers in here and keep an eye on the baby."

Chase followed Dori into the closet. "You'll be glad you did this now instead of waiting."

"I know you're right, but it still hurts."

Chase let his gaze roam over the shelves and rods full of clothes. "This closet reminds me of when I was a kid and saw Warren and Sally's closet for the first time. It was bigger than the bedroom I had in my mother's apartment. I'd never seen a closet like that except in the movies. It was huge, just like this one."

"You talk like they weren't even your parents."

"Sally Davis never was a parent to me, and Warren didn't do a very good job."

"If you feel that way, why did you side with Warren?"

"I already explained that, didn't I?"

"Yes, but it's hard for me to understand. I'm working on it."

"Good." Chase gave a mental sigh of relief that Dori didn't want to pursue the subject further. He'd had enough emotional upheaval for one day. "Now, show me that safe."

"It's in here." Dori went toward the far corner of the closet. She grabbed hold of the edge of one of the shelves that held several pairs of shoes and yanked it opened, revealing a hidden cedar closet.

The smell of cedar wood immediately filled the room

as Chase stood in the doorway and looked around. "I don't see a safe in here."

"That's because it's hidden, too." Dori knelt on the floor and carefully pulled back the carpet to reveal a foot-square metal plate with a hole in the center. She lifted the plate. "It's under here."

Chase stood over her and looked down at the numbered dial. "Do you know what's in there besides Marisa's jewelry?"

"Not really." Dori turned her head and looked up at him. "I saw some papers when Marisa let me borrow one of her necklaces for a party. I didn't pay much attention to them."

"Well, it doesn't matter right now. If I don't find the combination somewhere in Tyler's office, I'll have to hire someone to get it open." Chase stepped back into the main closet, glad to be in a larger area. He didn't want Dori to know about his claustrophobia. Or maybe it was her nearness that had him breaking out in a sweat. "I'm going to get to work on this other stuff."

"Me, too." She followed and closed the hidden door behind her. "I'll start with the shoes."

"And I'll do the ties and shirts." Chase went to work trying not to think of how much Dori affected him.

When he finished with the ties, he started looking through the shirts. He folded them in a neat pile. Then he moved on to the built-in chest in the middle of the closet. Opening the top drawer, he found several sweatshirts inside. He pulled the first one out. As he unfolded it, tightness filled his chest. The logo across the front was from the private prep school he had attended. He'd given Tyler this sweatshirt during one of his visits. Looking further,

Chase discovered two more sweatshirts and a ski sweater that he had also given to Tyler while he was in college. All of them were well-worn and faded. Breathing deeply, he closed his eyes. If Tyler had kept these things, why had he been so reluctant to make things right between them? Chase wondered why he had been so full of stubborn pride that he had thrown away the only good relationship he'd ever had. He could cry, but he wouldn't.

"Oh, you've found Tyler's ragbag drawer."

With a fierce ache settling around his heart, Chase turned at the sound of Dori's voice. "His what?"

"Marisa called this drawer Tyler's ragbag because he kept all this old stuff in here. He wouldn't get rid of it. One time she wanted to give it away, and he wouldn't let her. Told her to stay out of that drawer. Some of that stuff is so awful I'm not sure you can even give it away."

"I'll take care of it." Chase continued to look through the drawer. Had Tyler kept these things because it meant something to him or had it been old clothes that were good for working around the house or a winter game of touch football?

When he pulled out the last piece of clothing, he had his answer. Letters, newspaper clippings and old programs lay scattered across the bottom of the drawer. Pushing them into a pile, he brought them out and put them on top of the chest.

"What's that?" Dori asked, coming over for a closer look.

"Some stuff Tyler had at the bottom of this drawer."

"What kind of stuff?" Dori reached for an envelope.

Chase wanted to retrieve it from her. It was one of the letters he had written to Tyler. Chase recognized his own scrawled handwriting.

"Southboro, Massachusetts. Who did Tyler know in Southboro, Massachusetts?" She gave him a curious stare.

"Me."

"You?"

"Yeah, it's where I went to prep school. When Tyler went away to college, the Davises sent me to boarding school there. It was some exclusive, expensive school that lots of kids would have done anything to get into, but I looked at it as prison. I'd been sent away because they didn't want to deal with me."

"Are you sure? Maybe they just wanted you to have a good education."

"Maybe." Trying to change the subject, Chase picked up the letters. "These probably got dumped in a drawer and forgotten."

"No, Tyler and Marisa moved into this house just two years ago. So if that stuff was there, Tyler put it there."

"I didn't know guys kept stuff like this. I thought only women did."

Dori shook her head. "Oh no. When my grandfather died, we were surprised to find the things he kept in one of his drawers. He had all the birthday cards, letters and silly little things we grandkids had sent him over the years. Men can be sentimental, too. If you'd met my grandfather, you'd never suspect him as the kind to save those things, but he did."

Chase wished he were alone so he could sit down on the floor and weep. The ache around his heart felt as though a thousands weights were pressing down on his chest. The regret of all those wasted years heightened the grief, but he couldn't sit here and cry. Not in front of Dori. She would say he deserved what he had gotten because he had chosen not to associate with his brother. She would have no sympathy for the sorrow and guilt that troubled him.

Steeling himself against the hurt, he gathered up all the clothing and keepsakes from the drawer and stuffed them into one of the plastic bags. "I'll just take this with me."

"You're taking those old shirts and sweaters?" She looked at him as if he was crazy. "Why?"

"Because these are things I gave Tyler."

"When?"

"A long time ago."

"And he kept them?" Dori's tone of voice and the way she looked at him told Chase she might be starting to believe that he and Tyler had had a bond, even though it had been broken for years. Then Tyler's death had destroyed it forever. "Would you like to explain?"

Would he? Chase let the question filter through his mind. This was the good part, the part he liked to remember. He could talk about this. Show her what Tyler had meant to him. "I could." Most of it anyway. He probably shouldn't tell her some of the things the two brothers had done during Chase's high school years. Like the time Tyler bought Chase his first beer. That might tarnish her image of Tyler, her saintly brother-in-law, who could do no wrong. "What do you want to know?" Bad question. He wanted to snatch it back as soon as it was out of his mouth, but he couldn't.

"Everything."

"We don't have time for everything. I'll tell you about the stuff in the drawer."

"Okay."

Thankful that she didn't demand more, he smiled. "While I was in boarding school and Tyler was in college, we wrote to each other. It was cool for a fourteen-year-old to have a big brother at Harvard. He'd drive up for visits, especially my last two years when I played on the basketball team. That's what the newspaper clippings were about."

"You played basketball?"

Chase nodded. "Yeah, I still do. I'm in a league down at the gym where I work out."

"I suppose you intend to give Jacob a basketball as soon as he can stand."

Chase threw his head back and laughed. "Probably before."

"That's what I was afraid of."

"You mean you don't want him to play basketball?"

"No. I meant giving him a ball before he can use it." Pursing her lips, she put her hands on her hips. "You might have competition from my dad in a different sport. He's given all his grandsons footballs. Jacob is due to get his. Of course, a Dallas Cowboys jersey accompanies it. Do you like football?"

"As much as the next guy."

"Then you should fit right in with the men in my family."

Chase let Dori's last statement soak in. Was she beginning to accept his part in the baby's life? He could only hope. "Does this mean I'm invited to the next family gathering?"

"Do you want to be?" she asked, her gaze narrowing.

"Yes. I want to be part of Jacob's life." He held his breath while he waited for her reply.

"You have the right. You are his uncle." She let her arms fall to her sides as if she had resigned herself to the necessity of accommodating him. Not because she wanted to, but because she had to. In that familiar gesture, she tucked her hair behind her ear. "However you decide to be in his life, I won't stand in your way."

Insane as it was, he wanted to take her in his arms and kiss her until all she could think about was having him in her life, not just Jacob's. All these emotions were getting to him. He needed to get out of here. Despite the size of the gigantic closet, he felt closed in because Dori was like the forbidden fruit, something he shouldn't touch. He was letting himself get carried away with wanting more than she would ever be willing to give. More than it was wise for him to want. Maybe one day he could be her friend, but not if he did something as crazy as kissing her. Then she'd know for sure he was the cad she thought him to be.

Picking up the bag at his feet, he stepped toward the door. "I'm going to take this out to my car."

When he returned, Teresa was hanging up the phone. "Dori, that was Aunt Rosalia. She said she's coming down with a cold and can't come over to watch the baby while we go to church."

"That's okay, Mom. You go. I'll stay home. I can go in the morning."

Chase stepped into the room. "I couldn't help over-hearing your conversation. Dori, you don't have to stay home. I'm here. I can watch the baby."

"I don't know." Dori stared at him, her eyes full of doubt.

Would that ever go away?

"That's a marvelous idea," Teresa said.

Dori glanced at her mother. "I suppose."

"Good. Then it's all settled." Teresa looked at her watch. "We can work for another hour. Then we'll get ready."

"I'll take good care of him," he said, hoping to get rid of the distrust in Dori's eyes. Was her hesitation due to her concern that he might not know how to take care of a small infant? He wanted to ask, but why put her doubts into words. Or maybe his own as well.

At four-thirty, Dori and her mother left the house. Teresa had to nearly drag Dori away from Jacob. This child was more than just her charge. She wasn't only his guardian, but his mother as well. What he would have given for a mother like that when he had been a kid.

Jacob had been fed, bathed and changed. He'd been left in Chase's care in perfect condition. Now all he had to do was keep things in order for a couple of hours. Piece of cake. At least he hoped it was.

Chase took the baby into the family room and sat on the couch. Holding the infant in his lap, Chase reached for the remote control and flipped on the big-screen TV that sat in a built-in niche along one wall. "You want to watch TV with your uncle?"

Jacob waved his fists in the air. Chase wondered whether the baby recognized his voice. What did he know about kids? Maybe he should buy one of those baby books so he'd know all about stuff like that. It wouldn't hurt. He continued flipping through the stations until he came to an NBA basketball game. The play-offs. How had he forgotten? With everything that had happened in the past few weeks, it was no wonder that a mere game would be pushed to the back of his mind. He loved basketball. His game. Would he lose out to Jacob's other uncles when they taught their nephew about football? Jacob could learn both.

Chase placed Jacob against him so it appeared that he was watching the TV. "You see those guys on there? They're playing basketball. Your dad taught me how to play. When you're old enough, I'm going to teach you how to play."

With the baby on his lap, Chase watched the game for over an hour. Everything was going great until Jacob started crying. Chase walked the baby as he'd seen Dori do. The crying didn't stop. Chase rocked the baby and rubbed his back. That didn't help. The kid couldn't be hungry. Dori had fed him right before she left.

Chase wrinkled his nose. "Well, kid, I think I've got you figured out. Let's take care of that diaper. We wouldn't want you to get diaper rash, especially if your aunt blamed me. We men have got to stick together. Right? Right."

Chase carried the wailing infant back to the nursery and took off the offending diaper. He did the baby wipes, the powder and was about to put on the new diaper when suddenly something wet and warm hit him in the face and went down the front of his shirt. He grabbed for a baby wipe and used it on his face. "Ugh, kid, is this how you repay your old uncle for not realizing you had a dirty diaper?"

Laughter made Chase look up.

Dori stood framed in the doorway, her hand covering her mouth. She stepped into the room. "What happened to you?"

"I think you know. Why didn't you warn me about this?"

"I thought you knew. You're a boy." She laughed again.

"You think this is funny, don't you?"

"How could you tell?" Still laughing, she came to stand next to him. "Do you need some help?"

Yeah, he needed help but not with the baby. He needed help remembering not to touch her. Her close proximity had him thinking about her lilting voice, her sweet smell, and her disarming laughter, not a messy baby. He had to remind himself that despite her seemingly friendly manner, she was still wary of him. He'd better keep his hands to himself. At this point, if he knew what was good for both of them, he'd leave. "Yeah, you can take over. I'll change my shirt again. My nephew and his aunt are making it difficult for me to keep my clothes dry today."

As he turned to leave the room, something soft hit the back of his head. He spun around just in time to see a decorative pillow from the nearby rocker land at his feet. Chase looked at Dori. "Your aim is good. I'll have to remember that."

After Chase had changed his shirt, he went back to the baby's room. When he saw that it was empty, he headed for the family room. Seated on the couch, Dori held Jacob. Standing nearby, a big burly man with a mustache and dark brown hair liberally sprinkled with gray was talking with her. Chase recognized Dori's dad from the family photo.

As Chase stepped through the doorway, Dori looked in his direction. Their gazes met. A blush rose in her cheeks. Quickly she looked away. What had she been thinking? Had she felt the same spark?

"Chase," Teresa said, coming from the kitchen. "I want you to meet my husband, Luis."

The large man walked around the coffee table. He grasped Chase's hand and shook his arm vigorously. "I am very glad to meet you. Your brother was like another son to me. My daughter tells me you'll be looking after Tyler's estate."

Thankfully, before the man crushed Chase's hand and his arm dropped off, Dori's mother patted her husband on the shoulder. "Dear, you don't have to pump his arm off."

Luis stepped aside, and the tiny woman, who seemed half the older man's size, took Chase's hand in hers. She patted his hand. "He's right. I didn't tell you how much we all cared for your brother."

Chase didn't know what to say. Tyler had adored this family as well, but Chase felt awkward, realizing these people knew his brother better than he did. "He cared very much for you, too."

Before anyone could make a response to Chase's statement, the doorbell rang.

Teresa started for the front door. "I'll get it. That must be everyone coming from church."

Chase stood glued to the spot where he stood. Everyone? What did she mean? He didn't have to wait long for an answer as a whole troop of people of all ages filed into the room and gathered around the couch where Dori still sat holding the baby. The smiling and laughing group oohed and aahed over Jacob. In the pandemonium, Chase felt left out, cheated of his time with his nephew.

When the initial hubbub died down, Dori looked at him and smiled. "Everyone, I want you to meet Chase Garrett. He's Tyler's brother."

Heads turned his way. Then a plump, gray-haired woman babbling in Spanish grabbed him around the waist and hugged him.

In a fog of uneasiness, Chase heard Dori's voice. "Grandma, please speak English."

"That's okay. I speak a little Spanish. I caught most of what she said." Gently extracting himself from the older woman's embrace, he dug deep into his memory of the Spanish he had learned for business. He wanted to thank Dori's grandmother and mention how proud she must be of her great-grandson. "*Gracias. Usted debe estar muy orgullosa de su biznieto.*"

Dori's grandmother smiled. "*Si*, I'm so very proud of that little one."

Then in a flurry of introductions, Chase met Dori's brothers and sister, whom he recognized from the photo, as well as aunts, uncles and cousins. All of Dori's brothers, with their dark hair and eyes, were the image of their father only with a slighter build. Even Natalia, Dori's sister, who shared the same dark coloring, was tall like her father. Dori seemed to be the only one who had taken after her petite mother. He didn't know how he would keep everyone straight. Amazingly, Jacob had fallen asleep in Dori's arms and didn't twitch a muscle in all the commotion.

Little by little, Chase felt excluded from the conversation. No one intentionally left him out, but he wasn't really a part of this family. He was an outsider. He'd even been an outsider in his own family. When he was twelve, his mother had dumped him on his father. His stepmother had ignored him, and his father had sent him far away to boarding school when he was fourteen. Nobody had wanted him.

Yet, Dori had needed him today to take charge. Now she didn't. She had the love and care of all these people. What could he possibly do for her now? Besides, that's not the question he should be asking himself. She wasn't his responsibility, but seeing that she had the means to take care of Jacob was. That was his job. Nothing more.

The touch of a hand on his arm brought Chase out of his reverie. He looked down. Teresa stood by his side. "It's a bit overwhelming, isn't it? All these people."

Chase smiled in spite of his feelings of trepidation. She obviously sensed his discomfort. "Yes."

She smiled in return. "And this isn't all of them. The food hasn't shown up yet."

"Why didn't you tell me you were having company?"

"Because I didn't know."

"These impromptu family gatherings happen all the time. Don't let all these people intimidate you." Teresa steered him toward the side of the room. "They just decided to come over after church. Most of them haven't had a chance to see Jacob for any length of time. Everything was so crazy with Marisa and Tyler dying so unexpectedly."

Before Chase could comment, the doorbell rang.

"That's the rest of the group. I'd better answer the door." Patting his arm, Teresa departed, calling over her shoulder. "Enjoy yourself. They don't bite."

While Chase stood off to the side, Teresa directed the newcomers into the kitchen where they set up a buffet along one of the counters. In a few minutes, Luis said a prayer of thanks, and people lined up to get food. Feeling alone in a crowd, Chase joined the line. After he filled his plate, he glanced around the room. Folks sat at the bar in the kitchen, at the kitchen table, or on the couch with their plates on the coffee table.

Where should he go?

"Looking for a place to eat?" Luis approached. "Come into the dining room with me."

"Sure." Chase followed him through the arched doorway.

Several others sat at the dining room table, including Dori and the baby. Luis sat leaving the chair next to Dori empty. Chase had no choice except to sit there. When he took that seat, she smiled. Was she warming up to him, or was she putting on a good face in front of the family?

There had been an unexpected camaraderie between them when she had teased him about changing Jacob's diaper. Would it continue? Only time would tell.

While he ate, the conversation buzzed around him. He listened, content not to contribute. Finally, Luis turned to him. "You remind me of Tyler the first time he encountered this group. He adjusted. You will, too." Luis gave a big belly laugh. "In fact, it took me awhile to get used to this crowd myself. These are just my in-laws. Wait till you meet my side of the family. You'll have a chance at the baby dedication for Jacob at our church. We'll expect you."

"You couldn't keep me away," Chase blurted, then wondered what he had agreed to do. The Davis household had been staid and quiet. Now he lived alone in a fancy high-rise condominium with security to keep people out. If he was going to be part of his nephew's life it meant being part of this big, boisterous and loving family. Could he learn to deal with the crowd, the noise? Yes. Anything for Jacob. "Where and when?"

"Two weeks. Sunday morning at eleven o'clock. Covenant Fellowship Church."

"I'll be there." Chase glanced at Dori to gauge her reaction. She just sat there rocking Jacob. Had she heard the conversation? If she had, was she pleased he would be there? He pushed the question away. He was getting irritated with himself for always wanting her approval. Right now he had Luis and Teresa's approval. What more did he need?

"I hear you work for your father," Luis said, interrupting Chase's thoughts.

Nodding, Chase cleared his throat. Where was this topic headed? His relationship with Warren had deteriorated in the past few weeks. "You could say I work for my father. I'm chief financial officer for W.T.D. Enterprises."

Luis clapped Chase on the back. "I like to see a son working for his father."

That's the last thing Chase had expected to hear in this house. After talking with Dori, he had the impression Warren Davis was the devil incarnate in this family's thinking. As if to punctuate the shock of Luis's statement, a crack of thunder sounded outside. Finally managing to speak, Chase said, "I find the job challenging."

"That's good. I have this nice printing business. Do you think any of my sons would work for me?" Luis slowly shook his head. "No. They all want to go and do their own thing. Maybe my grandsons will work for me one day."

Despite the ache in his heart, Chase smiled. Here was another father who had wanted his sons to work with him, but they had gone their own way. And yet, Luis hadn't alienated his sons as Warren had. What was the difference? Caring. Closeness. Concern. This loving family created envy deep inside Chase. Could he ever have something like this in his life, or would he always be on the edge of the family circle? "Maybe they will, but everyone has to make his own decisions."

"How true. How true." Luis nodded his head. "Why did you decide to work for your father?"

Surreptitiously, Chase looked at Dori. She was looking out the dining room window at the darkening sky that opened up with a typical late May thunderstorm. What did she think of this conversation? She probably hadn't been listening. He also stared out the window at the roiling black clouds as if he could find the answer there. Had he chosen the wrong path? Why *had* he gone to work for

Warren? Tyler had been the reason in the beginning. Eventually, trying to win his father's approval had been the reason. "I wanted to follow in my brother's footsteps. Unfortunately, about the time I came on the scene, Tyler and Warren had come to a disagreement they couldn't overcome. I don't want that to happen with me."

"And you shouldn't let it." Luis clapped him on the back again. "Fathers and sons should stick together."

That last statement crashed through Chase's brain like the thunder overhead. What a surprise! Maybe he hadn't taken the wrong path. "I suppose."

"Family's important, don't you agree?"

How could he respond? He couldn't explain to this man what it was like to spend the first twelve years of his life not knowing who his father was. Then spending the rest of his life trying to win his father's love and losing his brother's love in the process. Sometimes he wanted to explain, just like the day he had met Dori. But when the opportunity to explain emerged, he couldn't bring himself to say the words that opened up all that pain. "Yes, sir, but sometimes relationships can't be repaired."

Luis shook his head. "I disagree. I tried to convince Tyler of that."

"Weren't you offended by Warren's rejection of Marisa?"

"Not offended. Unhappy, but if Tyler had just stuck with it, Marisa would have won over her father-in-law in time, just like Tyler did with me. I wasn't pleased to have my beautiful daughter run off to Las Vegas to get married. Especially to a man who didn't honor God. Thank the Lord Marisa's faith helped Tyler change his life. But there were other things besides Marisa that caused the split. She was just the final straw."

"I was always under the impression that Marisa was the one and only reason." Chase looked at Dori for confirmation. She averted her eyes.

"On the surface, yes, but so many other things entered in. Tyler confided in me." Luis tapped the arm of the chair. "That's one of the reasons he named you executor. Marisa thought it was time for him to mend the rift. With the birth of his son, he recognized it, too."

"I wished he'd called me sooner."

"We all do."

Me more than anyone. The words stuck in his throat. Sorrow burrowed deep in his heart as Chase glanced at Dori. Did that *all* include her? She was involved in an animated conversation with a woman, maybe an aunt, at the end of the table and wasn't paying attention to what her father was saying.

"Don't let it get you down, son." Luis placed a hand on Chase's shoulder. "You have a big part in your nephew's life. You'll be the one link to the father he'll never know. As he grows up, you can share your memories of Tyler with him."

"I'll do my best," Chase said, then excusing himself from the table. He had to get away. Despite Luis's good intentions, the conversation was tearing Chase apart inside. The thought of all the years he'd missed with Tyler and the recent trouble with Warren placed a heavy burden on his heart. He had to look forward. Dwelling on the past would only make things seem bleaker. He had to concentrate on the happiness, not the gloom. As he took his plate into the kitchen, a man Chase recognized as one of Dori's brothers approached him.

The man extended his hand to Chase. "I'm Javier. I

know we met earlier, but I'm sure it's hard to remember who everyone is. Some of us guys are going upstairs. You're welcome to join us."

Shaking Javier's hand, Chase smiled, glad for the invitation. "Sure. What's upstairs?"

"You haven't been up to Tyler's den?"

"No, I've only been on the first floor."

"You've got to see this."

"Show me the way," Chase said, following Javier through the house to a back stairway near the laundry room.

At the top of the stairs, they emerged into a huge room. One wall contained built-in oak bookcases and cabinets on either side of a big-screen TV, twice as big as the one in the family room. Several other men were sitting on a burgundy leather sectional. They waved as Chase and Javier walked back to the bar at the opposite end of the room from the TV. Chase sat on one of four barstools covered in the same burgundy leather while Javier went behind the bar and opened a small refrigerator.

"You want one?" Javier pulled out a Dr. Pepper, then looked at Chase. "Or I can I get you something else." He indicated shelves full of glasses and numerous cans of soft drinks.

"That's fine."

Javier stepped around the bar, handed Chase a glass full of ice along with the can of Dr. Pepper. Then he pointed to the pool table sitting near a wall of windows that looked out on the swimming pool. "Do you play pool?"

"Not in a long time," Chase said, remembering the last time he had shot pool during a ski trip they had taken the Christmas before Tyler married Marisa.

"Let's see what you remember." Javier pulled a couple of cue sticks from the rack on the wall.

Chase chalked the end of his cue stick. "I'm out of practice."

"That's what Tyler said when we played for the first time. Let's see how you play. You could be like your brother," Javier said with a laugh. "Tyler tried to hustle me when we played."

Chase smiled, thinking about all the things he'd done with his brother. "Tyler taught me everything I know."

"Then you ought to be pretty good. Rack 'em up."

After several games, Chase discovered Javier was better at pool than Tyler ever was. When they finished, they joined the others, who were watching another basketball play-off game.

Chase welcomed the camaraderie of the other men. They had accepted him without question. He speculated as to whether they thought he was wrong for having disassociated himself from Tyler. Could he fit into this family? Would they include him on a regular basis? This chance to play pool and watch the game with the guys brought Chase a sense of belonging. At the same time it brought him a mountain of regret that he hadn't done these things with Tyler when he'd had the chance. When they talked about Tyler and things he had said or done that Chase didn't know, the regret became Mount Everest.

Chapter Five

Dori watched Oscar the Grouch fly across the family room. Chase caught it and returned it to its rightful owner, her three-year-old niece, Laura. A flirt at three. Coyly, she smiled at him. He tickled her in the ribs, and she ran off laughing with the green monster tucked under her arm.

How appropriate for the green monster to show his face. Jealousy. Dori tamped it down. She didn't like herself much today since they had come back from the dedication ceremony for Jacob. Every relative she had ever known was in Tyler's house, and they all loved Chase. He wasn't part of this family, but he might as well be. Why was she the only one who still had doubts about his intentions? Had she let her bad experiences with Ramon and Scott color her judgment too much?

Yet, for all her distrust, every time he looked her way, her heart beat a little faster.

After lunch, Chase had discarded his jacket and tie and rolled up his shirtsleeves past his elbows. His hair was di-sheveled from a recent round of roughhousing with three of her nephews. Even when his hair was combed, he had this funny little cowlick right in front. It stuck up in an endearing way that made her want to comb it back into place. Breathtaking. Heartthrob. Too good to be true. The thoughts pumped through her brain like the pounding of her pulse.

She wasn't the only female under his spell. He charmed her mother and her sisters-in-law. They teased Dori, saying she should grab Chase before he got away. That's the last thing she wanted to do. He was even a big hit with her brothers, taking them to Rangers baseball games, where they sat in the W.T.D. Enterprises luxury box. Warren probably didn't know. Worst of all, her father was treating him like a son.

When she saw him in the family circle, she couldn't forget how these same people had welcomed Scott. He had worked his way into their hearts and then betrayed them, especially Tyler. Chase was doing the same thing. She had no doubt he was up to no good when he had told her he intended to sell Tyler's company. He wanted to get rid of his brother's legacy. Couldn't they see what he was doing?

"Is that Tyler's brother?" Dori turned to see her Aunt Rosalia leaning over the couch to talk with her.

"Yes, that's Chase."

"Oh, isn't he a handsome one. Just like his brother." Aunt Rosalia chuckled and patted Dori on the arm. "He would be a good one for you, Dori."

"Probably not. I think he has a girlfriend," Dori said, hoping to send Aunt Rosalia to meddle in someone else's love life, but wondering whether he actually did have a girlfriend.

"Too bad." She waddled away to talk with someone else.

Dori sat for a while longer watching relatives and

friends of the family mingle on this joyous occasion. Despite the overriding happiness of the event, Marisa and Tyler's absence dampened the spirit, at least in Dori's mind. Maybe she was letting all this stuff with Chase take away her enjoyment. But she couldn't shake the specter of Scott. She had brought a viper into their family, and he had struck with poisonous venom. Could it be happening again? Would anyone listen to her warning if she spoke out against Chase? At this point, she figured any warnings would fall on deaf ears, but she would keep a vigil, ready to come to the rescue if he made a wrong move.

Dori got up from the couch and went outside, joining two of her sisters-in-law as they sat by the pool. Several of their children cavorted in the pool like a school of porpoises.

"Who's got Jacob?" Patti, her brother Javier's wife, asked.

"I think his great-grandma Morales." Dori looked back into the house through the windows behind her. "I can't be sure. He's been passed around so much today because everyone wants to hold him. I can't believe how good he's been. All these people and he's loving it."

"He loves the attention," Patti said. "He takes after Marisa."

"I think you're right." Dori thought about Marisa, the life of every party. Sometimes, the hurting got better, but on a day like today, the sorrow seeped deep inside and settled like a large stone in the middle of her heart. How long before the pain went away? Getting up, Dori waved. "I'm going back inside. It's too warm to be out here in this dress."

"We've already changed our clothes. Why didn't you?" Patti asked, raising her eyebrows. "Trying to impress Uncle Hunk?"

Dori put her hands on her hips. "If you don't watch it, Patti, you're going to wind up in the pool with your children."

Patti threw her head back and laughed. "Easy now. We're just having a little fun."

"Not at my expense. Please. I'm going to change. Then I won't impress anyone." Walking around the pool, Dori used the side door to slip into the master suite.

As she walked through the room she could almost feel Marisa and Tyler's presence. At Chase's insistence, she had gone through all of their things and cleared out the drawers and closets, but this was still their room. She still preferred to sleep in the twin bed in the nursery. She convinced herself it was better for getting up in the middle of the night to tend to the baby if he awakened even though he had been sleeping through the night for the past week.

After changing from the dress she had worn to church, she put on a pair of blue knit shorts and a floral-print cotton T-shirt. As she left the room in search of Jacob, her mother approached through the living room. She carried a very fretful infant.

"I've been looking all over for you," her mother said as she hurried to Dori's side.

"Is something wrong?"

"Not really. I thought he might be hungry."

"I'll warm a bottle." Dori took the baby and headed for the kitchen.

"I can feed him if you like," her mother said, following close behind.

Shaking her head, Dori eased her way through the throng of relatives who stood talking in the kitchen. "No, you go on. I enjoy this time with him."

After Dori had warmed the bottle, she made her way to

the bedroom and sat in the rocker. She treasured this peaceful time with Jacob. With *her* baby. Maybe her unrest today came from everyone's reminders that this child was Marisa and Tyler's when she had come to think of him as her own. She wanted to make that a reality. But was she wrong to think about Jacob in that way? She wasn't trying to wipe out Marisa and Tyler's memory. She had to protect this child and make sure he knew she loved him enough to make him her son. She had set in motion her plan to accomplish that task.

In her quest to adopt Jacob, she worried about the past that might come back to haunt her. Could her previous mental health problems become an issue? With God's help, that aspect of her life was under control. Marisa was one of the few people who knew about those problems, and she had believed Dori would make a good guardian. So surely her adopting Jacob was something Marisa would have championed. Closing her eyes, she rocked back and forth. *Please, Lord, give me the wisdom to make wise decisions in this matter.* While she prayed, she heard the click of the doorknob. Her eyes fluttered open.

Chase stood in the doorway. "I'm sorry. I should've knocked. I'll come back later."

"It's okay." She continued to rock as the baby greedily drank from the bottle. "Did you want something?"

Chase shifted from foot to foot as he talked. "I was just looking for Jacob. Your dad wants to make his football presentation, so he sent me to find the baby."

"Tell Dad we'll be out in a little while."

"Okay," Chase replied, backing through the doorway. "After everyone leaves, will you have some time to talk? I need to go over some stuff with you."

"Natalia's spending the night, but if it's not too late, we can talk."

"That's fine." Turning on his heel, he closed the door behind him.

Half an hour later, Dori took Jacob into the family room. When her father saw her, he came to her side. "There you are. We want to do this before everyone leaves."

"Okay, the floor's yours, Dad. Do your thing." Dori handed Jacob to her father.

He balanced the baby in his large capable hands. He looked proudly at his grandson. Dori's heart warmed at the image. While family and friends gathered around, Luis produced a football and a tiny Dallas Cowboys jersey from behind the raised snack bar separating the kitchen and family room.

"May you be a Cowboys' fan in the tradition of the Morales family." Luis did his best to tuck the football that was almost as big as Jacob under his arm.

While everyone applauded, Chase stepped up beside Luis. "As long as we're making presentations here, I thought I'd like to make one of my own." He picked up a colorful bag from the floor near the snack bar and pulled out a basketball and a Mavericks jersey. "I think he should be a Mavs fan, too."

Spontaneous applause and laughter radiated from the group. With a nod, Luis laughed hardest of all. "That sounds good to me. A boy can't go wrong with that."

Dori stood off to the side, taking in the way Chase had insinuated himself into the family tradition. She'd made the mistake of telling Chase about her father's plan to give his grandson a football. Was she the only one who felt Chase was intruding, overstepping his bounds?

"I was going to get him a bat and Rangers jersey, a hockey stick and Stars jersey, too, but I decided to save that for Christmas." Chase put the ball and jersey back in the bag and handed it to Dori. "I'll let you take care of these."

Taking the bag, Dori read the entreaty in his eyes that said, "Don't shut me out." Something in her wanted to deliver that request, but at what cost to this family? "Sure."

For the rest of the day, Dori waited in nervous anticipation for everyone to leave. What did Chase want to tell her? Maybe he had decided against selling Tyler's company after all. That was a foolish hope. He had been adamant about his decision. Besides the uncertainty of what he wanted to tell her, the emotions of the day had played havoc with her mind. The prospect of the coming conversation had her thoughts wired. How could she deal with Chase when he made her feelings hopscotch from fear to loathing to something bordering on an attraction she didn't want to admit?

Later as she saw her parents out and closed the door behind them, the final click of the latch sounded like a warning in her head. Now she had to face Chase and his "stuff."

She went to the nursery, tiptoed over to the crib and peeked in at her sleeping baby. Tightness flooded her chest at the sight of him. Reaching out, she gently rubbed her finger across his cheek, then the tuft of soft dark hair that always managed to stick straight up on his head.

She'd do anything to make this child legally hers.

Anything.

Turning from the crib, she ran into Chase. She let out a startled gasp, and he grabbed her shoulders to steady her. Heat radiated from his touch. Her heart raced as she looked into his eyes. Her pulse pounded in her head, and her breath caught in her throat. She couldn't speak. The stone-like feeling that had sat in her heart earlier today dropped down into her solar plexus, but this time it didn't have anything to do with sorrow. Would she ever find her equilibrium with him?

"Are you all right?" he whispered.

She nodded and scurried from his grasp and out of the room. She wanted to get away from Chase. Her crazy emotions betrayed her every time he was near. She sat down on the chair in the living room, the scene of their first meeting in this house.

"I didn't mean to startle you," he said, sitting on the end of the couch closest to her chair.

"That's okay. I just didn't want to wake Jacob. He was sleeping so peacefully."

"He should. He had a big day. Where's Natalia?"

"She's on the phone with her boyfriend, Manny."

"Then you have time to talk now?" He leaned his elbow on the arm of the couch and looked at her, his gaze so intent she had to look away for fear he'd read something in her eyes she didn't want him to see. Like how much his presence disturbed her. Her insides churned.

When she finally felt under control, Dori looked at him. "Sure. What did you want to tell me?"

Sitting forward, he returned her gaze. "First I wanted to thank you for letting me share this day with your family. It meant a lot to me."

"You don't need to thank me. Jacob's your nephew. You had a right to be here." Lowering her gaze, she picked at a loose thread on her shorts.

Why did he have to be so nice and make her feel like a heel for wishing he would just go away? Her life would be less complicated if he weren't around. She wished he would get to the real point of this conversation, but she didn't want to sound abrupt by asking him what he wanted again.

He made no response. Looking away, he sat there fiddling with the decorative coasters sitting on the end table. The ticking of the grandfather clock in the corner of the living room seemed loud in the quiet. She waited, but still he said nothing.

Finally, he looked up. "I want to ask you something. Have you ever considered giving the baby a nickname?"

Where was this leading? "I don't know. What did you have in mind?"

"I was thinking of calling him JT. What do you think?"

"JT?" Wrinkling her nose, she shrugged. "What would Tyler want? Did he ever have a nickname?"

"Nothing that had to do with Tyler. That's all he was ever called around the Davis household, but at college his nickname was Torpedo."

"Why?"

"He never would explain it to me. It's just something his fraternity brothers called him. And something tells me you probably wouldn't want to know," he said with a laugh.

"So why do you want to give the baby a nickname?"

"Maybe it's just a hang-up of mine. I know a lot of people name their boys Jacob these days. But whenever I think of Jacob, I think of an old guy with a beard."

Dori couldn't help giggling. "Images from Sunday school?"

"Well, I didn't go to Sunday school, but maybe old Bible pictures are responsible for that image." He leaned back, obviously more relaxed than when they had first started talking.

Dori sat for a moment, realizing the amicable nature of their conversation. It reminded her of the night she had teased him about changing the baby's diaper. If they could just keep this tenor to their relationship, maybe it wouldn't be so bad. "No, it's not just your hang-up. That crossed my mind, too."

"So should we give JT a try?"

"JT Davis." Dori let the name roll off her tongue, then smiled. "You know I think I heard my dad call the baby JT once."

"Then we should be in pretty good company."

"Yeah. Is that all you wanted to talk about? The baby's name?"

Chase shook his head. "No. I've got some figures I want to show you. I could tell you weren't thrilled I intend to sell Tyler's company, so I wanted to show you why it's in JT's best interest. How did that sound?"

"Selling the company or calling the baby JT?"

"The name."

"Not bad. I could get used to it," she said, thinking how getting used to Chase was much more of a challenge.

"Good," he said, standing. "Let's go back to the study so I can show you my plans."

Dori followed him. He flipped on the overhead light, then picked up the chair from the corner of the room and set it behind the desk next to the swivel chair. Sitting in the swivel chair, he indicated she should sit in the other one. As she sat, he spread several files out on the desk. "Here's what I've got."

Dori reluctantly looked where his finger pointed. He started going through the assets and liabilities of the company, explaining this and that. All she could think about was how strong and virile his hands looked against the white paper. She closed her eyes. Why did these thoughts keep popping into her head? Had it been too long since she'd been on a date? That was it. She'd been out of circulation too long. It was time to remedy that situation.

"Dori, are you listening?"

She looked into his eyes. She couldn't hide the blush she felt rising in her cheeks. She grimaced. "I'm sorry. It's been a long day."

"Would it be better if I did this another time?"

Shaking her head, she picked up one of the folders and held it in front of her. "You can go over this stuff all night with me, and it'll never change my mind. To you this company is just a bunch of numbers. To me, it's Tyler's legacy to his son. Tyler put his life into it. How can you sell that?"

Chase placed his elbows on the table and steepled his hands in front of his mouth. He appeared to be thinking over what she had said. Would it make a difference, or was he so removed from his brother's life that he didn't see all that had gone into the building of that company?

Finally, he said, "You're right. I realize all the work that went into making Tyler's business, but in the end, it's just a thing. It's not Tyler. Keeping this company for JT won't bring his father back. The memories of Tyler are his legacy, not some company with his name on it."

Dori picked up a pencil and tapped the eraser on the desk. She hated to admit Chase was right. And hadn't she just been thinking the same thing about adopting the baby? That becoming his mother could erase Marisa's memory. But Dori knew she wouldn't let that happen, but she wasn't sure about Chase's intentions. "I still don't see why you have to sell it. You said things were going okay."

"Yes, they are, but there are estate taxes to pay. That will amount to a substantial sum." Chase opened up another folder. "Do you see this?"

Picking up the folder, Dori glanced through the papers inside. "You already have an offer?"

Chase nodded. "They came to me. I didn't go looking. After I checked out the numbers, I decided it's an excellent offer. We should take it now while things are going well."

"Why? Do you think it will change?"

Chase shrugged. "Who knows? Right now the company is doing great, but I don't know how well this guy who worked under Tyler will do. Can he run it as well as Tyler did?"

"Tyler hired him."

"Yeah, to be second in command. That doesn't mean he can run the whole show." Chase swiveled the chair in order to face her. "What if I just left the company as is, and in a year's time things went downhill? Then I couldn't sell it for nearly this price. Who loses? Me? No. JT does. I'm doing this for him. I can take the money I get from this sale and make more by investing it somewhere else."

She was losing this argument. Why did she feel the necessity of opposing Chase? The trust issue? "I think you're doing it for yourself."

Chase frowned. "How? None of this will be mine."

"Because someday, instead of showing JT the company his dad built, you can say, 'See the portfolio your uncle Chase built.'"

"You think I'm trying to wipe out Tyler's memory by selling?" Chase asked as the muscle worked in his jaw.

"Maybe." Feeling the need to put some distance between her and Chase, Dori got up and walked over to the built-in bookcases taking up one wall of the study. She picked up a book and thumbed through it, then waved it at him. "Are you going to get rid of these, too? You're slowly getting rid of everything that had anything to do with Tyler or Marisa. Next I'll find out you've put this house up for sale."

Shoving the chair back from the desk, Chase stood and stepped toward her. "Dori," he said, taking the book from her and laying it on the shelf, "what makes you think I'm trying to get rid of their memories?"

Dori couldn't think. Swallowing a lump in her throat, she took a deep breath and wished she could calm her racing heartbeat. He shouldn't have this kind of effect on her. He couldn't be trusted. "We've already cleaned out the closets and drawers and gotten rid of all of their things. Why their company?"

Chase grimaced. "How can I convince you I'm only doing what I think is in the best interest of JT? I want him to know his parents. He should know everything about them. But things aren't them. Can't you get that?"

"But some things are what memories are made of. You can't get rid of them all."

"I haven't." Chase sighed. "You remember that bag of old sweatshirts?"

Dori nodded. "Yes, you saved junk."

"Not junk. Memories."

"But isn't Tyler's company a memory, too?"

"Yes. But by the time JT is old enough to appreciate it, there won't be any part of Tyler or Marisa left in that company. But there will be memories in things like photos, videos, cards, and letters. Like the stuff your grandfather saved. Those are memories. And some memories are only up here." Chase reached out and gently tapped the top of her head. "Besides, we can't hang on to the past."

Closing her eyes, Dori slumped against the bookcase. Yes, some memories were only in one's mind. Like the memories she had of Chase and his interaction with her family today. She remembered how her father had accepted Chase more eagerly than he had accepted Tyler. Her father treated him like some kind of hero just because he could read a balance sheet. Just because he had taken charge of his dead brother's affairs. But he was no hero in her mind. He was like Scott, trying to destroy Tyler's company. Scott had tried to destroy it from within. Chase was doing it from without.

Tears stung the backs of her eyelids. She squeezed them tight, and a tear trickled down her cheek. She quickly wiped it away. When she opened her eyes, Chase was staring down at her. His scrutiny made the blood pound in her brain, leaving her light-headed. She wanted to dash from the room and leave Chase and all the conflicting emotions behind, but her feet felt glued to the floor.

"Dori, please don't cry." He stepped closer and placed a hand on her arm as if he knew she was ready to run away.

"I'm okay." She sniffled as she struggled to ignore how his touch made her weak-kneed. "I know you think this is the best thing to do, but it hurts to see Tyler's company go to someone else. It's like losing Tyler and Marisa all over again. Do you understand?"

"Not completely." Chase shook his head. "I was just hoping you'd give your approval to what I do. I want us to come to an understanding. I *have* JT's interest at heart."

"I want to believe that, but I keep remembering how you turned away from Tyler and Marisa."

With his hand at the back of his neck, he slowly shook his head as though he was trying to rid himself of her accusatory words. "Can we let go of the past, because I can't undo it. You've got to trust me."

Dori took a deep breath, willing herself to be calm. There was the crux of the problem. She didn't trust him. She didn't trust herself when he was around. "I'm sure you've figured out by now I'm not very excited about this arrangement. I'm used to taking care of my own affairs."

"Maybe that's the problem. We both are." Sighing heavily, he lowered his head and ran his hand through his hair. "What do you want from me?"

Tension crackled between them. It wasn't over the past, but the present. She drew in a shaky breath. Her pulse pounded in double time. Her gaze fell on his mouth. The only thing that came to mind. A kiss. Her body's betrayal frightened her, but she shook the thought away, steeling herself against anymore treacherous notions.

"Nothing. Absolutely nothing."

Chapter Six

Chase gazed into Dori's brown eyes. Moments before they had swum with tears. Now they sparked with opposition. Or was it something else? The attraction between them had been there from the first time he'd seen her in Brady's office. But Chase soon recognized she didn't like him much because of his estrangement from Tyler. From that moment on, Chase's goal was just to have her not hate him.

Then he'd met the Morales family. They had embraced him and made him feel welcome, but not Dori. She still held back. He loved his nephew. He loved this family. He wanted them to be his family, too. Now it was all tied together. Wanting to care for JT, wanting a family, wanting Dori. But she wanted nothing from him.

The need to kiss away the frown on her lips just about overcame his common sense. If he kissed her now, he was sure she'd slap his face. Letting sanity reign, he walked to the other side of the room. "All right, Dori, if that's the way you want it."

She opened her mouth as if she was going to say something, then closed it. Her lips painted a grim line across her face. She sidled away and walked toward the door. As Chase went back to the desk to sit down, she stopped in the doorway and turned. "You should know I intend to adopt JT."

The statement hit Chase like a bomb. As the implications exploded in his head, he jumped from the chair and strode across the room. Gently grabbing her arm, he pulled her to a stop. "When did you decide this?"

"A couple of weeks ago," she said, extricating herself from his hold.

"Do you think that's a good idea?"

"Why wouldn't it be? I'm a good mother."

"I didn't say you weren't. I was just thinking…" He paused. What *was* he thinking? He didn't know, but something about the idea of Dori's adopting JT didn't set right with him.

"Thinking that'll take away your power?" she finished for him.

Chase rubbed his forehead. "I don't have any power, at least not with how this child is raised. I have power over the money, and you don't want anything to do with that." This whole thing was giving him a headache. "Are you sure you want to be a single mother?"

"That's what bothers you?" Dori laughed half-heartedly. "What do you think I am now? I might as well make it legal."

Chase gazed at her. "I can't argue with that. If you're sure that's what you want, you should do it."

Tucking her hair behind her ear, she looked at him and blinked her eyes as if she didn't believe what she had heard. "I'm sure. I've already talked with Brady Houston about it. He's going to start drawing up the papers."

"Good."

"You don't care?"

Chase wished he could show her how much he cared. About JT. About her. The need to take her in his arms, hold her, and kiss her until she couldn't think of anything but him nearly overrode propriety. Why had he let this happen when he had told himself all along he'd be crazy to care? "I care. I want both JT and you to be happy. I'll do my best to help you. I won't ever stand in your way."

"Thanks," she said softly. Her smile portrayed her relief. "That makes me feel so much better."

"Me, too." He shoved his hands in his pockets to keep himself from touching her. He didn't want to do anything to destroy their fragile peace. "Do you mind if I stay and work?"

"No, as long as you don't mind letting yourself out and setting the alarm. I'm really tired. I'm going to feed JT, then go to bed." She touched his arm. "Do you know the code?"

"Six, five, six, seven?" He tried to ignore the way her touch tied his insides into knots.

"Yeah, that's it." She turned to go, then suddenly stopped and turned back to him. "Thanks again. Good night," she said, standing on her tiptoes and planting a kiss on his cheek. Then just as abruptly, she departed.

Chase stood there, watching her go. Touching his cheek where she had kissed him, he wondered what he was supposed to think of that. She had been almost belligerent during their discussion. Then he had agreed with her idea of adoption, and like magic, he had seen a trace of the Dori he had watched interact with her family. She leaned on them for support. He wanted her to look at him that way. That's all he wanted for now. This was a start. He could be her friend. Maybe he should have told her he cared before now. But he was sure she had no idea how much he cared. She'd probably run the other way if she knew.

He went back into the study and sat down at the desk. The muffled sound of female voices filtered into the study through the bedroom. Dori must be talking with Natalia. Today, when he had seen the two sisters together, he was reminded how he had pushed his own brother away. Picking up folders and spreading them in front of him, he vowed never to let that happen with JT. He attempted to focus on the numbers regarding the sale of Tyler's company. The numbers swam around in his head. Putting his elbow on the desk, he rubbed his forehead. How could he concentrate on figures when the only figure he saw was Dori's?

Looking up from the maze of papers, he made the mistake of looking at Tyler and Marisa's wedding picture. It didn't take much for Chase's mind to imagine Dori and him in the picture instead of Tyler and Marisa. Chase shook his head. His mind was playing tricks on him now. Hoping to send his thoughts in another direction, he turned on the computer to check stock quotes for the week. He had to get his head on straight, or he would never get any work done.

Getting online and checking stocks kept him busy for a long while and kept his mind from roaming into fruitless territory. With supreme effort he concentrated on the task at hand. He wanted to get a good price and at the same time protect the jobs and livelihood of the people who worked there. Too often when a company was sold, good people were let go. He didn't want that to happen. An hour later, he closed the folder, satisfied that he would be ready for that meeting.

Pushing back the chair, he raised his arms over his head and stretched. He brought his arms down and laced his hands behind his head. As soon as he relaxed, Dori's image filled his mind. Every time his mind wasn't occupied with work, he was thinking about her. What kind of hold did the Morales women have over the Davis men? Marisa had enchanted Tyler, and now Dori had Chase under her spell. Well, technically he wasn't a Davis, but he would be if his father had ever given him his rightful name. Would Dori's adopting JT change his name? Chase wasn't sure about the legal implications.

Was that what bothered him about Dori's plan to adopt JT? No. What bothered him was her being a single mother. Life hadn't been easy for his single mother. She just got too tired of it all. Thinking about her, Chase tamped down the misery her memory gave him. Loretta Garrett had been a tall blonde. Her ambition to be a movie star got in the way of her being a good mother. So she had dumped him on his father.

Would being a single mother someday become too much for Dori? Did she plan to go back to work? What were her ambitions? Could he talk to her about it without ruining the progress he'd made with her tonight? What would happen if she ever married? How could he ever compete with her husband for time with JT? The questions swirled in his mind like the mobile over JT's crib. They made him dizzy with frustration.

Chase didn't want to think about any of it, but his mind overflowed with grief, anger and pain. He had held the tears in too long. At twelve, left in a strange household with a father he didn't know, he had been afraid to cry. As an adult, he had refused to cry because real men didn't do that. But he ached inside.

Folding his arms across each other on the desk, he put his head down on them and let the tears come. He cried for the loss of his mother. He cried over the loss of Tyler, his father's betrayal, and the thought of JT growing up under the influence of another man.

The dam had finally broken.

When Chase awoke the next morning, his head hurt and his neck ached. Sitting up, he looked around. Bright light streamed in through the arched window to his right. Stretching, he stood up, then rubbed his hands over his face. The abrasive stubble beneath the palms of his hands told him he must look a wreck. He glanced at his watch. Six o'clock. Was Dori awake? What would she say about his falling asleep in the study?

Maybe he could sneak out, and she would never know the difference. But what if she knew he'd been here all night? Then she'd think he was rude. It didn't make a difference. She thought he was a barbarian anyway. Why was he afraid to face a tiny woman who probably didn't weigh much more than one hundred pounds soaking wet? The answer: she had him tied in emotional knots.

Releasing a slow breath, he went over to the desk and picked up his folders. He tossed them in his briefcase. As he made his way toward the front of the house, he saw the nursery door closed. Dori wasn't up. The quiet house told him Natalia was asleep as well. As he approached the front door, he noticed the little red light shining on the keypad for the alarm. The alarm was set. So sometime in the night, Dori or Natalia had set it. In order to leave the house, he would have to put in the alarm code. The beeping sound could wake them. He didn't want to do that because Dori was probably tired from getting up with JT during the night.

Chase decided to wait until he knew she was awake before making an attempt to leave the house. He returned to the study and began looking through the drawers in Tyler's desk for the combination to the safe. Chase discovered files for the hard copies of things he had already seen on the computer. He found files for insurance, health benefits, bank statements and operating instructions for everything from refrigerators to the pool heater. Opening a second drawer, he saw a leather-bound Bible and picked it up. Tyler's name was written in gold script letters in the lower right-hand corner. A dozen paper markers stuck out of the top.

Chase held the Bible in his hands. What might he learn about Tyler from this book? Carefully, Chase opened the cover. Topics with scriptures listed below them filled the originally blank sheets at the front of the Bible. He perused the topics. Love, forgiveness, truth, wisdom, joy, faith and grace were just a few. Turning to the next page, he read it. "Presented to my loving husband, Tyler, by Marisa with all my love. May God bless you always." Chase rubbed his hand over the words as if somehow the love that radiated from the page could somehow touch him. He wanted what Tyler had had.

A loving family.

Chase had a Bible that sat on a shelf in his condo. He couldn't remember the last time he had opened it. He couldn't remember the last time he had truly prayed. He had gone through the motions at church from time to time, but a real personal involvement with God hadn't existed. Maybe that's why he had been afraid that Tyler might preach that day when he said he'd become a Christian.

Chase let the Bible fall open to one of the markers. He studied the page. Psalm 133:1 was underlined. He read it aloud. "How good and pleasant it is when brothers live together in unity."

Quickly, he turned to the next marker and found an underlined passage in Proverbs. The next marker indicated two verses in the fifth chapter of Matthew, and he found another in Matthew in the sixth chapter. The following marker took him to the book of Colossians. He read the underlined scriptures. All of them spoke of brothers and forgiveness. He rested his elbow on the desk and put his hand to his forehead. Closing his eyes, he let the significance of these passages roll through his mind. Tyler must have been reading these before he came to see Chase. These verses had surely prompted Tyler to seek reconciliation with his brother. Regret inundated Chase knowing that although he and Tyler had made amends, they never had the chance to be with each other again.

With a heavy sigh Chase opened his eyes, and he noticed one last marker. Turning to it, he found the fourth chapter of I John. Again, Chase read the underlined verses aloud. "We love because he first loved us. If anyone says, 'I love God,' yet hates his brother, he is a liar. For anyone who does not love his brother, whom he has seen, cannot love God, whom he has not seen. And he has given us this command: Whoever loves God must also love his brother."

Chase closed his eyes again. He prayed silently that he would do his best in this job as executor and trustee and that somehow he could get Dori on his side. And he prayed that God would take away the ache in his heart and help him understand why Tyler had to die before their reconciliation was complete.

When Chase finished praying, he opened his briefcase and carefully placed the Bible inside. It was a connection with Tyler, and Chase wanted to study it further at home. He glanced at his watch. An hour had passed. He decided to see if Dori was awake. When he approached the nursery, the doorway stood open. That meant Dori was up. Wanting to see if JT was still in his crib, he stepped into the room. The crib was empty, and Dori's bed was unmade. What would she say when she found out he was still here?

As he made his way toward the front door, the smell of brewing coffee wafted his way from the kitchen. How would she greet him if he went back there? The need to talk with her again about her plans to adopt JT played across Chase's mind, but he didn't want to upset her. He'd already done that once, and he didn't want to have a repeat performance.

Chase opened the front door, and the alarm set off a beep. He quickly punched in the code. At the same time, he heard Dori's voice. "Trying to sneak away without saying good bye?"

He turned, steeling himself against the emotional impact of seeing her disapproving gaze. Instead, she stood there smiling. She looked almost delighted to see him. "No, I was just taking my briefcase to the car."

She leaned on the doorframe as he started down the front walk. "When you're finished come back to the kitchen," she called after him. "You can have some breakfast if you want."

"I'll be back in a minute." He opened his car and threw the case on the front seat. Closing the door, he caught his reflection in the car window. His hair was sticking up in at least a dozen different directions. Hoping to find a comb somewhere in the car, he opened it again. His search was futile. His attempt to comb it with his fingers only made it worse. What difference did it make? She had already seen him in this state, and she had smiled. Maybe that's why.

When he came into the kitchen, Dori was standing behind the snack bar cutting up honeydew melon. Natalia stood nearby with a cup of coffee in her hand, her eyes twinkling. She appeared to hide a smile as she took a sip of her coffee. "Good morning, Chase."

"Good morning," he replied as he wondered whether she was smiling about his disheveled appearance.

"Did you sleep well?" Dori asked.

"What do you think?" he asked, rubbing his neck. "My neck is stiff, and my back's sore."

She continued to work, not looking at him while she talked. "I thought about that when I saw you sleeping in there. I can't believe you slept like that all night."

Chase sat on one of the stools at the snack bar. "When did you realize I was there?"

"About three-thirty, when JT woke me and wouldn't go back to sleep. I saw the light and went to turn it off." Dori set the plate of sliced melon on the counter. "When I saw you, I didn't know what to do with you. So I let you sleep."

Chase thought about how foolish he felt after falling asleep in the study, but he felt so much better this morning, despite his stiff neck. "Speaking of JT, where is he?"

"In his swing." Dori pointed to a spot near the windows in the eating area of the kitchen. "He likes to sit in there in the mornings and look out the window after he's been fed. Sometimes, he falls asleep."

"Do you care if I get him out?" Chase asked, getting up and walking over to the swing.

"No. Do you want some coffee or juice?"

"Coffee." Chase picked up the baby and held him up in the air with his arms extended. JT kicked his legs and waved his arms. "Did you keep your aunt awake last night? You've got to quit doing that. She needs her beauty sleep."

"Thanks." Dori set a cup of coffee on the table.

"I meant that in the kindest possible way."

"I'm sure you did." Laughing, Dori sat down in the chair closest to the swing. "I was going to warn you about holding him up in the air like that right after he's eaten, but after that remark about beauty sleep, I'm not sure I should."

"You mean I shouldn't hold him like this?"

"Not unless you want a face full of something warm, wet and smelly," she replied with a laugh. "Why do men pick up babies and hold them up that way? My dad and brothers do that, too."

"Must be a male thing." Chase lowered JT and placed him back in his swing. "Have they ever gotten a face full?"

"Javier did once with one of his own kids," Natalia said as she put the coffee cup on the table and helped herself to a piece of melon. "Gotta run. Don't wanna be late for my first day of work. I'll stop by later."

Chase pulled out the chair opposite Dori and sat down as they said goodbye to Natalia. Taking one of the bowls on the table and pouring himself some cereal, he thought about the enjoyment of having someone to share breakfast with. He liked having someone to talk to in the mornings. In his condo the only companionship he had was the morning news anchor on TV. Being with Dori like this made him wish this were something he could do every morning. What would it be like to share his life with a woman who loved him? He shook the thought away. His thoughts were on a one-way track to disaster if he didn't change their direction. His mind was too far ahead of reality. First, he had to make her his friend. And the way things were going that would be no easy task.

"When do you have to go to work?" Her question startled him from his thoughts.

"I'm not going to work today. I took vacation time this week, because I need the time to tie up all the loose ends with the estate." He watched the curiosity reflected in her eyes as he ate a spoonful of cereal.

"If you were taking vacation time, why did you stay and work late last night?"

"I have a meeting this morning at eleven to finalize the details on the sale of Tyler's company. I wanted to get everything in order." Chase held his breath while he waited for Dori to berate him for selling the company.

Staring at him, she put her elbows on the table. "I hope things go well. I think you're doing the right thing."

"Thanks," Chase replied, surprised by her acquiescence. He had been in enough negotiating situations to know her body language didn't quite match the civility of her words. But maybe it was a start in making them friends rather than enemies. He wasn't going to mention her change of heart and ruin the whole thing.

This morning she was certainly amiable. Despite his reservations, agreeing to her idea to adopt JT had been a step in the right direction. Taking a swig of coffee, he wondered how he could talk to her about the adoption without making her angry.

"Do you know when the sale will be final?"

"No," Chase said, shaking his head. "The other party will want to go over all the books. It may take several months before the signatures are on the dotted line. I've been involved in this kind of thing many times, and you never know what will happen. Sometimes the whole thing falls through."

"Do you think this one will?" she asked, looking at him speculatively.

Chase shrugged. "Are you hoping?"

"I prayed about it last night, and I've decided not to worry. I'm going to leave it in God's hands. He knows what should happen with Tyler's company."

"That's a good way to think about it. Leave it in God's hands." Hoping to change the subject before things deteriorated, he said, "I wanted to spend some time with JT this week since I'm on vacation. So if you have something you want to do, I could baby-sit."

"Are you sure you're up to it after what happened the last time you baby-sat?" Dori pinched her lips together, obviously trying to suppress her laughter.

Chase chuckled, and she joined in. "Don't worry about me. I'm a fast learner."

"I'm glad, but you'll have to fight it out with Grandma. I have a couple of job interviews this week, so I've already made baby-sitting arrangements with my mother."

"Job interviews?"

"Yes, I can't live on my good looks forever."

Chase smiled, thinking she could. "Haven't I been giving you enough money for the baby?"

"There's plenty of money for JT, but I have my own obligations, like car payments and my student loans from college." Dori finished her cereal and put her spoon in the empty bowl.

"Is that why you were so upset about my selling Tyler's company, because you wanted to go back to work there?" Chase couldn't believe how obtuse he had been.

"No. My position was filled when I left to take care of Marisa. Tyler had intended to create a new job for me. When he died, I knew that possibility was gone." Dori got up and checked on JT, who was still content to rock in the swing. After picking up the dirty dishes, she went into the kitchen. She looked at him over the counter. "Anyway, I don't want to do what I was doing before. Not now that I have JT."

"What do you want to do?" He wished he could help her somehow. Would she welcome his help or think he was intruding where he wasn't wanted? He picked up his own dirty dishes and put them in the sink.

"The interviews I have are for positions where I can do a lot of work from home. I'd keep in touch with the main office using the computer." She busied herself, putting dishes in the dishwasher and wiping the table and counters clean.

As he stood next to her, the familiar scent of her perfume reminded him of how much she had come to mean to him in such a short time. He wanted her to need him. He could help her now. How could he convince her to accept his help? He could pad JT's expense account, but she'd never use that money for herself. Could he give her some of his money? He had more than he could ever use in a lifetime, and he had no one to share it with. He'd trade it all for what Dori had. A loving family. Isn't that what Tyler had done, and yet, it was returned to him in double measure.

"Well, I hope the interviews go well. If they don't work

out, I could check around for you, I have lots of contacts. Just let me know." Chase held his breath while he waited for her reply. Would she welcome his offer? He remembered Teresa telling him how much Dori liked doing things for herself.

"Thanks. We'll see how these go." She closed the dishwasher, then went to pick up JT. He gurgled and cooed as she held him.

Chase took in the picture of mother and child silhouetted against the morning sun shining in through the wall of windows. Mother and son. He was beginning to think of Dori in those terms. JT's mother. He hadn't brought up the subject of adoption. Maybe it was best left alone. Voicing his concerns wouldn't change her mind. But somehow he wanted to be part of that picture.

Chapter Seven

Chase hesitated at the door to Warren's office. The summons to see his father had immediately put Chase on the defensive. What did Warren want? Since Chase had returned from vacation, he and Warren had barely spoken to each other. After Tyler's death, and especially after the scene in the lawyer's office, the lines of communication between them had completely broken. Confronting Warren late on a Friday afternoon was the last thing Chase wanted to do. He took a deep breath and opened the door. Warren sat at a cherry desk inlaid with mahogany. Behind him a wall of windows looked out on the Dallas skyline in the distance.

As Chase approached, Warren stood and walked around the desk. "I've heard things are going well with the deal in China."

"Yeah. It's all right in here." Chase laid the bound report on the desk. "Did you want to talk about any specific aspect of the deal?"

Warren picked up the report and thumbed through it.

"I can look at this later. There's something else I want to tell you."

"What's that?"

"My attorney brought this over today." Warren handed Chase a folder.

Chase opened it. He recognized it as a DNA report, showing that JT was Tyler's son. Why was Warren showing this to him? Chase tried to remain nonchalant. "What about it?"

"Looks like I have a grandson."

"I didn't doubt it." Chase walked to the window and looked out. "Does this mean you won't contest Tyler's will?"

"No point in it now."

Chase turned around. "I'm glad you've finally come to your senses."

"That's right. I'm going to get custody of my grandson."

Warren's pronouncement pierced Chase's heart. He had intended to confront Warren about his actions before and after Tyler's death. But Warren's performance at the reading of the wills made Chase believe it would be a futile effort. He had left everything unsaid. And now, Warren wanted to wreak more havoc on the Morales family. "What makes you think you could do that?"

"There are ways." Warren rubbed his hands together. "I've been informed that Ms. Dorinda Morales intends to adopt that child. That will never happen as long as I can help it. Those people robbed me of my son. I'm not going to let them rob me of my grandchild."

"How can you say that? They didn't rob you, you robbed yourself." Stepping closer, Chase glared at Warren. "Doing this will only hurt you and your grandson. You're going to lose all the way around."

"Does this mean you're going to walk out on me, too?"

Chase thought about the question. Why would he want to stick by his father? A father who was more interested in a grandson he couldn't have than in the son who had stood by him for years. Then Chase remembered Luis's words: "Fathers and sons should stick together." In the short time he had known Luis, he had acted more like a father to Chase than Warren ever had, and somehow Luis's advice gave him his answer. "No, I'm not going to walk out, but I'm not on your side when it comes to a custody battle. You're going to lose."

Without looking back Chase left the room. Out in the hall he released a long sigh. Why hadn't it occurred to him what Warren might do? He could have warned Dori. It wouldn't have made any difference. Dori and Warren had been on a collision course ever since they had met. What could Chase do to stop it? He had to tell her. When he did, she would probably put him in Warren's camp. The little bit of her trust he had gained would be washed away in the turmoil to come.

Chase rushed to get through with his work. The week had flown since he had been back from vacation. Late on a Friday afternoon, he was eager to get out of the office. He had someplace to go. He could hardly wait to see JT. While Chase was on vacation, he'd spent countless hours with JT while Dori had run her errands and had her interviews. This week Chase hadn't seen JT at all. Chase missed that little boy more than he had ever dreamed. He missed Dori, too.

Before JT and Dori had come into his life, he had often stayed at the office until eight or nine o'clock at night. There had never been any reason to leave. Maybe he should call Dori. No. This news had to be delivered in person. What could he say that would make what he had to tell her less frightening? He thought about how Tyler had wanted to introduce Chase to her. Now he and Dori knew each other because of a tragic accident, and she viewed him as the man who had parted ways with his brother. Chase wished he could change all of it. He could never bring Tyler back, but Chase wanted more than anything to change Dori's mind about him. This news about Warren wasn't going to help.

As Chase stepped into the elevator that took him to the parking garage, he removed his coat and tie. Every time he got in an elevator, he had a touch of claustrophobia. Tyler used to kid Chase about it. Tight places gave him a sense of panic. Now Chase was panicked over the thought of Warren gaining custody of JT.

On the drive to Tyler's house, Chase considered his options for telling Dori about Warren's plans. Maybe bringing her a little gift would serve as a peace offering. Something had to help. As Chase passed a grocery store several blocks from the house, he stopped.

Once inside the store, he immediately found some colorful rattles for JT, but he didn't know what to get Dori. Walking the aisles, Chase passed any number of items he could possibly buy for her such as candy or flowers. None of those seemed right. What did she like to do? His gaze fell on the racks of books near the checkout. She liked to read. Not knowing what kind of books she liked, he asked a female clerk what she would recommend and bought that. After paying for the merchandise, he drove the short distance to Tyler's house.

Chase picked up his purchases and went to the front

door. Before he rang the bell, the door opened. Natalia stood there holding JT.

"Hey, Chase," she said, stepping aside so he could go in. "How's it going?"

"Fine," he said, closing the door. "Where's Dori?"

"She's not here. I'm baby-sitting."

"I thought she would be here."

"When did you talk to her?"

"Monday." Chase followed Natalia back to the family room.

"That explains it. She didn't accept the date until Wednesday."

"Date?" Chase asked, feeling an empty sensation in his gut.

"Yeah, can you believe it?" Natalia bounced JT on her hip. "It's so cool. I finally convinced her to go out with this guy from the place where I work. He's really good-looking, but way too old for me, but not for Dori."

"And how old is that?" Chase asked, wondering how old was too old in the eyes of a twenty-one-year-old college student. Besides, he wanted to size up the competition.

"He must be thirty-eight or thirty-nine, about the same age as your brother was." Natalia put JT in his carrier, then went into the kitchen. "You can have some of this casserole. If you want, you can heat it in the microwave."

Chase set the bag from the grocery store on the couch and went into the kitchen. "So where's Dori going on her date?"

"I think a movie and dinner." Natalia shrugged as she put her plate in the microwave and punched the buttons. "Dori told me you were coming over sometime tonight to see JT. I hope you don't mind, but I invited my boyfriend over to watch TV. We were going to watch upstairs. Is that all right with you?"

"Sure." Berating himself for the crazy ideas he'd had, Chase filled a plate with casserole and waited to put his plate in the microwave. He had imagined spending a quiet evening with Dori, maybe watching TV. Then when the time was right he would have told her about Warren. What had made him think a pretty woman like Dori just sat at home on the weekends? "I'll just hang out down here until it's time to put JT in bed."

The microwave beeped, and Natalia took her plate out. Chase put his in. While it heated, he got the rattles out of the sack. He hunkered down beside JT and held one out to him. "Here you go, JT. Something to entertain yourself." Chase watched as the baby closed his little fist around the rattle, then started banging it against the side of the carrier. "You like that, huh?"

"He likes anything that's noisy." Natalia sat at the table as the microwave beeped again. "Chase, your food's ready."

He went to the kitchen and retrieved his plate from the microwave. Opening the refrigerator, he peered inside. He sure could use something cold to drink. None in here. "Are there any colas upstairs?"

"Probably," Natalia said, looking up from her plate. "Not in the mood for iced tea?"

"I'm never in the mood for that. Don't like the stuff." Chase headed for the back stairs.

Taking the stairs two at a time, he wished he didn't have this empty feeling inside that even being with JT didn't fill. Hadn't he hoped just to be Dori's friend? Yeah, but he'd been counting on something more. Was there some way he could hang around until Dori got home?

What was he going to do? Punch her date in the face? Hardly.

He should have asked her out himself instead of relying on his estate work and family get-togethers as an excuse to see her. Would she have gone? Somehow he doubted it. She still didn't completely trust him. Afraid of rejection, he had let someone else take the initiative he should have taken. Was he going to stand back and let another man win her heart? Not if he could help it. But what would telling her about Warren do to his chances of getting a date?

When Chase came back downstairs, a big hulking guy with jet-black hair sat at the table next to Natalia. "Chase, I want you to meet Manny Alvarez."

Manny stood up, towering over Chase. He extended his hand. "Nice to meet you."

"Chase Garrett. I'm JT's uncle."

"Yeah, Natalia told me," Manny said, resuming his seat.

Natalia slipped her arm through Manny's and gazed at him with adoration. "Manny plays football for A&M."

"What position?" Chase sat down across from the young couple, opened his cola and took a swig.

"Offensive tackle."

"You guys going to have a good season this year?"

"Yeah, we should. We got a lot of guys coming back." Manny wolfed down several bites of casserole while Natalia continued her worshipful gaze.

Chase wished that could be him with Dori hanging on his arm, a look of devotion on her face. He needed a plan. He couldn't just sit back and let her get away. Taking another swig of his drink, he decided he had to be here when she got home tonight. He looked at Natalia. "You know, if y'all want, you don't have to stay here unless you really planned to just hang around and watch TV. I don't mind baby-sitting."

Manny looked at Natalia. "It's up to you, babe."

"You know, Jen is having that party. I wanted to go, but I promised Dori I'd watch JT if she'd go out with Pete."

"Go to your party," Chase said, hoping they would take him up on his offer. "I'll watch JT. No problem."

"Okay." Natalia got up from the table and took the dirty dishes to the kitchen. "The party won't get started till after eight. So we'll just hang here until then."

"Whatever you want is fine with me." Chase drank the last of his cola, then took his plate to the kitchen.

While Natalia and Manny went upstairs, Chase settled in a recliner in the family room with JT on his lap. Grabbing the remote control, he flipped through the stations on TV until he came to a baseball game, the Rangers against the Yankees. He watched the game and lectured JT on the finer points of pitching and batting.

JT responded to Chase's voice with a gurgle. The baby kicked his feet and waved his arms. Chase's chest swelled with love. He wanted this child to be his. He wanted Dori to be his. How was he going to make that happen? There had to be a way, but this other guy was intruding and ruining Chase's plan for a slow assault on the wall of distrust she had built against him. Now his only choice was to bring out the battering ram, but he didn't have one. He had to come up with one fast.

An hour later, after Natalia and Manny left, Chase went upstairs with JT to watch the game. Chase grabbed another cola before he sat down again with the baby in his lap. Just as the game was over, JT began fussing. Chase decided he must be hungry and went downstairs to get the bottle

Natalia had shown him. He warmed the bottle in the bottle warmer. Afterwards, he went back upstairs and got himself another cola.

"You and me, bud. You with your drink and me with mine," he said, sitting down on the reclining portion of the sectional.

While JT drank his bottle, Chase found a West coast baseball game on TV. As he watched the game, his mind buzzed with thoughts of Dori. Was she enjoying her date? Would the guy ask her out again? His heart raced while he thought about the possibility. What would happen when they got back? Maybe deciding to baby-sit so he'd be here when she returned had been a stupid idea. Here he was tying himself in knots again.

When JT finished his bottle, Chase burped him and settled the baby back in his lap under one arm. Chase kept glancing at the clock on the VCR. As it got later, he worried that Dori was having too much fun. While he sat there stewing, JT had fallen asleep. Not wanting to wake the baby, Chase settled back in the lounger. Closing his eyes, he tried to ease the tension building in his head as he thought about Dori and her date.

Dori walked to the front door with Pete. Fishing her keys out of her purse, she turned to him when they got to the door. "Thanks for a great evening."

"I enjoyed it, too." He helped her open the door. "I'd really like to see you again. A friend of mine is giving a party tomorrow. Would you like to go with me?"

Dori hesitated. True, she had had a wonderful time tonight. It was fun to go out again. Pete was witty and nice. What could it hurt? "Yes, I'd like that, if I can get a baby-sitter."

"Maybe Natalia can watch JT for you again."

Dori laughed. "I doubt that she'd agree to two nights in a row. Call me tomorrow around noon, and I'll let you know."

"Okay. Great." Pete gave her a quick, gentle kiss. "Talk to you tomorrow. Good night."

"Good night," Dori said, slipping inside.

After shutting the door, she leaned against it and closed her eyes. As she stood there, she wondered why she had agreed to go out with Pete again. He was a great guy, but there was no spark. Opening her eyes, she went into the nursery and looked in the crib. JT wasn't there. Why hadn't Natalia put JT in bed? Irritation knitting her brow, she walked toward the family room. It was empty. Maybe Natalia was in the game room watching TV. Dori made her way up the stairs as she called Natalia's name. There was no answer. Panic gripped her while she took the stairs two at a time.

When she came around the corner, Chase was asleep in the lounger with JT tucked in the crook of his arm. Chase's head lolled off to one side. His cowlick made that one section of hair stick up on the left side. Her heart tripped at the sight. She wanted to reach out and smooth it down.

Why had she reacted that way? Because he was holding JT. No other reason. But Chase made her feel things she hadn't felt all evening with Pete. She hadn't lied when she said she'd had a good time. The date was fun, but something was missing. Even Pete's good-night kiss hadn't ignited any excitement. It had been like a great evening with one of her brothers. Why did Chase make her pulse race and her stomach curl when she couldn't or wouldn't trust him?

Now he had fallen asleep here again. Would he wake up when she took JT away? As she walked closer she saw the baby bottle sitting alongside an empty bottle of cola on the end table. Seeing the baseball game still on the un-watched TV, she smiled. Just two guys sharing a drink and watching a game. She erased the other thought that came to mind. Her two guys.

Chase wasn't hers, and she didn't want him to be.

She walked over to the lounger. Why was Chase still here and what had happened to Natalia? Dori hoped she could pick JT up without disturbing Chase. Very carefully, she slipped her hands beneath the baby and lifted him up. He made a jerky movement with his arms but didn't awaken. Chase shifted his head, but never opened his eyes. She decided to deal with him after she put JT in bed.

After JT was safely tucked into his crib, she went back upstairs. The volume barely audible, the TV still flickered in the dimly lit room. Picking up the remote from the coffee table, she pressed the power button. The screen went black. The only light came from the small Tiffany lamp on the bar. Turning, she looked at Chase still sleeping in the lounger.

Maybe she should let him sleep here again. At least this time, he was in a more comfortable position. She looked at her watch. Midnight. This wasn't three-thirty in the morning, and he could get up and go home at a reasonable hour. She debated with herself about the wisdom of either option. Finally, she decided to send him home.

"Chase," she called gently as she shook his shoulder. "Wake up. Wake up."

He twisted in the chair and batted her hand away with his arm. Dori furrowed her brow. He must be a sound sleeper. She'd be completely awake by now if someone had shaken her and called her name. She tried again.

This time he sat straight up in the chair. Shaking his head

and blinking his eyes, he stared at her. He ran his hand through his hair and shook his head again. "Dori, why are you here?"

"I live here. Remember? Or do you think you do now?"

He glanced around the room. "Oh, man." He rubbed his hand across his forehead and down one side of his face. "I'm still at Tyler's. Where's JT?"

"I put him to bed."

"What time is it?"

"A little after midnight. How come you're here? What happened to Natalia?"

Chase pushed the footrest of the sectional down, then stood. Still rubbing the sleep from his eyes, he looked at her. "I was really out. Give me a minute."

"Sure," she replied, suddenly feeling light-headed as she stood near him. A pulse pounded in her head, and her heart raced at the sight of him in his rumpled slacks and dress shirt. Breathing deeply, she was glad he was probably still too sleepy to notice her reaction to him. "Are you okay?"

"I've got a headache, but I'll get over it." He shook his head again. "I'm sorry. What'd you ask me?"

"Why are you still here, and what happened to Natalia?"

Chase rubbed his temples. Being awakened from a deep sleep had him completely disoriented. He was sure he'd been dreaming about Dori because she occupied his dreams while he slept as well as his daydreams. With a sigh, he replied, "I'm baby-sitting. I told Natalia I'd be glad to sit with JT so she could go out with Manny." Chase gave a lopsided grin. "I hope you won't fire me because I fell asleep."

"Not this time," she said with a chuckle. "I'll give you another chance if you want it. I need a sitter tomorrow night."

"Tomorrow night, huh?"

"Yeah, Pete invited me to a party."

A sinking sensation settled in the pit of Chase's stomach. "Is Pete the guy you went out with tonight?"

Dori wrinkled her brow. "How did you know?"

"Natalia told me," Chase said, wondering how he managed to talk so calmly when all he wanted to do was take Dori in his arms and kiss her until she forgot all about Pete.

"Well, what do you say? I told him I'd let him know if I came up with a baby-sitter."

What did he say? He could tell her he couldn't, but what would be the point? She would just find someone else. Besides, this way he could see what was going on. Best of all, he would be with JT. "Sure. You can count on me. What time?"

"I'll have to let you know on that. I'll call you after I talk to Pete."

"Okay," Chase said while a sense of dread invaded his fuzzy mind when he recalled what Warren had told him. How and when was he going to tell Dori? Not tonight. It was too late, and his mind wasn't clear. Things were not looking good. Then tomorrow, she was going on another date. Maybe after a good night's sleep, he could formulate a new plan. His old one had been blown to smithereens. "I'd better be going. Is it okay if I look in on JT before I leave?"

"Sure." Dori smiled at him, then turned to leave.

As Chase followed her down the stairs, he couldn't help thinking how her smile lit up the room. Had she smiled at him because she appreciated his concern for JT, or had she smiled because he had agreed to baby-sit so she could go out with some other guy?

When they reached the nursery, Chase opened the door,

and they tiptoed inside. They stood side by side gazing into the crib. JT slept with his little arms flung up toward his head. Stroking the top of his head, Dori smoothed down the patch of dark hair that stood on end.

Then she turned her gaze on Chase. Reaching up she touched the hair that was combed back from his forehead. "He has a cowlick just like you."

For several seconds, Chase didn't breathe. Did she know how her touch affected him? Finally, releasing a long, slow silent breath, he marshaled every ounce of his willpower to keep from touching her. She stood so close, and it would be so easy to gather her in his embrace. Instead, he held his arms rigidly to his sides. He had always cursed that section of hair that wouldn't comb right, but never again.

Finally, she stepped away, but Chase still wanted to hold her more than ever. How much longer was he going to be able to keep his distance if she kept doing things like that? He had to devise a plan of attack. He could come over early in the morning and tell her about Warren, and maybe that would ruin her date. That could backfire. Then she would lean on Pete for moral support and make Chase out to be the bad guy again. He could wait and tell her he had something to discuss with her on Sunday.

No matter what scenario he came up with, there was always some drawback. Right now he was stewing in his own juices. He had done what he promised himself he wouldn't do. He had let the smile of a pretty woman turn him inside out.

He had let himself care too much about Dori.

Chapter Eight

As Chase walked to the front door of the house, he chided himself for helping Dori go out with someone else. Only one word described him.

Chicken.

He rang the bell, and Dori immediately opened the door. Wearing a floral-print sundress, she held JT in her arms. The sight of them made Chase's heart ache. This was the family he had never had. This was the family he wanted.

Walking in, he wondered whether she had been watching for him. What wishful thinking. Why would she be pining to see him, when she was going out with another guy?

"Hi," she said as she went into the living room and sat down on the couch. "Did you get rid of your headache?"

"Yeah, I was just out of it last night." Smiling, he followed her. She remembered. Unlike the previous times they had sat in this room together, Chase sat on the couch beside her. As an excuse to be close, he played with JT while she bounced him on her lap. "How did your interviews go?"

"I think they went well. Of course, that was just the first round. I'll see if I get any calls for a second interview."

"I hope it all works out for you."

"I'm sure it will."

"Remember if you need any help, just ask me."

"Okay."

JT grabbed hold of Chase's finger as he let his gaze rest on Dori. "You know I can't have the woman who's going to be my nephew's mother going out with just anyone. I have to put my stamp of approval on this guy."

Dori's laughter trilled off the vaulted ceiling. "You sound just like Dad. Pete's taking me to church before we go to the party so Dad can meet him."

"Luis is checking him out? Whoa, this is only the second date." Chase hoped his uneasiness over this situation wasn't obvious to Dori. He was trying to joke about it, but the underlying possibility that she might have found someone after only one date made him sick inside.

"That's what I told Dad. I'm just trying to humor him."

"Humor me, too."

"Poor Pete. He didn't know he'd have to meet the approval of the baby-sitter."

"When you sit for free, there ought to be some compensation."

"And checking out my dates is compensation?" Dori smiled. "Funny that you should mention compensation. I have a little something for you."

Chase furrowed his brow, and curiosity captured his mind. "What? I was only kidding."

"Well, I'm not. Hold JT and I'll get your surprise." Dori deposited JT in Chase's arms.

His heart thumped as Dori disappeared into the nursery. Only a man who wasn't quite right in his mind would baby-sit so the woman he cared about could go on a date with another man. He had to think of something else. While Chase bounced JT on his knees, the baby grinned and gurgled. Chase's heart overflowed with love for this little boy. No matter what happened with Dori, at least JT would be part of his life. While Chase agonized over the situation, Dori returned carrying a huge wrapped present with a big blue bow sitting on top.

"Here it is." She set the package at his feet.

"What did you get me?"

"Open it and find out." Laughing, she looked as though she was truly excited to give him this gift.

Chase returned JT to Dori. "You didn't have to get me anything for babysitting."

"This isn't a gift because you're baby-sitting. This is…is…a…'Sorry I've been so prickly' gift." She smiled wryly as she gazed at him over the top of JT's head.

What could he say? She had been prickly at times, but he understood why. She had seen him as Tyler and Marisa's enemy. He must be making progress in erasing that image. This was a sign that she was beginning to like him. Did he dare voice that thought? Why not? "So maybe you're thinking I'm not such a bad guy after all?"

She gave him an impish smile. "Yeah, maybe."

"At least I'm making progress."

"You are."

"I'm glad you feel that way." Chase wondered how long that thinking would last when he told her about Warren. There was no sense in thinking about that now. He'd enjoy her good graces while they lasted and hope for more.

He ripped open the paper to reveal a box with the picture of an infant car seat. She shouldn't be spending her money on him. He could have bought this for himself. But this was her goodwill gesture. He couldn't refuse to take it. He tore open the box. Even though this gift meant a softening of her thoughts toward him, the best present would be having both Dori and JT in his life forever. Could that ever happen?

Chase pulled the carrier from the box and set it on the couch. He smiled at Dori. "Thanks. You really didn't have to do this, but thanks. Being with JT is payment enough."

"I wanted to do it. This way you'll be prepared to take JT with you when you want to go somewhere."

"I'm glad you thought of it. Thanks again." Chase picked up the car seat. "I'm going to put this in my car right now."

After installing the car seat in the backseat of his car, he returned to the house. His heart was lighter. She was telling him that she had definitely accepted his role in JT's life.

He hoped that thought would take his mind off his fears that Dori really did have an interest in another man. Chase's insides churned with nervous anticipation as they waited for Pete's arrival.

When the doorbell rang, Dori handed JT to Chase and went to answer it. He slowly followed Dori and hovered in the background as she opened the door. A tall, thin man with dark hair and a mustache stepped inside. Dori immediately made introductions.

"Nice to meet you, Chase," Pete said, giving Chase a firm handshake, then patting JT on the head. "Hey, JT. Are you going to let me borrow your mom for the evening?"

Chase took in Pete's question. The other man had called Dori JT's mom. Pete was winning points while Chase fumbled the ball. All he had ever done was question whether Dori was wise to adopt JT. Even though Chase had agreed to stand by her decision, he hadn't given her the full endorsement she needed. Now what would she think when he told her about Warren?

Watching Pete's interaction with JT, Chase wanted to find some fault in Pete, but Chase couldn't. How was he going to win this battle?

"Well, we'd better get going," Dori said, then kissed JT on the top of his head. "You be good for your uncle Chase." Dori looked up at him. "There's a bottle in the refrigerator if you need it."

"I can handle it. Now, Mom, did you write down your cellphone number in case of emergency?" Chase hoped she caught that reference even if it was probably too late to score any points.

"Yes, it's all written on the pad by the phone in the kitchen." Suppressing a smile, she winked at him. "Try not to fall asleep before you put JT to bed."

"Okay." Chase smiled in return, but inside he ached. What kind of fool was he for letting the woman he cared for walk out the door with another man?

While Chase watched JT, he tried not to think about Dori and Pete. He wanted to enjoy the evening with his nephew. But at every turn, images of Dori holding JT crept into his mind. She wanted to be JT's mother, and he wanted to be more than JT's uncle. He understood Dori's most urgent wish.

After Dori adopted JT, what if she married? Where would that leave him? Just an uncle? He couldn't settle for that. His mind swirled with the implications. Hoping to put his mind on other things, Chase decided to take JT for a swim. After putting JT into his crib, Chase changed into the swim trunks he had brought with him, then stripped JT of everything except his diaper. As they left the air-conditioned house, the hot air outside hit Chase like a blast from a furnace. The late afternoon sun beat down on the patio, making the concrete blistering hot beneath his feet. He quickly carried JT to the steps going into the pool. The cool water relieved the burning sensation on the bottom of Chase's feet.

Holding JT out in front of him, Chase slowly walked down the steps into the shallow end. He carefully lowered JT into the water and watched the baby's reaction. He didn't seem to mind. It was probably like bath time to him. Or maybe Dori brought him into the pool on a regular basis. He didn't know, but he wanted to. He wanted to be part of JT's everyday life.

After the swim, Chase changed JT's diaper on a nearby lounge chair. Then balancing him in one arm, Chase pulled up another lounge chair. He placed the towel on one of the lounges and sat on it, with JT on his lap. It wouldn't take long to dry off in this heat.

"Just you and me, JT. No women to disturb us now," Chase said, thinking how Dori disturbed him every time she was in his presence.

As the sun sank lower in the sky, shadows crept across the patio and pool. The smell of cooking steaks on a neighbor's grill wafted across the fence. Chase's stomach growled. What was he going to eat? He could take JT out for supper.

Chase dressed JT, packed his diaper bag, strapped him in his new car seat and was ready to go. Driving to a neighborhood eatery, he figured it was early enough for him to beat the crowd. After he walked into the restaurant, the hostess, cooing over JT the whole time, seated Chase almost immediately. The waitress who took his order did the same. Two women at a nearby table oohed and aahed over JT.

If Chase was looking for a way to pick up women, this was it. But he didn't want just any woman. He wanted Dori.

When they got back to the house, Chase fed JT, then read him several of the little books that Dori had sitting in a basket by the couch. He remembered hearing how important it was to read to children, but did that make sense for a nearly three-month old? Pointing to the pictures and telling JT what they were, Chase supposed it made as much sense as the pitching and batting instructions he had given JT last night. A daily talk with his boy was something he could get used to. How to make it come true was his only problem.

Marry Dori. That's what he had to do. If only it were that simple. What would it take to convince her? Did he dare use Warren as the enemy that he could fight better than anyone else?

A desperate situation called for desperate measures.

After putting JT to bed, Chase checked the intercom before going to sit by the pool and sat in a lounge chair. The setting sun cast a warm, red glow across the Texas sky. Heat still radiated off the concrete patio. But despite the heat, Chase decided to turn on the spa, then went inside to change into his swim trunks again. When the spa was warm he eased himself into the water. What was Dori doing now? How could he convince a woman who didn't love him or trust him to say 'I do?' He sat in the swirling, bubbling water while his mind swirled and bubbled as well. When his fingers began to resemble prunes, he finally got out of the spa. After getting out, he jumped into the pool. As he surfaced, he wished his thoughts could be as cool and clear as the water.

After he dried off, he pulled a T-shirt over his head and relaxed on one of the lounge chairs. He shouldn't think about Dori, but as he pushed the thoughts away, they only became more abundant. A door opened. He looked up. Dori emerged from the master bedroom onto the pool deck.

She walked across the patio and sat on the lounge next to him. "Hi. How was your evening?"

"Fine." Chase smiled, relief filtering through his whole body. She was home early and without Pete. Did that mean the date hadn't gone well? Did he dare hope? "Home so soon?"

"Yeah, Pete got paged. Some kind of computer problems at his office. He had to leave in a hurry. In fact, he sent me home in a taxi." Kicking off her shoes, she eased herself back in the lounge chair. "I see you're still awake."

Chase chuckled. "I'm wide awake tonight. JT and I had a great time. I took him out to eat. He charmed every woman he met. I taught him everything he knows, of course."

"Of course." Nodding, she gave him a questioning look. "Speaking of women, did you buy a book for a lady friend or do you read romances?"

Chase gave her a puzzled frown. "What are you talking about?"

"I found a book in a grocery sack on the couch. I thought it belonged to Natalia, but she said it was in a bag you brought in the other night. Do you know anything about it?"

"Yeah, I bought it for you. I was going to give it to you last night. But you weren't here, so I forgot about it."

"Why did you buy a book for me?"

"The truth?" He watched her nod. "A peace offering."

"A peace offering?" Her brow knit with concern. "What did you do?"

"It's not what I've done, but what I'm going to tell you."

The furrows on her brow deepened. "Don't tease me, Chase."

"I'm not teasing." He wanted to touch her, make her understand that everything was going to be all right. "I have some news you won't like, so I thought I'd break it to you gently with a little gift."

"What is it?" Dori grabbed his arm.

Her beseeching look took him back to that day in the lawyer's office when she had learned that he was Tyler's brother. She hadn't wanted his help then. Would she want it now? Would she accept what he had to offer? Even with all the thinking he had done while sitting in the spa, he hadn't put together what he was going to say.

"I wanted to tell you yesterday, but I didn't know you had a date."

"Quit beating around the bush. You're scaring me. Has something happened to Tyler's company? Is the money all gone?" She sat forward in the lounge and continued to furrow her brow.

"No, this has nothing to do with the finances. You don't have to worry about JT's trust fund."

"Then what is it?"

Chase rubbed a hand across his chin. "I talked with Warren the other day. He got the DNA tests back."

"That should be good news for us."

"Uh…yeah. He's not going to contest the will."

"Then what's the problem?"

"He's going to fight the adoption, and sue for custody." Even in the dim light, Chase saw the color drain from Dori's face.

"How could you let this happen?"

"You think I had something to do with this?"

"How did he find out if you didn't tell him?" She stared at him.

"I don't know. He has ways of getting information."

"Why does he want to do this?" Dori got up and shoved her feet into her shoes. Then she stood there and stared at him some more.

"He has this notion that he wants his grandson," Chase said, hoping she would listen to reason.

Dori laughed derisively. "That's unbelievable. He wants his grandson. Well, he rejected his grandson, and now it's too late."

Chase stood and grasped the top of her arms. "Listen to me, Dori." She looked up at him, her eyes swimming with tears. It nearly undid him inside. "A judge would be crazy to take that child from you and give him to Warren."

"Warren will hire detectives and find out about my past. He'll use it against me. I know he will. He'll say I'll be an unfit mother." Dori covered her face with her hands and sobbed.

"Come over here and sit down." Chase led her back to a lounge chair, and she didn't resist. It was as though her will had been zapped right out of her.

Sitting down beside her, he put his arm around her shoulders. He let her cry. He felt a little guilty for taking advantage of the situation, but not that guilty.

Finally, she wiped her eyes and nose with the edge of a nearby towel, then looked at him. "What am I going to do?"

Marry me, he wanted to say, but he had to lay the groundwork first. "What could be so terrible in your past that Warren would use it against you?"

Dori sniffled. She released a loud sigh, then blurted, "I was treated for depression. Several years ago, I tried to commit suicide." She closed her eyes.

Chase swallowed hard. What could have brought Dori to that kind of low? What did judges do with that kind of information? Would it be held against her? He didn't have a clue. "You want to talk about it?"

Dori opened her eyes and stared into space. She rubbed one hand up and down on her arm as though she was trying to warm herself.

"Dori?" Chase took her hand and rubbed it. It was cold despite the hot evening air. "Talk to me, please."

Finally she looked at him, her eyes full of fear. "They'll say I'm unstable and won't let me keep JT."

"How long ago did this happen?" he asked, hoping she would open up to him. He understood what it was like not wanting to talk about the past.

"Six years ago."

"And you've been fine ever since?"

She nodded. "I feel so ashamed. I don't want anyone to find out. Now it will all come out for everyone to know."

"Then you're telling me nobody knows about this?"

Dori shook her head. "Mom, Dad and Marisa knew. That's all."

"If they're the only ones who know, how do you think Warren could find out? Medical records are private."

"You know."

"Dori, I'm on your side." He grasped her shoulders and turned her to face him. "I've seen what a terrible father Warren is. Why would I want him to have JT?"

Dori swallowed hard and closed her eyes. "All kinds of reasons. You might want to get on his good side."

"Have you heard *anything* I've said? I've already told Warren I would fight him on this."

Dori sighed and looked heavenward. "I don't care what you do. He'll find out. He has power and money."

"But you have love and caring. That wins every time." He took her hands in his. "I love JT, and I want him to have the best parent. And you are the best."

"Why should I believe what you're saying? You chose Warren over Tyler. How do I know you aren't just making me think you're on my side?"

For a second, Chase felt like Dori had slapped him in the face. What would make her understand? "You don't know the whole story."

"What's there to know? Tyler and Warren had a falling out, and you sided with Warren. I think that says it all." Dori stared at him, a challenge in her eyes.

"That says very little."

"It says enough about where your loyalty lies. With a hateful man."

"I want you to understand."

"Then help me understand."

"Okay." Chase hesitated as he summoned the courage to open up to her. How far back did he need to go to make her understand? He didn't want to share the feelings he'd had as a twelve-year-old boy left in a strange city with a man he didn't know was his father until that day. He had to relate to terms she understood. "Let me put it to you this way. What would you have done if Marisa had told you to choose between her and your mother?" Chase crossed his arms. "Who would you have chosen?"

Dori shook her head. "That's not a fair question."

"That's what Tyler wanted me to do. Choose between him and my father."

"But both my mother and Marisa were warm, loving women. There's not a clear choice between them like there is between Warren and Tyler. They were like night and day. Tyler was loving. Warren was hateful."

"But he's the only father I knew. I'd spent twelve years trying to show him I was worthy to be recognized as his son. I thought working side by side with him would finally prove that point. And there was Tyler telling me if I wanted to be his brother, I had to throw away any chance to know my father."

"You really wanted to be recognized as Warren Davis's son?" she asked as her eyebrows disappeared under the fringe of bangs.

"Yes. He's not the complete ogre you seem to think he is. He's far from perfect, but he's a well-respected businessman. At least he didn't ask me to choose between him and Tyler."

Dori couldn't help noticing the defiance in Chase's eyes. The muscle worked in his jaw just as it always did when something bothered him. She had to admit she was beginning to see things differently. He had put his struggle into terms she could understand, deciding between a parent and a sibling. "Why was Tyler so insistent?"

"He was angry and Warren wouldn't relent. I couldn't

reason with either one of them, and I was furious with Tyler for putting me in that position."

"So you chose the path of least resistance."

"Hardly. Tyler was the only one who took the time to get to know me when I moved into the Davis household. He recognized me as a brother. Turning away from him was one of the hardest things I've ever had to do." Chase rubbed the back of his neck.

"Then why did you do it?"

"I told you the first time I came over here. Stubborn pride. His and mine."

"I can't relate to the Tyler you're talking about. There was nothing stubborn or prideful about him. He treated everyone with respect and went the extra mile for his employees."

"That's the Tyler I knew, too. But when it came to standing up for Marisa against our father, something snapped." Chase sighed heavily. "Several months after our argument, the feud was still alive and well between Warren and Tyler, but I still tried to talk with him. He told me I'd made my choice and it was too late to make amends."

Unable to meet Chase's eyes, Dori gazed at the patio. She didn't want to believe it. Was he just telling her this to make himself look good? There was no one here to dispute his claim. Maybe it was the truth. Chase's explanation made sense of Tyler's decision to name Chase executor. Maybe after all those years, Tyler had come to realize his mistake.

Had she made a mistake in judging Chase too harshly? Her family had accepted him. Could she trust him? Her past experience told her she wasn't a very good judge of men. "Why did Tyler change his mind after all those years?"

"The birth of his son made him realize he needed to

make things right with me. He told me he wanted to be right with God." Chase's multi-colored eyes gave her a challenging look. "I found Tyler's Bible, and I've been reading it. He had several passages marked that talked about forgiveness and brothers. So I know it was uppermost in his mind. He saw the importance of family relationships. He saw what you and Marisa had."

Logically, Dori acknowledged the truth in his statements, but she wasn't sure she could admit as much to him. "Tyler told you about Marisa and me?"

Chase hesitated. "Well, not exactly, but he mentioned you, and later, your mother filled in the blanks for me. I see how much you loved your sister."

"I did. I miss her so much." Tears stung Dori's eyes as she tried not to cry. She couldn't cry anymore. Crying wasn't going to solve any of her problems. Hanging her head, she blinked back the tears. "I'll do anything to keep her baby safe."

"Believe me, Dori. I feel the same way."

"You don't have a problem with my taking care of JT now that you know about my past?"

"Not from what I see now." Chase put a finger under her chin and lifted her head until their gazes met. His gaze seemed to bore right through her. "Did you know your dad was the one who convinced Tyler to mend the rift between us?"

Her heart raced at his touch while she read the sadness in his eyes. "I don't know what to believe." Shaking her head, Dori let Chase's explanation filter through her mind. "Did Tyler tell you that?"

"No, your father did."

Dori sank back in the lounge chair. Her mind was on

overload with too many things to process. "Why didn't anyone tell me?"

"Did you ask?"

"No."

"Then why would anyone tell you? It was personal between Tyler and me."

Chase's words chastised her. She had become too judgmental, never giving him credit for all the good things he'd done for her and JT. Yet, in the back of her mind, that nagging doubt kept her from completely trusting Chase. Maybe it wasn't so much the idea of trusting him, but trusting herself. And where had she put God in all of this? "I'm sorry for doubting your good intentions."

"Apology accepted." He smiled and touched her arm.

Dori didn't say anything for a moment as she took in Chase's words. Tyler had had a change of heart regarding God, but what about Chase? "Then you don't share Tyler's former disdain of God and religion?"

"No, but I'll have to admit Tyler's death has made me realize my relationship with God isn't what it should have been." Chase gave her a curious glance. "What about you? If you had faith in God, why would you try to take your life?"

"That was the whole problem. I didn't. Just like Tyler, I had turned away from God during my college years. Tyler and I used to commiserate with each other at some of the family gatherings during the early years of their marriage. We were the two black sheep. I didn't go to church at all. Tyler went to please Marisa, but he was just going through the motions."

"When did things change?"

Dori released a heavy sigh. "After I got out of the hospital. Lots of people were praying for me. They knew about the depression, not the suicide. Marisa prayed especially hard. I had sessions with a Christian counselor, and she helped me see what I had refused to let my family tell me. I realized that God loved me and sent His son to save me. I know my change of heart had an effect on Tyler, too."

"Will you tell me why you wanted to end your life?"

"Is it necessary?"

"No, but I'd like to understand, too, so I can help. Otherwise, I'll always wonder."

Dori looked out into the yard beyond the pool. The light from the alley cast long shadows, making eerie shapes on the ground. They reminded her of the dark shadows she had pulled herself out of in fighting her depression with the help of her family and finally learning to rely on God to see her through the rough times. She needed to remind herself of that again. Another crisis was about to hit her life, and she couldn't see it through without her faith. She had come a long way from those days. Now she was strong and ready to fight any demons that came her way with God's help. Chase wanted to help, too. Shouldn't he know what happened? What would he think when she finished telling him the story?

Taking a deep breath and releasing it slowly, she turned to look at him. Her heart tripped, and she swallowed a lump in her throat before she could speak. "It's not an easy story to tell."

"I'm sure it's not. But I want to understand. To help you if I can. Take your time."

"Well…I…when I was a college junior, I met Ramon. He was a year older than me. We got engaged when he finished his undergraduate work. We planned to get married when he finished graduate school. In the meantime, I graduated and went to work for Tyler. We planned a huge, elaborate wedding. Ramon called me a week before the wedding and said he couldn't go through with it." Dori released a harsh breath. "I was heartbroken."

"That's why you tried to commit suicide?" Chase interrupted, his brow furrowed in a question.

"No. I got over it. Then I met Scott on the rebound. He was just what I thought I needed to heal my broken heart and mend my shattered ego. He was a smooth talker, and he charmed everyone he met. I convinced Tyler to hire Scott as a consultant. He came into the company and seemed to work miracles, but he was selling information to our competitors. He didn't care about me. He only used me to get inside Tyler's company."

"Being jilted twice was more than you could handle?"

Dori shook her head. "No, just let me finish."

Grimacing, Chase shrank back in the chair. "Okay."

"Sorry. I didn't mean to sound so harsh. This isn't easy."

"I understand."

Dori sighed heavily, then continued. "Scott's betrayal nearly cost Tyler his company. And it was my fault. I thought Tyler and Marisa were going to lose everything because of me. My love life was in shambles. The company was in shambles. I couldn't face them. I hated myself. I was such a fool. I just wanted to end it all. I thought everyone would be better off if I weren't around. So I took a bottle of pills."

"How did you survive?"

"Marisa knew I was distraught and came to see me. She found me and rushed me to the hospital. They pumped my stomach. Marisa saved me." Dori sniffled and wiped the tears out of her eyes.

"That's why you were so close?"

"Even before that I would have done anything for her."

Searching Chase's face, Dori looked for understanding. "I can't let Warren have Marisa's baby."

"You won't have to."

"But what will happen when this all comes out?"

"I don't know, but I think I have a solution. Marry me."

Chapter Nine

Chase held his breath while he watched Dori's face. Her wide-eyed expression of dismay told him what she thought of his proposal. Why had he just blurted it out without explaining first? Would she even listen now?

"Marry you?" Dori shook her head as the expression of dismay turned to one of disbelief.

"Are you rejecting my proposal?"

"You're serious?"

"I am."

Dori stared at him. "Why would you want to marry me?"

How could he answer? What explanation would satisfy her and make her see this was the solution? He had to explain his plan. "I want to help you. It doesn't have to be a real marriage."

"Oh, and how is that supposed to help me?"

"The court might look more favorably on a married couple adopting a child than a single woman."

"So all that stuff you said about me being the best parent doesn't mean anything?"

"No, you're a wonderful mother to JT. Even though adoption laws don't preclude single parents anymore, why not pull out every weapon we've got to fight Warren?"

Dori didn't say anything. She looked as if she was thinking over what he had said. "So what's in this for you?"

"I get to make JT my son."

Dori's eyes beamed with skepticism. "So you can divorce me and fight for custody?"

Chase's heart sank. After all they had shared tonight, she still didn't trust him. For a moment he wanted to walk out. But if he did that, Pete would be all too willing to step into Chase's place. He couldn't give up. He had to fight for what he wanted. "You've got it wrong, Dori."

"So what's your plan? You want to be in a loveless marriage for the rest of your life? The church frowns on divorce."

"I know that, and I know how important the church and your faith is in your life. I've thought of that, too."

"Oh, you've thought of everything?"

No, not everything. He hadn't thought about how this plan could lead to heartbreak. "I've tried. Listen to my plan."

Dori grimaced. "I suppose it won't hurt."

"Okay. Here it is. We draw up a prenuptial agreement with all the financial stuff. The most important part involves custody of JT. I'll grant you custody, but I want liberal visitation rights. We can go to Las Vegas to get married. The marriage will remain unconsummated. Then after the adoption is final, we can get the marriage annulled."

Dori didn't say anything for what seemed like years. Finally, she got up and walked to the door. With her hand on the knob, she turned and looked at him. With her silhouetted against the inside lights, he couldn't read her expression. His heart pounded while he waited for her to say something.

"I can't do that, Chase," she said, then went inside, leaving him sitting there by the pool.

He grabbed his towel and followed her. The air-conditioning in the house made him shiver, but not as much as the thought of her rejecting his proposal. "Dori, think it over. Give the idea a chance."

Standing in the kitchen in front of the refrigerator, she shoved a glass under the water dispenser and filled it. Lifting the glass to her lips, she looked at him over the top of the glass as she drank. The color had returned to her face, but she looked shell-shocked. "A deer in the headlights" was a perfect description of the look in her eyes. When she finished drinking, she set the glass on the counter and walked back into the family room. "Your plan can't work. I can't live with a marriage like that. When I get married I want it to last forever. I've had enough heartache. I don't want any more."

Chase didn't know how to combat her argument. He searched for an answer, but he couldn't think of a thing. "I see what you mean. It was a crazy thought. I just wanted to help."

Dori threw her head back and looked at the ceiling. When she lowered her head, her gaze settled on Chase. "I'm sorry for the way I reacted. I know you were trying to help." She rubbed her finger across her bottom lip. "I just don't know what to think. Let me change clothes. Then we can talk about it." She headed for the nursery.

"Okay," Chase called after her as he let Dori's statement soak in. She actually wanted to discuss his crazy idea. What had changed her mind? Did he dare hope she would agree? Then he wondered how he was ever going to deal with an unconsummated marriage. Crazy was the right word for his scheme.

When they returned to the family room, Dori sat at one end of the couch while Chase sat at the other end. With a stricken look on her face, she crossed her arms and stared at him. "While I was changing, I thought about what you said. I'm so afraid of what Warren will do that I'm terribly tempted to agree to your...your..."

"Wild proposal?" Chase finished as he slid across the couch to sit near her.

She nodded. "It goes against everything I've ever wanted, but Marisa saved my life. The least I can do for her is to keep her little boy safe. Do you really think our getting married would help? Don't you think people will wonder why we're suddenly getting married?"

"Didn't Tyler and Marisa get married out of the blue?"

"No. They dated for a few months. But Marisa told me they knew after only a few dates that they were in love. They eloped because they realized neither family was receptive to their marriage. My parents eventually came around, but your father never did." Dori narrowed her gaze as if to say, "And neither did you." But the fact that she didn't say it was a point in his favor. "What will your father say about this?"

Her question rolled through his mind. Did he dare hope she was agreeing to his plan? He was afraid to ask. "I don't have any idea what he'll say, but he can't tell me what to do."

"Will he disown you like he did Tyler?"

"That estrangement was mutual. You only looked at it as Warren disowning Tyler. They disowned each other. It was a family feud." Putting his elbows on his knees, Chase leaned forward and clasped his hands in front of him almost as if he were praying. "The only thing you need to concern yourself with is whether he will actually try to gain custody of JT."

Dori returned his gaze. "You mean you think there's a chance he won't try to do it?"

"Yes, if we're married."

Dori slowly shook her head. "I don't know, Chase. I'm so tempted to do this for JT, but it just doesn't feel right."

"Why?"

"Because everyone would assume we're in love."

"I'm not sure you know what to think. First, you tell me you think people will be suspicious. Then you say they'll think we're in love. Which is it?"

"Both."

"Well, the way I see it, I think you'd better sleep on it. We'll make a decision tomorrow. Agreed?"

"All right."

Chase stood up. "I'm going to head home after I look in on JT. Then I'll call you tomorrow and see what you've decided."

"What if I haven't made up my mind by then?" she asked as she followed him to the nursery.

"I figure if you haven't agreed by tomorrow, you won't ever agree. This isn't a love match. It's a business agreement. We come to terms or we don't." Opening the door to the nursery, Chase hated saying the marriage was only a business deal, but Dori wasn't ready for anything else.

She joined him near the crib. "Doesn't it bother you that JT will have divorced parents? Have you thought of that?"

"Technically, we won't be divorced. We'll be annulled," he said with a wry smile.

"You think this is funny?"

"No. I'm completely serious. It just sounded funny."

Dori leaned over the crib and lightly stroked JT's arm. He didn't stir. "I love watching him sleep."

"Me, too." Chase put his arm around Dori's shoulders and breathed a mental sigh of relief when she didn't tense up or move away. "I want to do what's best for him. We can't let Warren have JT."

Dori looked up at Chase. "I do agree with that."

"Good. Then maybe we've made some progress."

"I don't know about that. I still have lots of doubts running through my mind."

"We won't get rid of it all tonight. I'm going to take off." Chase turned to go, then stopped. "You know, if we get married, you won't have to go back to work. You'll be free to stay home with JT if that's what you want."

"That's what Marisa would have done," she said, then walked out of the room.

He closed the door and followed her to the front hall. He wasn't quite sure how to take her last statement. Her tone of voice had been tinged with irritation. Had he offended her by suggesting that she need not go back to work? When he got to the front door, he turned and put a hand on her shoulder. "Maybe you want to go back to work, and that's fine, too. I just thought I'd mention it."

"I'll take it all into consideration."

"Good night. We'll talk tomorrow." He stepped outside. While he stood there, he kept thinking about giving Dori a kiss, but that was out of the question. If she agreed to his plan, would he be able to survive a no-touch marriage? He would have to until he made her see the marriage could work for real. Having the family he wanted depended on it.

"Good night." She stood on her tiptoes, put her hand on his upper arm and kissed his cheek. "Thanks for wanting to help me."

"I'm here to help. That's my job," he replied, trying not to let her know how much the brotherly kiss had affected him.

When he reached his car, he looked back at the house. Dori still stood silhouetted in the doorway. He waved. She waved, then stepped inside the house and closed the door. If they decided to go through with this marriage, would she one day close the door on him for good? Would he be trading one unloving family for another? He didn't just care about Dori. He was falling in love with her, too. The thought of putting his heart on the line again for rejection scared him, but the thought of losing JT scared him more. Could they possibly fall in love? Or was this whole thing a recipe for heartache?

Whatever the outcome, JT would be his son, and that would be worth it all.

The next morning Dori awoke after a restless night. As she went to feed JT, she remembered the bizarre visions of Chase that had filled her dreams as he changed from friend to hideous monster. She had no doubt they symbolized her fears about the choice she had to make. What would she tell him when he called? A night's sleep hadn't resolved anything.

After feeding and dressing JT, she took him out to the patio and put him in his swing while she ate her breakfast by the pool. The morning sun sparkled off the water. Nearby, the noisy drone of a lawn mower explained the smell of freshly mowed grass carried by a stiff Texas breeze.

As she ate, she weighed all the options. None of them

appealed to her. She wavered back and forth until she was mentally seasick. A marriage of convenience was not what she wanted. Why did Chase's saying this was a business deal bother her so much? What could she say to her family and friends?

When she finished eating, she picked up her Bible for her morning devotion. She had tried to pray about this decision, but she feared talking to God about it. Was she prepared for the answer God would give her? She wasn't sure she was prepared no matter what solution God might give.

She looked at JT who kicked his little legs as the swing moved back and forth. He was such a happy baby. She wanted him to stay that way. What choice would be best for him? The pros and cons battled in her mind like wrestlers on a mat. "Oh, JT, if only you could talk. Maybe you could tell me what to do."

After she put JT down for his morning nap, Dori attempted to make her decision. She listed every advantage and disadvantage. When she looked at the list, the disadvantages greatly exceeded the advantages. If she looked at the list, the decision should be easy. She should tell Chase no, but the advantages, though fewer, outweighed the disadvantages.

The one advantage of keeping JT away from Warren took precedence over a dozen disadvantages. But if she went through with this plan, was this what God wanted for them?

While Dori doodled on her list, the doorbell rang. Her heart jumped into her throat. Was that Chase? She glanced at the digital clock on the microwave. Ten o'clock. He said he'd call first. Getting up, she took a deep breath as she went to answer the door. She breathed a sigh of relief when she opened the door and saw Natalia.

"Hey, Dori, how's it going?" Natalia bounced into the front hallway.

"What are you doing here?"

"Can't I come to visit my sister?"

"Yes, but you're hardly ever out of bed before noon on a Saturday."

Natalia waved an envelope, then handed it to Dori. "I just had to show you. I'm going to study in Barcelona spring semester next year."

"Oh, Natalia, I'm so happy for you." Dori took the letter out of the envelope and read it. "A scholarship. How wonderful!"

"I know. I can hardly wait." Natalia nearly squealed in her excitement.

"What do Mom and Dad think?"

"They said I could do it as long as I got the scholarship." Natalia hugged Dori. "I'm so excited."

Dori grinned. "I can tell. Come into the family room and tell me all about it."

Dori sat down with her sister on the couch and listened while Natalia gave her the details regarding her study-a-broad program. When Natalia finished talking, she leaned back on the couch and flung her arms up over her head. "I'm so happy I could burst."

"Well, don't do that. It would be too messy."

Natalia grabbed the decorative pillow from the couch and threw it at Dori. "Don't get smart with me. If you're not nice, I won't invite you to visit me. I'd love to have you come to Barcelona while I'm there."

"That sounds like fun, but we'll have to see what I'm

doing next spring." What would Natalia think if she knew Dori might be married to Chase by then?

Tossing the pillow back at Natalia, Dori got up and went to the kitchen. "I'm going to have a soda. You want one?"

"Sure."

When Dori finished making the drinks, she turned around. Natalia was studying a piece of paper. Dori's stomach did a flip-flop, and she rushed toward Natalia. "Don't read that."

"Too late." With a big grin on her face, Natalia waved the paper in the air. "Looks like I'm not the only one who's got exciting news."

Dori set the drinks down on the table and tried to snatch the paper away from Natalia. "Please give it to me."

"Only if you tell me what's going on."

"Okay," Dori said with a grimace as she sat down at the kitchen table.

Natalia took the chair across the table from Dori. "I didn't know you two had a thing going. And I can't believe you even have to think twice about saying yes to Chase."

"It's not what you think."

"This looks pretty clear to me. Marry Chase. Don't marry Chase." Natalia shoved the paper across the table to Dori.

"Chase did ask me to marry him, but there's nothing going on between us."

Wide-eyed, Natalia looked at Dori. "You'll have to explain that one."

Dori reached across the table and grasped the hand Natalia had on the table. "You have to promise you won't tell anyone about this. What I'm going to tell you has to remain between you and me."

A puzzled frown painted Natalia's face. "Why?"

"You'll understand when I tell the whole story. Just promise me."

"Okay, I promise." Natalia nodded. "You know I never told anyone about the time while you were in high school when you sneaked out of the house to go to that party Mom and Dad said you couldn't attend."

"I know I can count on you." Dori patted Natalia's hand, then launched into the events of the night before.

When Dori finished, Natalia just stared. "Wow, are you saying he asked you to marry him just to keep Warren Davis from getting JT?"

Dori nodded. "Yeah, he said it straight out. We sign the papers and treat it just like a business deal. That's all it is to him."

"Is that all it is to you?"

Dori closed her eyes and thought for a moment. When she opened them, Natalia gave her a curious stare. "I thought it was until I started thinking of all the reasons why I should or shouldn't agree to do this."

"Your list looked pretty lopsided to me."

"What do you think I should do?"

"I think you should marry him."

"Marry someone I don't love?"

"Are you sure about that? I've seen the way you look at him, Dori."

"Like how?"

"Oh, that moonstruck look," Natalia replied with a shrug.

"You're imagining things."

"Am I?"

Dori sighed. "Okay, I'll admit I find him incredibly attractive, but that's not love."

"If you give it a chance, it could turn into love."

"But that's not what he wants. He wants JT, and I come with the bargain." Dori swallowed a lump in her throat as tears threatened, but she blinked them away. "It's just like Scott. He's using me to get what he wants."

"Oh, Dori," Natalia said, rushing around the table to put an arm around Dori's shoulders. "Chase isn't like Scott."

"I want to believe that. The more I get to know him, the more I realize he's not the awful person I thought him to be. He's explained a lot of things about him and Tyler. But I've been such a poor judge of character in the past that I'm not sure I can trust my own feelings."

"Get over the past, Dori. He's trying to be a hero now. Let him. Maybe you'll even fall in love."

"He doesn't want that."

"Marry him, then make him want it."

Dori closed her eyes again. Could that possibly happen?

Chapter Ten

Chase sat in his car in front of Tyler's house. He clutched the steering wheel as if somehow it could be a lifesaver in a sea of his own doubt. He wasn't sure what awaited him today. Could Dori bring herself to accept his proposal? He hoped she wouldn't feel awkward discussing a marriage that wouldn't be real. And how did he feel about a marriage in name only? It was not what he wanted. He wanted a real marriage. A real family. But that's not what he was getting here.

Then his thoughts fell on the story of Rebekah and Isaac that he had read a few days ago in Tyler's Bible. That story told of an arranged marriage that turned into love. Could this happen with Dori and him? Did he dare believe they could fall in love someday? His thoughts were getting too far ahead of reality. He had to convince her to get married in the first place. And judging from her response last night, it wouldn't be easy.

With his hands still gripping the steering wheel, he bowed his head and closed his eyes. *Lord, if this marriage is what you want for Dori and me, let her agree to my proposal. Please give me wisdom in dealing with this situation.* Opening his eyes, he took in the beauty of the cloudless blue sky and the sun glinting off the hood of his car. All a part of God's creation. Remembering that God was in control, Chase emerged from his car with renewed determination.

As he strode to the front door, he thought about all the times he had gone up this walk, wondering what kind of reception he would receive. Even though she had warmed to him over the past few weeks, he still speculated about their upcoming talk.

Before he was halfway up the walk, Dori opened the door. "Hi."

"Hi," he replied, thinking this was a good sign. Her greeting seemed almost shy. He had to treat this like business. They would sit down and decide whether they could go through with his plan. Then they could draw up their prenuptial agreement before they went to see Brady Houston. Chase cautioned himself again for jumping too far ahead in the scenario as he followed Dori into the house.

"Let's go back to the family room. I just put JT down for his afternoon nap." She went through the double doors. When they were standing at the end of the couch, Dori stared past him as she spoke. "I can't agree to your plan."

Chase's heart sank while irritation flooded his mind. She still hadn't looked him in the eye. "Then why'd you ask me to come over? You could've told me on the phone."

She fiddled with the fringe on the throw pillow that sat in the corner of the couch. Picking up the pillow and holding it to her chest, she finally met his gaze and blurted out, "I...I don't want to get married in Las Vegas, and I'm not sure I want an annulment."

Chase let her hurried words sink in. Did this mean, she wanted to marry him and make it a real marriage? He was afraid to ask, but he had to take that step. "What *do* you want?"

Her chocolate-brown eyes widened as she stared at him. "I'm not sure, except for one thing. I have to keep JT from Warren Davis. If marrying you will help, then that's what I want."

Chase walked away toward the kitchen. He couldn't bear to watch the tortured expression on her face when she talked about marrying him. He ached inside. What had he expected? That somehow overnight she had come to care for him? Letting the ache subside, he reasoned with himself. She hadn't said no, so this was his chance to have a family.

He gathered his courage and his pride, then turned to her. "Tell me what you have in mind. You don't want to get married in Las Vegas. Does that mean you want to get married here?"

"No," she said with a shake of her head.

"Then where?"

"Lake Tahoe."

"That's fine," he replied, still wondering about her plans.

"Then you said you didn't want an annulment. What did you mean by that?" He held his breath as he waited for her answer.

She tucked her hair behind her ear in that familiar gesture. Sighing audibly, she turned away toward the windows that looked out over the pool. "I...I can't go into this with the idea that we'll just throw it all away when the adoption is final."

"You want a real marriage?" When she shook her head, Chase wanted to close his eyes against the reality of her response.

"No," she said turning back to him. "How can we when we don't love each other?"

Chase sighed. "Good question. So what do you want the marriage to be?"

"In name only. We make a family for JT. After the adoption is final, we can decide what we want to do with the marriage. Can you live with that?"

"So we go into this as if we're business partners. We make a deal, sign the papers and after the adoption reassess the plan. Is that what you have in mind?"

"Yes, if that's the way you want to look at it."

"I do," he said, knowing he wanted more, but maybe this is what he would have to accept for the time being. Besides, wasn't she holding out a possibility for something different in the future? He held on to that thought as he motioned her toward the kitchen. "Let's sit at the table so we can put our plan on paper." Chase pulled out a chair. "Do you have a pen and paper?"

"I'll get it." She went to the small built-in desk in the corner of the kitchen. When she returned, she put the pencil and paper on the table, then sat on the chair next to him. She still didn't look at him.

"Dori, are you sure you want to do this?"

"I said yes. I wouldn't have said it if I didn't mean it."

"You don't seem very happy."

She flashed him a fake smile. "See. I'm happy. Let's just get this over with."

Chase drummed the pen on the table. "I'm not going to do this if you're going to go around looking like a martyr.

We can't have long faces. We're supposed to be in love. Or did you forget about that part?"

"No. I didn't forget. I'm sorry. I'm nervous about all this. Let's just get started."

Wanting to make sure she was completely happy with the arrangement, he let her rule the discussion. However, when he mentioned the prenuptial agreement, she silently shook her head.

"We need this. You want a business deal, and a prenup should be part of that deal."

"So, in other words, you're making sure I don't take half your money." She finally lifted her gaze to his with a defiant look that seemed to say, "Go ahead. Deny it."

Chase felt as though she had socked him in the stomach. Was she doing this to test his resolve? Before he spoke, he weighed his words carefully. "I already told you why I think we should have such an agreement. Protecting JT is the only thing I want. I don't care if you take half my money. That's Texas law anyway. Here, let's put it at the top of the list." He grabbed the pen and paper and wrote it in big bold letters across the top. **Dori gets half the money**.

She snatched the paper and crumpled it in her hand. Shaking her head, she gazed at him. "I'm so sorry. Forgive me. You're trying to help me, and I'm being a shrew. I just can't forget what your father thought of Marisa when she married Tyler. He said she was only after his money."

"Look at me, Dori. I'm not my father. Remember we're doing this to keep JT away from him. That's what we have to remember. We're doing it all for JT."

"I know, I know." She nodded as her eyes brimmed

with tears. She blinked, and tears trickled down her cheeks. She used the back of her hand to rub them away. "Forgive me?"

"Of course. Now let's make that agreement." As they talked things over, he agreed to whatever she said and wrote it down. It bothered him that she wanted so little. He had so much to give.

When they finished, she touched his arm. "Thank you for understanding. Thank you for helping me."

Chase smiled. He felt a whole lot better. "Sure. I'll contact Brady Houston tomorrow. He can draw up the prenuptial agreement and the adoption papers at the same time." Chase picked up the paper, folded it and put it in his pocket. "Dori?" She looked at him. "I think we should include a lump sum of money for you in addition to the child support in the agreement."

Blinking, she opened her mouth as though she was going to say something. Closing her mouth, she vehemently shook her head.

"Dori, listen to reason."

"I don't want to feel beholden to you for anything."

"Why would you feel beholden to me?"

She shrugged. "I just would. Child support will be enough. You've been very generous with that. Let's just go with what we've already agreed on. I understand how you want to take care of JT because he'll be your son. But you don't owe me anything. You're making enough of a sacrifice to help me."

"I asked you to marry me. You didn't come up with the idea. You're making more of a sacrifice than I am. You're giving up a budding relationship with Pete."

Dori placed her elbows on the table and stared straight

ahead. She didn't say a thing for a moment. Finally she looked at him. "If that were the case, I wouldn't agree to marry you."

"You aren't having second thoughts?"

She looked him directly in the eye. "No. I'm ready to go through with this just as much as you are."

"There's one more thing to discuss. The wedding."

Dori shrugged. "You make the plans. It makes no difference to me."

Chase wished it did. She was doing this for JT. She didn't care about the marriage. It meant nothing to her. "After I find out when Mr. Houston can meet with us, then we'll set a date. In the meantime, we need to spend time together so it won't seem strange when we run off and get married. Okay?"

"What…what did you have in mind?"

"A few dates."

"I suppose."

"Don't sound so enthusiastic."

Sighing, Dori tilted her head back. "I'm sorry. I'm still nervous. I feel like I'm getting ready to act in a play, and I haven't learned my lines."

"We don't have to know the lines. This is improv."

"You can say that again." Dori smiled. "Please be patient with me."

"I'll try. You'll have to be patient with me being patient with you," he said with a chuckle. "We can make this work."

"Yeah, I think we can."

"Good. Do you want to take JT to Lake Tahoe, too?"

"I hate to leave him. What do you think?"

"It's up to you." Chase tapped his fingers on the table.

"We should spend a few days out there and enjoy ourselves, take in a few shows and just relax."

"I didn't think of that." Dori shook her head. "We can't do that with a baby."

"We can get someone to watch him. How about your mom?"

"Oh no. If she finds out, she'll make a big fuss and say we can't get married in Tahoe. She'll want a big church wedding. We don't need that."

"Then who?"

"I could ask Natalia. Maybe she can get off work for a long weekend. Besides, there's something I need to tell you."

"What's that?"

"Natalia knows we're planning to get married to keep JT from Warren."

"How does she know?" Chase narrowed his gaze.

Dori quickly explained. "She promised not to tell. We can count on her to keep our secret."

The crack of a bat and the roar of the crowd filled the air. The batter rounded second base. Dori joined in the applause and glanced at Chase. He was on his feet cheering along with a number of people from the accounting department, their spouses and children. He gave a high five to the teenager sitting beside him as the lead runner for the Rangers crossed home plate to put the home team ahead of the Boston Red Sox in the bottom of the eighth inning.

Chase was sharing a good time with his employees. They all seemed to respect him. Maybe because he was the boss, but she had sensed a true admiration in their interaction with him during the whole evening. Her relationship with him had taken on a new tone, too. A more comfortable feeling. Like tonight. She and Chase and JT almost felt like family. A reality in only a few days, but a reality in name only. At times like this, their prospective marriage seemed right, but at other times doubts and fears gathered in her mind like the players around the pitcher when he was in trouble. Would their marriage bargain bring them trouble?

The Rangers ended the game with three quick outs for the Red Sox in the top of the ninth inning. Dori JT and Chase joined the jovial crowd exiting the ballpark.

"Did you have a good time?" Chase walked beside her as he held JT in a carrier.

Dori nodded, unable to find her voice. His nearness did crazy things to her insides. In less than a week he was going to be her husband. How could she deal with that when he made her heart race and her stomach jittery? That wasn't part of the bargain, nor did she want it to be. Somehow she had to get her head on straight. They were doing this for JT. Her personal feelings didn't matter.

"You're awfully quiet. Like JT. I can't believe what that kid can sleep through. The noise from the game hardly stirred him." Chase gave her shoulders a squeeze.

"I don't have much to say. Thanks for inviting me to the game. It was fun," she replied, trying to ignore the way his touch jumbled her insides.

"I'm glad you enjoyed it. I didn't know if you were much of a sports fan." He punched the remote to open his car as they approached it. The lights flashed and the horn beeped.

"I grew up with three brothers who loved sports. And you know what a sports fan my dad is." She took JT out of the carrier and put him in the car seat. "So I'm no stranger to sports, but I'm not a rabid fan."

"Well, I'm glad you indulged me."

"No problem." She got into the car and buckled her seatbelt. "It was only fair that I went with you to the ballgame after you took me to the arboretum."

He settled into the driver's seat. "The concert was entertaining."

"You mean you didn't like the flowers?" she asked with a giggle.

He joined her laughter as he started the car. "Let's just say the concert made the flowers more beautiful."

As they drove away from the ballpark toward Dallas, Chase maneuvered through the heavy traffic. In the darkened interior of the car with the hum of the motor for accompaniment, Dori reflected on the amicable nature of their conversation this evening. It made her heart lighter. Marriage might not be so bad if they could keep their relationship like this. Chase had appeared lighthearted and nonchalant about their upcoming marriage for the past two weeks. So why did she still have doubts?

Despite her worry, so far their so-called dates had turned out better than she had ever anticipated. Although JT had gone with them, the outings to the arboretum and the ball game resembled dates more than any of their other activities. Going to church, the Fourth of July family picnic and trip to see fireworks were more family affairs than dates. Even the dinner date at Chase's golf club had included her three brothers and their wives, who had all joined them for a golf outing earlier in the day. Sometimes, she wondered whether Chase was afraid to be alone with her.

"Has anyone said anything to you about us?" Chase's question interrupted her thoughts.

Dori thought back over the last two weeks. Maybe that's why he had included so many people. He wanted the others to notice them being together. "No. I thought for sure at least one of my sisters-in-law would have said something. They teased me about you when you first started coming around."

Chase glanced at her. "They did?"

"Yeah. You were quite the topic of conversation. Your ears weren't burning?"

"No," he replied with a grin. "What did they say?"

"You really want to know?"

He grimaced. "Maybe. If it's good."

"Oh, it was good, but maybe I'd better not tell you or you'll get a swelled head."

"That good, huh?"

"Could be."

"You're not going to tell me?"

"Okay. I'll tell you this much. They gave you the nickname Uncle Hunk." Dori snickered, then waited for his reaction.

"So you think that's funny?"

"Don't you?"

"No, I think it's quite an accurate description."

She laughed out loud as she relished their jovial exchange. "Oh, you have a big head already."

"You found me out."

"A good thing since we're getting married in a few days." Although her comment was meant to continue their good-humored conversation, it reminded her of the reason for these dates. Was she ready?

"Are you ready for that?" Chase asked, voicing the question as if he had read her mind. He parked in front of the house and cut the engine. He looked at her in the dim light.

She took a deep breath. "I'm not packed yet if that's what you mean."

"I wasn't talking about packing." He got out of the car and opened the backdoor to get JT out of his car seat.

"I know." She sighed, wondering whether she would ever be ready for this marriage. "I'm as ready as I'll ever be."

"You don't sound too sure," Chase said as he carried a sleeping JT up the front walk.

Dori stopped and unlocked the door, then turned to face Chase. "I'm still getting used to the idea, but I'm ready to do whatever it takes to protect JT."

Placing JT in her arms, he seemed to give her a questioning look as if he wasn't quite sure he could believe her. "Good. I've got a lot of stuff to get done at work before we go. So I won't see you again until I pick you up Friday morning at nine. That should give us plenty of time to check in for our flight."

"You can count on me." The conviction she mustered in her voice was as much for herself as it was for him. "I'll be here waiting for you."

Dori watched the heat waves rise from the highway as the limousine sped toward the airport. Worry about whether she was doing the right thing gathered in her mind like a vulture circling its prey on the Texas prairie. Trying to shake away the negative thoughts, she ran her hand over the smooth leather seat. She reminded herself that she was doing this for JT. She glanced at Chase, whose expression remained unreadable as he sat near her in the spacious vehicle. He didn't seem the least bit apprehensive about their upcoming nuptials.

He obviously had spared little in travel expenses. Now she wished she hadn't left all the wedding arrangements up to him. Men didn't care about weddings. So what had he planned? Did she dare ask?

"Would you like something to drink?" He picked up a glass before she had a chance to answer.

"Water."

"Okay." He put ice and water in a glass and handed it to her. Then he poured himself a cola and took a drink as he settled back in his seat. "Are you all right?"

"I'm okay. Why do you ask?" She set her glass in the holder.

"This." He reached over and took her hand.

"What are you doing?" she asked as her heart hammered.

"I'm holding your hand."

"Why?"

"Do you realize when you're nervous or upset you keep tucking your hair behind your ear. You were doing it just now."

"I was?"

"Yeah. You took a drink, then tucked your hair behind your ear." Still holding her hand, he grinned. "I've seen you do it dozens of times. I noticed when we first met." He patted her hand as he released it. "Now why don't you tell me how you're really feeling? You don't have to do this if you don't want to."

Gazing at her lap, Dori wondered whether she was always this transparent. The thought of telling him how she really felt had her insides tied up in knots. She had never been motion sick before, but she was feeling that way now.

Finally, she lifted her gaze to meet his. He sat there staring at her. She swallowed a big lump in her throat. "Is telling me I don't have to go through with this your way of getting out of marrying me?"

He continued to stare at her as the muscle worked in his jaw. His eyes narrowed. His brows knit. "Is that what you think I'm trying to do? Why would I spend money on a limo and first-class tickets if I wasn't planning to go through with this?"

"I…I didn't think you'd agree to everything I suggested. Why would you do it?"

He didn't say anything, but the muscle continued to work in his jaw. Breaking eye contact, he leaned back and stared straight ahead as he released a heavy sigh. "For JT. We're doing this for JT. I want him to have what I never had. A mother and a father who both love him."

"You had a mother and father."

"Yeah, biologically. But my mother got tired of me and dumped me on my father, who didn't want me either. Some mother and father. Tyler treated me like a brother. I owe it to him to make sure his son has the life he deserves."

"But even Tyler turned away."

"He came back in the end. We just didn't have the chance to act on our reconciliation. That's why it's even more important for me to look after his son." His gaze radiated determination. "But if you change your mind just let me know. You can back out any time you want, but I'm committed. You're the only one who can stop our getting married."

Dori let Chase's adamant commitment to this plan roll through her mind as she took a long drink of the water.

The clinking of the ice in the glass sounded like a warning in her mind. He had told her everything was up to her. He wasn't going to change his mind. He had put it all in her lap.

She cast a glance in his direction. He drank his cola while he looked over some papers he had pulled out of his briefcase. Business as usual. Why did he have to be so calm when her insides bubbled like his cola? She had to talk to him about the wedding and find out what he had planned.

"Chase."

He glanced up. "Yeah."

"Could I ask you a question?"

"Sure."

"What exactly have you planned for the wedding?"

"I thought you didn't care." He looked at her with one raised eyebrow.

"I…I'm only concerned that you've kept things simple. That you didn't make elaborate plans."

"And why would you think that?"

Dori waved her arm around. "The limo. Flying first class."

"I like to be comfortable. I hate shoving my six-foot-two body into a coach seat."

"Oh, of course." Dori felt like a fool, and she hadn't even mentioned her major worry.

"You'll like the wedding package I purchased. The hotel has arranged it. We have a suite for three nights. We have dinner reservations in the restaurant at the top of the hotel our first night. And I got tickets for a show the second evening."

"What about the vows?" Dori blurted.

"What about them?"

"Have you thought about them?"

"Like which ones we use?"

"Yeah, what are you planning to say?"

"I picked the traditional vows. Is that a problem?" Chase asked with a shrug.

Dori nodded. "I can't stand before God and promise things I don't mean."

"Then what vows would you like to make?"

"I don't know," she said, closing her eyes and shaking her head. She didn't want to look at Chase. Looking at his handsome face only confused her more.

"Dori," he said, touching her arm, "if it's this difficult for you, let's just call it off."

She opened her eyes and stared at him. "We can't. We have to do this for JT."

He nodded. "That's what I'd like to think. Think about the vows. Rewrite them to your liking."

"What do they say? I can't remember."

Chase gave her a wry smile. "You're worried about something you can't remember?"

"Don't laugh at me." She put her fingers to her temples and rubbed them.

"I'm not laughing, just smiling."

"Same thing."

"You're going to make *me* laugh." He opened his briefcase and brought out a folder. He searched through it until he brought out one piece of paper. "Here they are. The vows."

"You have the vows?"

"Natalia found this on the Internet for me." He held the paper up and began to read. "I blank, take you blank to be my wedded husband." He glanced at her. "That's your part. So far so good?"

She couldn't help smiling. "Yeah."

"Okay, let's go on. To have and to hold, from this day forward, for better, for worse." He looked up again. "Are you okay with that?"

"Fine," she said with a nod.

"Okay. On we go. For richer, for poorer, in sickness and in health." He tapped the paper with his finger. "This must be the problem. Even though I'm loaded with money, you don't want to take care of me when I get sick."

Dori sighed and glared at him. "Don't make fun of me. This is serious."

"Okay, I'm sorry. I'll get serious." He held the paper in front of him. "To love and to cherish, till death do us part. And hereto I pledge you my faithfulness."

"That's the part."

"The part you can't live with?"

She nodded. "How can I say 'to love and to cherish, till death do us part' when we're not in love?"

Chase didn't say anything. He just stared at the paper in his hand. Finally, he turned toward her. "Do you hate me?"

"No," she cried, knowing how badly she had treated him in the beginning. "How could I think of marrying someone I hate?"

"Sometimes you make me feel that way."

"I know. I'm sorry. I've discovered that you're really pretty nice."

"Nice enough to love as a friend?"

"Yeah," she replied with a nod, but she was unable to look him in the eye.

"Then think of it that way when you say 'to love and to cherish.'" He laid his hand gently on her arm. "Okay?"

Nodding again, she raised her gaze to meet his. As he

smiled, the dimples appeared in his cheeks. She resisted the urge to reach out and run her finger across them. At that moment, she realized she hadn't been worried about what she meant when she said 'to love and to cherish,' but what he meant. Natalia was right. Dori knew with a certainty she had fallen in love with a man who saw her merely as a friend, at best, or a business deal, at worst.

After they arrived at the airport, they checked their bags and made it through security without any delay. Chase took her to an airline club where he got her something to drink and a snack before he made business calls on his cellphone. She tried to read her book to pass the time, but she couldn't help thinking about her decision to go through with this marriage. Her husband-to-be proceeded to go about life as usual while she fretted about what this meant for her future. How would her family react? What would they decide when the adoption was final? The questions rolled through her mind until nausea twisted her stomach.

She had to remember she was doing this for JT. Somehow everything would work out if she put her trust in God. She had prayed to God that He would give her a sign. Chase would agree to her terms, no questions asked. He had. Even the prenuptial agreement that she hadn't wanted had been written in her favor when it came to protecting her rights where JT was concerned. So now she had to trust that God had given her the answer she hadn't expected.

When the announcement for their flight came over the loudspeaker, Dori followed Chase out to the concourse. Unlike his earlier concern, he seemed oblivious to her turmoil. Still on the phone, he talked with co-workers who had no idea he was about to elope. As they got ready to board the plane, the airline agent took Dori's boarding pass. Was it a first-class ticket to heartache?

Chapter Eleven

Chase watched Dori as she walked into their hotel suite. She went immediately to the panoramic windows and looked out. Then she turned to him with a look of awe. "The view's fabulous. Wow, the lake's beautiful."

"You picked Lake Tahoe."

"I know, but I never dreamed it would be this gorgeous."

"I'm glad you like it." Chase walked across the living room toward the door leading into the bedroom. "This room's yours. My room's on the other side of the living room."

Dori disappeared into her bedroom, and Chase made himself comfortable on the couch. Staring at the lake, he told himself that being in the bedroom with her would only serve as a reminder that he wasn't going to share a bed with his wife. He'd agreed to it, and now he had to live with that reality.

"What's this?" Dori's voice shook Chase from his thoughts.

Getting up, he turned toward her. She stood in the bedroom doorway as she held up a hanger containing a white dress. His heart hammered. "Oh, wow. We don't have our luggage, but they've already delivered the dress."

"Who?"

"The hotel."

"And why did they deliver this?"

"Natalia said you didn't have time to look for a dress. So I asked her if she liked this for you. She did." He crossed the room. "You don't have to wear it if you brought something else. It's up to you," he said with a shrug.

"So Natalia put her stamp of approval on this?"

"Yeah." Had he done the wrong thing this time? Everything had been going so well up to this point.

Dori looked at the dress, then at him. She smiled. "It's nice. I'll try it on to see if it fits."

Shaking his head and smiling, he watched her retreat into the bedroom. And here he thought he was able to read her moods. He returned to the couch, kicked off his shoes and put his feet on the coffee table. Lacing his hands behind his head, he gazed at Lake Tahoe nestled amongst the alpine beauty of the Sierras. Looking at the majesty of God's creation, he prayed for help with this marriage made for the sake of one little boy. Selfishly, Chase prayed that God would somehow let Dori learn to love him. He loved her. That realization became clear today while he read the wedding vows to her. He loved her not just as a friend, but as the woman with whom he wanted to spend the rest of his life.

Had he really thought this through? Was he trying to kid himself into thinking this would work? He had a marriage in name only and one that might last but a few months. He wanted more than that. An impossible dream? He pushed the worrisome thoughts from his mind. He had prayed that if God wanted this marriage for them, Dori would accept his proposal. She had. Now he had to believe this marriage is what God intended.

A knock on the door interrupted his thoughts. Opening the door, he discovered the bellhop on the other side waiting to deliver their luggage. "You can just leave the bags here," Chase said, then gave him a generous tip.

He stared at Dori's suitcase. What had she brought? She still hadn't inquired about the wedding other than her worry over the vows. He had to make himself realize she just didn't care. It didn't make any difference to her what he had planned. He had asked Natalia to help him plan the wedding when she had helped him pick out the dress. She had gone over all the stuff he printed off the Internet about Lake Tahoe. He had told her to plan something first class when it came to an elopement, but Natalia wasn't Dori. And Dori was the one who counted.

While he stewed over his plan, Dori reappeared, wearing what she had worn earlier. He tried to act like it didn't matter to him. "Did the dress work?"

Smiling, she nodded. "It's lovely. Thank you. You picked that out by yourself?"

Relief washed over him, and Chase let out the breath he'd been holding. "Natalia helped."

"What else did she help you with?"

For a moment, he almost imagined that a little jealousy came with that question. But he gave himself a mental shake back to reality. "Everything. I had no idea what to plan. I ran things by her, and she helped with all the details to make sure I wasn't doing anything you'd absolutely hate."

"Natalia has a tendency to be a romantic."

"And you're not?"

Shaking her head, Dori shrugged. "This isn't about romance. I believe you said it best. This is business."

"Well, I hope you don't mind mixing a little pleasure with our business."

Her eyes narrowed. "Just what do you have planned?"

"I thought maybe you'd prefer a surprise since you hadn't asked." He picked up her suitcase. "I'll take this into your room, then I'll let you know what's on the business agenda."

She followed him. "I didn't know there was anything to ask about. We get married, and that's it."

He set the suitcase near the bed. "First, we have to get the marriage license. We can do that now."

"Doesn't the hotel do that for you?" She gave him a puzzled frown. "That's what Marisa told me when she and Tyler eloped."

"Not in this case." Chase ushered her into the living room. "We're not getting married in the hotel."

"One of those little wedding chapels?"

"No."

"Then where?"

"In California."

Dori placed her hands on her hips. "Now you're teasing me."

"No, I'm serious." He glanced at his watch. "The clerk's office closes at four-thirty. So we'd better go. I'll get the car. Meet me out front."

When Chase brought the Lincoln Town Car he had rented around to the front of the hotel, he wondered whether he had made a mistake in not taking Dori with him when he didn't see her waiting. Maybe she had decided to back out. That scenario was constantly on his mind. At every turn, he feared she would look at him with those big brown eyes and tell him she couldn't go through with it. He took in a deep breath and let it out slowly when he saw her emerge through the hotel door. His heart pounded as she joined him in the car.

"Did you think I wasn't coming?" she asked breathlessly.

He didn't speak for a moment while he mulled over a good response. Could she read the worry in his expression? He didn't want her to know how anxious he had been. He smiled, trying to show that he wasn't concerned. "I haven't been here long."

"Sorry I was so slow. I think the elevator stopped at every floor on my way down."

"No problem." He started the car and pulled out onto the main highway. "The clerk's office is just up this main road a couple of miles across the state line. There's stuff on the seat that tells you about the wedding."

"This stuff?" she asked, picking up the folder that lay between them.

"Yeah." He kept his attention on the road even though he wanted to watch her reaction. Out of the corner of his eye, he saw her looking at the glossy promotional materials she had pulled from the folder.

"Chase?"

"Yeah."

She held up one of the pictures and tapped it with her index finger. "We're getting married on a yacht?"

"Yeah."

"Is that all you can say?"

"Yeah."

"Why? Why something so extravagant?"

"I wanted to make this a special day for you."

"Why?"

"Is that all you can say?"

She laughed. "No, but I don't understand why you'd do this when this marriage is only a business arrangement."

"When I go into business with someone, I do my best to gain customer satisfaction." He glanced her way, wishing he had the courage to tell her the real reason he wanted to marry her. Just beginning to realize himself that he loved her, he didn't want to scare her away with an unwanted declaration of love. But he was glad now for the special wedding he and Natalia had planned. He prayed the time would come when Dori would welcome his declaration of love.

She released a long sigh. "Well, this is more than I ever imagined."

"Is it okay?"

"Yeah, more than okay."

"Good. I'd hate to get off on the wrong foot." He slowed the car as he spotted the clerk's office. "We're here."

While they waited in line behind two other couples, Chase couldn't help noticing how they talked, laughed and constantly touched each other. Despite Dori's obvious delight over the wedding plans, she kept her distance. They stood like strangers waiting to get a driver's license instead of a marriage license. When their turn came, they showed their identification, paid the fee and signed in the proper places. In minutes, they possessed a license to get married.

"OK, we're all set," Chase said as they emerged from the clerk's office.

"Are we?" Dori tucked her hair behind her ear.

Chase's heart plummeted. He wasn't going to comment

on the gesture. The offer for her to back out was on the tip of his tongue, but he wouldn't give in to it. She would have to say the words, not agree with something he said. He had given her that opportunity earlier. He wouldn't make it easy for her now. He wouldn't give her the chance. "Questions?"

"Do we really know what we're doing?" She stopped beside the car.

"Yes. We're trying to protect a little boy."

She gazed at him with misery in her eyes. "I know that, but are you sure you're doing the right thing?"

Despite the pounding of his heart and the fear that curdled his insides, he looked her square in the eye. "Yes, I am."

"Chase, I'm scared."

"Of me?"

She shook her head. "No, you're my friend, but that license made it all so real. What if we can't make it work?"

Without hesitating Chase gathered her in his arms. She didn't resist, and that gave him hope. She felt so right in his arms. "With God's help we will. I promise."

Stepping out of his embrace, she gazed up at him. "I'm so sorry. You're trying to make this wonderful, and I'm like a big black cloud at a picnic. You won't hear another negative word from me. I promise." Then she stood on her tiptoes and planted a kiss on his cheek. "Let's go back to the hotel. I want to call Natalia and see how JT's doing."

"Good idea," he said, still remembering the touch of her lips as he opened the door for her. Every little thing she did left a brand on his heart.

On the way back she continued to study the information about the wedding. "So a limo takes us to the yacht?"

"That's right. We need to be ready around three-thirty tomorrow afternoon. Then we cruise over to Emerald Bay for the ceremony. It's on the California side of the lake. That's why we had to get a California license."

"The captain marries us?"

"Yeah. Then the crew serves us supper on the cruise back. And speaking of the marriage ceremony, what name do you want to use? Your given name's Dorinda. Why don't you use it?"

"Dori's always been easier," she replied with a chuckle. "Natalia's responsible for my being called Dori. When she was a baby she couldn't say my name. She called me Dori. And haven't I always been Dori to you?"

"Yeah." Smiling wryly, he nodded. "I made an appointment for you at the spa and beauty salon tomorrow morning. Take advantage of whatever they have to offer."

"So you're telling me I have carte blanche in the salon?"

"Yeah."

"Let's see. I can get a pumpkin peel or body polishing." She giggled as she studied the brochure for the salon. "Maybe I'll shine bright orange after that."

Chase grinned. "I kinda like you the way you are."

"You mean you don't want me to get a seaweed wrap?" She laughed.

"You do whatever you want." Her laughter made his heart lighter. He wished he could capture this joyful moment and make a thousand more like it. He only wanted her to be happy, not the tortured soul who had walked out of the clerk's office. "Pamper yourself."

After they got to the hotel, he dropped her off and went to park the car. Dori was just hanging up the phone when he walked into the room. As he approached, she looked up. "Natalia says hi. JT's doing fine, but my mother knows we've eloped."

"How?"

"Natalia said she forgot to put away our travel itinerary and phone numbers that were on the kitchen desk. Mom saw them."

"How does she feel about our eloping?" For the first time he realized he hadn't given enough consideration to the reaction of Dori's family about this sudden marriage. She was concerned about what her parents would think.

"Disappointed."

Chase's heart twisted. "Under the circumstances, I'm sorry she's not going to have a son-in-law she approves of."

Dori stood and walked over to him. Putting her hand on his arm, she gazed up at him. "Chase, it's not you. She likes you, but she's not happy about having another daughter elope. But she'll understand. You're going to be part of our family now."

Relief washed over Chase. He liked the idea of being part of a family who cared about each other. He had to make this work. He would hate to lose not only Dori, but her family as well. "That's a load off my mind. So JT's doing okay?"

"Yeah."

"How are you doing being away from him?"

"Okay," she replied with a nod. "But I didn't know I would miss him this much."

"Yeah, the little guy has a way of worming his way into your heart." Chase smiled wryly. Could he worm his way into Dori's heart?

The lake shimmered in the sunlight as the yacht cruised across the glassy water. The mountains provided a background of green against the blue sky and water. Standing at the bow, Dori clutched the railing. The breeze ruffled the chiffon flounce on her dress around her legs. Wearing a black suit, Chase stood beside her. She cast a surreptitious glance in his direction. Closing her eyes for a moment, she breathed deeply. The handsome man beside her, the lilting notes of a Jim Brickman CD playing over the yacht's sound system and the beauty of the surrounding countryside made this wedding the stuff of dreams. She wanted to pretend it was all real, but she couldn't let herself fall into that trap. She reminded herself that the absence of her family and the absence of true love dashed the dream.

All of this had been Natalia's fantasy for her, but that was the problem. It was a fantasy. Maybe Natalia had thought a romantic wedding might somehow change the reality of the situation. Chase was going through with this to make JT his son. She had to remember that fact. The thought made her shiver.

"Are you cold?" Chase's question brought her thoughts to an abrupt halt.

"Maybe a little," she replied with a slight nod.

"You want to go inside?"

"No, it's too beautiful to go inside." Crossing her bare arms, she rubbed them with her hands.

"Here, let me keep you warm." Chase stepped behind her and gathered her close against him. His arms encircled her. "Better?"

Unable to speak, she nodded. Closing her eyes, she leaned back against him and drank in his warmth. Her heart raced and ached at the same time. If only this were true love. If only.

Chase held her until the captain dropped anchor in

Emerald Bay. Then Chase took her hand and led her to the stern where the ceremony was to take place.

"Ready?" He gazed at her with concern as if he wasn't sure she would actually go through with this.

"If you are," she said, wondering whether he was seeking a last minute way out.

"I'm ready." The conviction in his statement laid to rest any doubts about his intentions. He handed her a cluster of yellow roses and baby's breath. "Here's your bouquet."

"Thank you." Smiling, she tried not to think about the yellow roses that stood for friendship, not red for love.

In minutes, surrounded by flower arrangements, they stood before the captain. Against the backdrop of sparkling water and the alpine beauty of the mountains, Dori and Chase repeated the vows they had talked about on the ride to the airport. As Dori repeated the phrase "To love and to cherish," she meant every word in the truest sense of its meaning. Not just in the sense of friendship as Chase had suggested. If only he felt the same way. If only.

The captain pronounced them husband and wife, then said, "You may kiss your bride."

Gazing at her new husband, Dori read the question in his eyes. She answered that question as she stood on her tiptoes and placed her arms around his neck. He drew her close. Their lips met. She closed her eyes and let the fantasy wash over her. Just for this moment, she would pretend he loved her and they would live happily ever after. His mouth covered hers, and she responded to his kiss with every ounce of her being. She wanted it to last forever.

When the kiss ended, Dori looked up at Chase. Surprise registered on his face along with a lopsided grin. He pulled her close again and whispered in her ear, "You can kiss me like that any time."

As a sinking sensation hit her stomach, she strained to smile. What had she done? She wouldn't think of what Chase might conclude from that kiss. Then having the photographer ask to take more pictures of them kissing did nothing to help.

While the yacht made its way back, the photographer took pictures from different locations while he had them holding hands, kissing, cutting a small cake and eating the meal served by the crew. The photographs would preserve all the day's memories. If only the pictures could make their love real. If only.

Dori observed Chase during the meal. He seemed to be enjoying every bite. He appeared to have no qualms about what they had just done. Why couldn't she enjoy the day as much as he was? She wondered whether her lack of appetite came from worry over the life they were about to embark upon. She shook away the pessimistic feelings. JT needed them. That's what this marriage was all about. There was no reason to worry.

"Don't you like pheasant?" Chase asked as he stopped eating.

"It's delicious."

"You've barely touched it."

"I know. I think I have a nervous stomach. That's all."

He reached across the table and took her hand. "It's going to be all right, Dori. We've done the right thing."

"You seem so sure. Why?"

"Because I promised myself I'd do everything in my power to make sure Tyler's little boy has a wonderful life. I want him to have all the things I never had." Chase took

Dori's other hand in his. "Love for JT is something we share. It's the reason for this marriage."

Dori nodded. She wished for so much more, but sharing a love for JT was a start. "You're a very sensible man, Mr. Garrett."

"And you're a very sensible woman, Mrs. Garrett." He gave her hands a squeeze. "We'll make a good team."

Dori liked the sound of her new name. Mrs. Garrett. Dori Garrett. While she let the names roll across her mind, she prayed that God would give her the wisdom to deal with this marriage made for the sole purpose of securing a little boy's happiness.

While they rode in the limousine back to the hotel, she looked at the man who was now her husband. She had feared feeling awkward with him, but nothing had changed except she now bore his name. He was still her friend even though she wished for more. Being his friend was better than nothing.

"We have tickets to a show when we get back," he said, interrupting her thoughts. "We can change before we go."

"What's the show?"

"Some country group. I hope you like that kind of music."

"I don't mind it," she replied, knowing anything would help distract her from thinking about the wedding night she wasn't going to have.

But after the show as they rode the elevator up to their room, Dori's head was filled with lyrics about searching and waiting for love, aching hearts, regrets and love gone right and wrong. She didn't need these reminders of all the pitfalls of love. She had created one big pit of her own and fallen into it.

When they got to the room, Chase unlocked the door

and opened it. He held it open as she went in. She quickly headed for her bedroom. Stopping in the doorway, she turned to look at him. "I'm going to call it a night. I'm tired. My body's still on Central time."

He stared at her for a moment. "Before you go to bed, I've got something for you. A wedding present."

"You shouldn't have done that." She had gotten him nothing. This wasn't a real wedding. They didn't need presents.

"But I wanted to." He rummaged in his suitcase until he found an envelope. Standing, he opened it and pulled out a piece of paper. "This is for you."

She took the paper and read it. When she had finished, she looked at him. "What does this mean?"

"I bought Tyler's house, and the money from the sale goes into JT's trust. I'm signing the deed over to you. It means you own it."

"But why? You didn't have to do that."

"I know, but I wanted you to have the assurance that no matter what happens, you will always have that house."

She could only stare at him. He thought he was being kind, but instead he was telling her that he didn't expect the marriage to last beyond the adoption. His gift was breaking her heart. "I'm sorry. I didn't get a wedding gift for you."

"I didn't expect anything. I know this marriage is about one thing—JT." Chase dropped his gaze to the floor. "I want you to be happy. Will you be happy with this arrangement?"

Dori's heart hammered as she stared at the man who was now her husband. Her husband, the man she loved. But she couldn't tell him. How could she be happy when she loved a man who didn't love her? And yet, he thought he was making her happy by arranging a marriage to protect JT. What kind of sacrifice were they both making? She didn't want to think about the future and what it might bring. How could she answer his question? There was only one answer because her happiness depended on JT's happiness. "Yes, yes, I'll be happy."

"You don't sound too sure. Why?"

"I'm sure. JT's future depends on it." She looked away quickly, fearful of what he might read in her eyes.

"What about our future, Dori?"

Had he guessed about her feelings? Or had that kiss on the yacht given him the wrong impression about the marriage being in name only? She couldn't ask. As Dori swallowed the lump that had formed in her throat, she turned to stare at him. There was no mistaking the look in his eyes. With her heart pounding so loud she was sure he could hear it, she shook her head. "I can't answer that, Chase."

"I know, but we'll have to figure that out sometime." He shoved his hands in his pockets.

"Good night, Chase." Her heart pounded, and it took every ounce of willpower to turn and walk into the bedroom alone. She closed the door and leaned against it. She let the tears flow as she flung herself on the bed and buried her face in one of the pillows. She could tell by the look in his eyes that he wanted her, but he didn't love her. How was she ever going to deal with loving a man who didn't love her? Had she trampled all over God's plan for her life?

Chapter Twelve

Dori drank in the sight of Tyler's house. No, now it was her house. She didn't want to deal with the implications of that gift. As the limo pulled up to the curb, she prayed that Natalia had succeeded in getting all the relatives to go home. Although no cars were parked out front, lights burning in the front rooms made Dori suspect otherwise. Everyone could have parked in the drive at the back of the house.

While Chase paid the limo driver, she walked slowly to the front door. Finding the door locked, she knew Natalia had managed to clear the house for their homecoming. Dori said a silent prayer of thanks as she found her keys and unlocked the door. As she stepped inside, Natalia hurried into the front hall from the family room.

"How are you?" Natalia asked, giving Dori a hug.

"Good."

"I want to hear everything."

"Not tonight. I'm tired." Deep down, Dori wished she could share all her thoughts and worries with her sister, but Chase's presence wouldn't allow it. "How's JT?"

"Sleeping, but he'll be up bright and early." Natalia put a hand on one hip. "I'm the one who's tired. You didn't tell me I'd have to get up at six in the morning, or I'd never have agreed to this job."

Shrugging, Dori grinned. "You should've taken a nap when he did."

"Who could take a nap when Mom was over here constantly wanting to know if I'd heard from you. I deserve a medal for getting Mom and Dad to leave tonight before you got here, but all your nieces and nephews left you a little surprise. I convinced them that you newlyweds would want to be alone." Natalia gave Dori a speculative look. "Is there any truth to that statement?"

Before Dori could answer, the door opened and Chase stepped inside while he and the limo driver set the suitcases on the floor.

"Hey, Natalia, how's my new sister-in-law?" Chase gave her a big hug. "I see you survived?"

"Barely! That kid gets up too early," she said with a chuckle. "I'm glad you're back."

"Me, too. I want to see that kid."

"He's sleeping. So I'm going to get out of here and let you guys have a family reunion."

"Thanks for everything," Dori, said, giving Natalia another hug. "We'll talk tomorrow."

"I'm parked out back. So I'll just let myself out. See you tomorrow."

"Okay." Dori watched Chase as Natalia disappeared through the family room door. His expression was somber. Did he feel as awkward as she did now that they were alone? She had just spent eight hours traveling halfway across the country with him and spent three nights together in a hotel suite. So why did she feel so nervous?

"I'll have to get you a key for the house and a garage door opener," she said, trying to cover her nervousness.

"Yeah, that would be good." He locked the front door and set the alarm.

"Well, at least Natalia was the only one here to greet us. We can be thankful for that. I don't think I could deal with my family tonight," she said with a sigh.

"Better your family than mine. Let's check on JT." Chase picked up one of the suitcases sitting by the front door. "I'll take your suitcase to the nursery for you."

"Okay," she said, thinking how stilted their conversation sounded.

They quietly tiptoed into the nursery. Chase set the suitcase by her bed. While she watched JT sleep, Chase joined her. He gently stroked the baby's head. She watched the loving action with a pang of regret. In the past, Chase had often put an arm around her shoulders as they stood watching JT but not tonight. Chase hadn't touched her in any way since their wedding. She missed his casual, friendly contact like a pat on the arm, a hug or a hand on her shoulder. She didn't realize how much they meant until they ceased. Although she longed to touch him, she resisted the urge. Living in the same house with him wasn't going to be easy. She wanted with all her heart to share the physical side of marriage, but she couldn't do that without Chase's love.

Despite all her misgivings, she wanted the best for her sister's child. For the child that would soon be hers. While Chase stood there with her, not saying a word, she knew they had done the right thing. No matter what happened between Chase and her, keeping JT from Warren Davis was worth the sacrifice.

"Do you want to see the surprise your family left?" Chase's question interrupted her thoughts.

"Sure." Dori leaned over and kissed the top of JT's head, then looked at Chase. "I love that little guy."

"Me, too."

Dori followed Chase into the family room. When she stepped farther into the room, she saw a huge banner strung across the fireplace mantel. Big red letters spelled out CON-GRATULATIONS and the artful images of children danced around the letters. She stopped for a moment and looked at it. She loved her family, and it made her heart ache to think Chase and she didn't share that same family love. The reality of this marriage hit her with full force. Telling her parents over the phone from Lake Tahoe had been pretty easy, but now that they were back how was she going to manage?

Chase walked across the room. "At least this is all we have to deal with tonight."

She turned to look at him. "That's true. But believe me, this is only the beginning. Wait until tomorrow. We'll be smothered. My mother will be here first thing in the morning."

Chase took the banner off the mantel and rolled it up. "You can deal with your parents tomorrow, and I'll deal with mine. I'm sure Warren will have some choice words for me when he finds out we've gotten married. I might get lucky, and it won't be tomorrow."

"Well, I wouldn't want to trade places with you. I'd rather talk with my parents rather than your father."

Chase snapped his fingers. "And here I thought you'd be willing to trade places with me."

"No, thanks," she said, glad they could joke about this now. Maybe things with Chase wouldn't be as awkward as she had first thought. "I'm really tired. I'm going to bed."

"Me, too," he said. "Where do you want me to sleep?"

The question hung in the air while all the awkwardness returned like a cat pouncing on its prey. She remembered the look in his eyes that night in the hotel room, but tonight his expression was blank, no love, just nothing. She longed for some emotion from him. Even dislike would be better than nothing. He was acting like a polite houseguest in his own home. But this is what she had asked for, and he was giving it to her.

"The master bedroom is all yours."

Grimacing, he shook his head. "No, I'd feel strange in there."

For an instant, she caught a flicker of regret in his eyes, or had she imagined it? "So I'm not the only one who feels like that room still belongs to Marisa and Tyler."

"I guess you could say that," Chase said with a shrug.

"If you don't want that room, you can take your pick of one of the rooms upstairs. There are linens on all the beds. Help yourself."

He headed for the front hall. "In that case, I'll get my suitcase and head upstairs. We both need to get a good night's sleep so we can survive the onslaught of relatives tomorrow."

"You don't have to convince me." She followed him into the foyer.

He picked up his suitcase that sat on the Oriental rug. As he passed by, he leaned over and kissed her on the cheek. "Good night."

With her heart beating in double time, she placed her

fingers where he had kissed her. Without a backward glance, he climbed the stairs. The kiss left an imprint in her heart. After he disappeared from sight, she turned away wondering why he had kissed her. After not touching her in any way for two days, what kind of message was he trying to send with that kiss?

The next morning, Chase went to the office bright and early. Dori had already been up when he had come down to the kitchen. Having someone there at breakfast felt strange. He had tried to read the paper, but he couldn't concentrate. Finally, he left because being with Dori and not being able to act on his feelings for her made him nearly crazy.

While he worked, his mind buzzed with thoughts of Dori and what their marriage meant. He accomplished little because his mind alternated between dreams of Dori and nightmares of Warren. Finally, Chase decided to confront his nightmare. He would tell Warren about getting married. That way, he would be in control of the situation. Warren would have nothing prepared when he received the announcement.

Chase dialed Warren's direct line. "Hello, Warren, this is Chase. If you have a free moment, I've got something important to tell you." Chase paused as Warren indicated he was free. "Great. I'll be there in five minutes."

When Chase walked into Warren's outer office, he remembered the day Warren had told him about his plans to thwart Dori's adoption of JT. What would come from this meeting?

The secretary nodded when he stopped by her desk. "He said you could go right in."

"Thanks." Chase opened the door. Warren was on the phone, and motioned for Chase to take a seat.

When Warren finished on the phone, he looked up at Chase. "What do you have to tell me?"

Chase stood and walked to the desk. "I got married this weekend."

Warren came around the desk and slapped Chase on the back. "I guess congratulations are in order. You'll have to introduce me to your bride."

"You've already met her."

"Well, which one is she?"

"Dori Morales."

Warren stepped back and glared at Chase. "What are you trying to prove here, boy? That gal is nothing but trouble, just like her sister. What are you thinking?"

"I'm thinking this will stop you from trying to gain custody of JT." Chase glared back. "You're the one who's trouble, trying to take a little baby away from his mother."

"That woman isn't his mother."

"She's the only mother he has now and a good one, too."

"There are things you don't know about that little gal, Chase. She tried to commit suicide."

"She told me you'd try to use that against her. And I was dumb enough to tell her I didn't think you'd be able to get that information. She knows you better than I do."

"So she told you. Probably trying to make you feel sorry for her. I can see you bought it hook, line and sinker. Besides that, she's probably after your money."

Chase laughed halfheartedly. "You're wrong there. We signed a prenuptial agreement."

"Well, at least you got smart on that account." Warren went back behind his desk.

"The thing I got smart about is marrying her. My name goes on those adoption papers now."

"So you think you can stand in my way?"

"Yes."

Leaning forward, Warren placed his hands on the desk. "You've got guts. I like your spirit, boy. Just like your brother, and over a woman, too."

Chase felt as though his heart had stopped for a moment. This was the first time Warren had ever referred to Tyler as his brother. Chase didn't know what to say. He took the coward's way out and said nothing. Taking aim at Warren over JT's adoption was enough confrontation for one day. "This isn't over a woman. It's over what's best for a little boy."

"Well, I like a good fight. May the best man win."

Smiling wryly, Chase nodded. "And I'm that man. You're going to lose big time. If you were smart like you say you are, you'd forget about gaining custody of JT and be a real grandfather to him. Otherwise, you're going to be a lonely old man without a family to turn to when you need one."

"Don't talk to me that way."

"It's time somebody did." Chase turned and headed for the door.

"If you weren't my son, I'd fire you," Warren called after him.

Chase almost turned around, but somehow he kept going as his pulse pounded in his brain. What was Warren trying to do? He hadn't ever acknowledged with words that Chase was his son. Why today? To soften him up? Take him off his guard? Warren was a shrewd negotiator. Chase couldn't let his guard down for a moment. He wouldn't let Warren get to him with the words he had wanted to hear since he'd been twelve years old.

When Chase arrived home, Dori was in the kitchen with her mother. He set his briefcase by the door. This was a performance for his new mother-in-law. "Hi, sweetheart. I'm home."

Dori immediately put down the knife she was using to slice mushrooms and hurried to greet him. She flung her arms around his neck and whispered in his ear, "Nice greeting. Kiss me."

His heart raced as his mind grasped what Dori was doing. Pretending for Mom just as he had with his greeting. Her idea was better. Putting his arms around her waist, he pulled her close, bringing her off her feet. The familiar scent of her floral perfume assailed his senses as he kissed her gently on the lips, then set her back on the floor. This pretending was going to kill him. He dreamed of kissing her like this dozens of times, but without the audience. Unfortunately, without the audience there would have been no kiss. "I guess you missed me," he said, grinning. "How was your day?"

She smiled and put her arm through his as she led him toward the kitchen. "My day has been fine except for dealing with my mother. Maybe you can talk some sense into her."

"What's this about?" Chase gazed at Teresa who was stirring something in a pan on the stove.

She stopped stirring. "No, you talk some sense into your wife. We want to have a little reception for you with the family. Now what's so bad about that?"

"A little reception to her is hundreds of people. She'll invite every person who has a drop of Morales or Juarez blood. You don't know how these things can mushroom. You've seen how many people are in the immediate family alone." Dori's eyes opened wide, imploring him for help.

He wanted to please her. How could he respond?

Luis came into the eating area through the door that led out to the pool. "Well, if it isn't my new son-in-law."

"Hello, Mr. Morales."

"Mr. Morales?" Luis boomed. "Dad. Call me Dad." He grabbed Chase's hand and shook it. "Congratulations. We're glad to welcome you to the family. My only regret is not getting to walk my daughter down the aisle." He turned to address Dori. "Why do you girls keep eloping?"

"To save you money, Dad." Dori stood on her tiptoes and gave her father a peck on the cheek.

Teresa joined the group. "Luis, convince them they need to have a reception."

Feeling the acceptance of this family, Chase put a hand on Teresa's shoulder. "We appreciate what you want to do, but we don't need a reception. We certainly don't want any gifts. We have everything we need."

"But we need a celebration to welcome you into our family." Teresa crossed her hands over her heart. "You don't know how happy this has made us. So surprised, but so happy. We loved your brother Tyler. And we love you just as much. You'll be like our own son. Like Luis said, we want you to call us Mom and Dad."

A tightness settled in Chase's chest, and he couldn't speak for a moment. Warren's acknowledgment, Dori's kiss and Teresa and Luis's acceptance into the family were all the emotional bombs Chase was prepared to take in one day. He wanted to be alone for a moment to collect himself, but he couldn't run out of the room. Instead, he took a slow, deep breath. "I'd like that. I'm proud to be part of your family."

"And we are proud to have you. That's why we want to have the reception. Don't you see?"

Chase nodded. "Yes, and I think it's a wonderful idea."

"Chase, how could you do this to me? I thought you were on my side!" Dori bellowed.

He went over and put his arm around her waist, using this situation as another chance to touch her. "I am, dear."

She looked up at him with a question in her eyes. "Then how could you agree with her?"

"Listen, I think we can work something out that will make everyone happy."

"What could that possibly be?" Dori's face was painted with skepticism.

"Why don't we wait and have a big celebration when the adoption is final. We can do it all at once."

Teresa clapped her hands together. "Oh, that's a wonderful idea. And that will give me more time to plan. What a smart son-in-law I have."

"Thanks, but your daughter's the smart one. She picked me for a husband." Chase pulled Dori close and kissed her again. He had promised himself he wouldn't touch her unless it was necessary, but that promise evaporated when he had kissed her hello tonight. He wanted to taste her delicate sweetness. One kiss had whetted his appetite for more. All the signs pointed to trouble ahead.

After dinner and an evening discussing plans for the big celebration, Dori walked her parents to the front door. Chase followed behind, carrying JT. Closing the door after her parents, Dori turned to Chase as she leaned back against the door. She didn't know whether to be pleased or angry with him. "I hope you're satisfied with yourself."

"As a matter of fact, I am. I thought I handled that pretty

well. Your parents went home happy, and we don't have to have a reception. Just as you wished."

"I didn't want one at all."

"At least this way, the emphasis will be on JT and not on us. Right?" Chase raised his eyebrows in question.

What could she say? He was right. But there was a problem. One she didn't want to face. How could she live with this man and continue to hide her real feelings? "Just listening to my parents tonight makes me think this was all a mistake."

Chase's gaze searched her face. "We haven't made a mistake."

"Why are you so sure?"

"Because I told Warren about our marriage today. I thought it would be best for him to hear it from me rather than someone else." Chase readjusted JT in his arms when the baby started to fuss.

Dori held out her hands. "Let me take him. He's hungry. I'll get him ready for bed. Then you can tell me about Warren."

Chase placed JT in Dori's arms, then kissed him on the top of the head. "Good night, my little slugger. Hit a few homers in your sleep."

"Dad won't like it if you turn him into a baseball player instead of a football player."

Chase laughed. "Dori, this is baseball season. When it's football season, I'll tell him to throw some touchdown passes and when it's basketball season, a three-point shot."

As Dori took JT to the nursery, she thought about this situation. How was she going to survive being with Chase day after day when he didn't love her? Chase's kisses affected her more and more each day.

What would happen if they went beyond a gentle brushing of the lips? She closed her eyes and inhaled a shaky breath at the thought. When she was honest with herself, she wanted to experience his kisses. She wanted to share the tender bliss of a real marriage. But she couldn't do that without his love.

When JT was asleep in his crib, Dori tiptoed out of the nursery. She found Chase in the family room watching a baseball game on TV. She sat down on the couch with him, and he turned off the TV with the remote.

"You didn't have to turn off the game on my account."

He set the remote on the end table. "That's okay. It was a lopsided game anyway. Besides, I wanted to tell you about my meeting with Warren."

"What did he say?"

"He said he's going to fight us. I tried to talk him out of it, but it didn't make much of an impression." Chase moved toward her on the couch and took her hands in his. "He knows about the suicide attempt."

The news made Dori's heart sink while Chase's touch made her heart race. "How can he be so cruel?"

"I don't know, Dori. I've never understood him. He's my father and yet a stranger." Chase's beautiful kaleidoscope eyes radiated with sadness.

Dori wanted to take away that sadness. Warren's fight with her not only hurt her, but Chase and JT as well. What must it be like to have a father who was a stranger? Thankfully she didn't have to know. "Is there any way you can convince him not to do this?"

"I tried, but he won't listen. I told him he was going to wind up a lonely old man without a family."

"Does that mean you've turned your back on him, too?"

"No, he's still my father, and I hope someday he'll act like it." Chase paused as if he was thinking about something. "You know what he did today? He called me his son for the first time in my life. I don't know why he did it, but I can't turn my back on him now."

"Then why is he trying to fight us?"

Chase released a halfhearted laugh. "When you hear how he called me his son, you'll probably understand. He told me I shouldn't talk to him that way. Then as I'm leaving he calls out, 'If you weren't my son, I'd fire you.'"

Dori's heart broke for Chase. "How mean can he get?"

"I'm not sure he meant to be mean. My suspicion is that he was trying to use it to soften my resistance."

"Well, whatever the reason, I think he's awful."

Dropping her hands, Chase slid closer on the couch and put his arm around her. He gave her a wry smile. "Remember, he's your father-in-law."

"Something I'd like to forget." Dori leaned against Chase. He was touching her again and not because they had an audience they had to impress. She couldn't read anything into it, but she wanted to. She wanted to hold him in her arms and take away his hurt. The hurt of having a father like Warren Davis. Her own family was such a contrast.

"I hope you still don't hold being Warren's son against me. I hope we can be friends. I know you didn't like me for a long time, but I hope that's all changed."

Changed. Yes. More than she had ever dreamed. "Yes, we can be friends."

"You don't sound very sure." Chase's eyes were filled with a question.

"I'm sure." Sure that she wanted to be more than friends. That's why she wanted this marriage to be real, full of love.

But for now, she had to be satisfied with having Chase as a friend. A friend who was on her side when it came to protecting JT against Warren. Yet, she worried about how she was going to deal with loving Chase when he didn't love her.

Taking his arm from around her shoulders, he turned to face her. "Thanks. That's important to me. Will you be my friend no matter what happens?"

"Why are you asking that?"

"A lot can happen."

Dori's heart beat faster as she stared at him. Her pulse pounded throughout her body. What was he trying to say? "You promised to keep the bargain we made regarding this marriage."

"Yes, but you don't have anything in writing." Chase stared at her. "Maybe that's something you should've put in the prenuptial agreement. What if I change my mind?"

"I couldn't put our plan in a prenuptial agreement. I didn't want Mr. Houston or anyone to know. This is just between you and me. If it isn't in writing, then no one else could find out. Besides, I didn't think I needed it in writing. I have your word." Dori realized she had come to trust Chase. He had given his word, and she had believed him.

"I'm glad you've come to trust me that much. When it comes time to decide what we want to do with this marriage, maybe the best thing is to leave it up to God."

Dori swallowed a lump in her throat, then breathed deeply. "Are you asking what God wants for us?"

"Yeah," he said, nodding. "Keep that thought."

"Okay," Dori said, knowing she had fought her attraction for Chase by trying to hate him and assign him motives. How had she ever disliked him?

Chapter Thirteen

Dori stood in the family room and stared at Natalia, who perched on one of the stools at the breakfast bar. "I suppose you're here to find out about the wedding."

Natalia nodded. "I thought I'd never get you alone so I could hear all about it. You have to tell me everything. I've been waiting all week. Mom said your pictures are beautiful."

"So you've talked to Mom?"

"Yeah, she's eagerly planning this party for you and Chase." Natalia gave Dori a questioning look. "How do you feel about that?"

"It doesn't make any difference. There's no stopping her."

"The pictures are in that album on the coffee table." Dori put JT in his swing and turned it on.

Natalia hopped down from the bar stool and retrieved the album. Sitting on the couch, she opened the album and placed it in her lap. She gave Dori a speculative glance. "You both look happy."

"Who wouldn't be happy standing on a yacht surrounded by the splendor of that lake and the mountains? The pictures don't capture half of the beauty. It was a fairy tale."

"And does this fairy tale have a happy ending?"

"What are you asking?" Dori wondered how much she could tell Natalia.

"Did anything change between you two while you were gone? You seemed pretty eager to be alone that night when you got back."

"Nothing's changed. It's not a real marriage."

"I was hoping it would be." Natalia looked up from the album.

"Is that why you made the elaborate wedding plans?"

Natalia shrugged. "It wasn't my idea."

"Then whose idea was it?" Puzzling over Natalia's statement, Dori knit her eyebrows.

"Chase's."

"He told me you made the plans."

"I did," Natalia said with a nod, "but he said, 'Don't consider the expense. Make it wonderful for her.' And those were his exact words."

"But why would he do that?"

"I'd say he cares for you. Don't push him away."

"I don't have to. He leaves early in the morning to work out before he goes to the office and comes home late. I rarely see him," Dori said, afraid to reveal her real feelings for Chase.

"Maybe that's his normal routine."

"Could be, but I think he's trying to avoid being alone with me."

"Why?"

"It's obvious. He married me for one reason and one

reason only. He wanted to make JT his son. That's the only thing we have in common."

"And how do you feel about the whole thing?"

Dori couldn't hide her feelings from Natalia any longer. "I know one thing. You were right. I love him."

"Then what's the problem?"

"He doesn't love me." Dori sighed heavily. "It's business."

"But he spent a lot of money on this wedding," Natalia said, nodding her head. "He must care."

"Believe me, Natalia. It's business. Like entertaining clients. You know. Give them the best."

"Well, he can certainly do that. You do realize your husband is a multimillionaire, don't you?"

Dori nodded. "But money can't buy love."

"Chase, I want to see you in my office. Now." Warren's commanding voice resonated over the phone.

"I'm on my way." Chase hung up the phone and grabbed his suit jacket as he left his office. Glancing at his secretary, he said, "I'll be in Mr. Davis's office."

Chase walked to the elevators. What did Warren want now? They had said nothing personal to each other since that day a month ago when Chase had told Warren about his marriage. Did other people notice the strain he was under? Seeing JT every night was the highlight of his life, but being around Dori and not holding her was driving him crazy. At first he left for work early and came home late, but it only took him a few days to realize when he did that, he didn't get to see JT.

Thoughts of Dori constantly crossed his mind. While she puttered around the kitchen each morning, she hummed as she fixed their breakfast. It took every ounce of his willpower not to go over and put his arms around her. As Chase stepped off the elevator, he shook away thoughts of Dori. He needed to get ready for his meeting with Warren. He sensed this meeting was about more than business just by the tone of Warren's voice.

When Chase went into the office, Warren greeted him with a handshake. "How's married life treating you?"

Surprised by the question, Chase took a minute to collect his thoughts. "Great. It's nice to have someone to come home to every night." Without a doubt, despite everything else, that part was true.

"Well, good." Warren took a seat at a conference table to the left side of his desk. He motioned for Chase to sit down beside him. "I've heard the deal you had going to sell Davis Import and Export has fallen through. Is that right?"

"How'd you know?"

"Not much happens in the way of business around this town without my knowing about it."

Shaking his head, Chase realized what a stupid question he had asked. "Yeah, I wasn't thinking." Blame that on Dori. "You're right, the sale fell through at the last minute. The buyers lost their financial backing."

"If you still want to sell it, I have a buyer."

"Who?"

"Me."

Stunned, Chase didn't respond. What was Warren going to do? Try to get a steal on the company because he thought Chase was desperate to sell? He'd let the company go into bankruptcy before he'd sell it to Warren. "I'm not interested."

"You haven't heard my terms. How can you turn me down?"

"Because I don't like the way you treated Tyler. It would be an affront to his memory for you to have that company."

Warren slapped the tabletop with his hand. "You are getting bold. I let you get by lecturing me the other day, and now you think you can tell me anything. I'm beginning to see that behind those numbers you spout to me all the time, you've got some gumption. I like that."

Chase glanced at Warren. The man was grinning from ear to ear. He was serious. Chase realized he should have stood up to Warren years ago and told him what he had thought. "Good. Then maybe you ought to listen to me on this. I won't let you ruin Dori's reputation by bringing up her past in a custody battle that you'll never win." Glaring at Warren, Chase wished his father could be reasonable. "I don't know how I'm going to stop you, but I'll try everything in my power to do it."

Leaning back in his chair, Warren put his elbows on the arms of it and steepled his hands in front of him. "So you'll do anything, huh? Sell me Tyler's company."

"Why do you want it? So you can destroy it as you did your relationship with Tyler?

"No, I want something of my son's." Chase heard the anguish in Warren's voice. "Don't you think I grieved for Tyler? I have a profound regret, more than I can ever tell you, that Tyler and I were estranged when he died."

For a moment, Chase's heart went out to Warren. But when Chase thought about all the pain Warren had caused, Chase steeled himself against any sympathy he might feel. "It's too late. You can't bring Tyler back by buying his company."

Warren slapped his hand on the table again. "Didn't you

hear what I said? Sell me the company, and I won't try to gain custody of Tyler's son."

"His name is Jacob." Chase scowled at Warren. "Do you think you can get the company for a little bit of nothing because I said I'd do anything to keep you from ruining Dori's reputation?"

"No, I'll give you the same deal you were ready to make with the other buyers."

Chase rubbed his hand down his face. "Did I hear you right?"

"Yes, I'll put it all in writing. The custody stuff and everything." Warren stared at Chase over the top of his hands that he had once again steepled.

Chase released a harsh breath. Dori wouldn't approve of what he was about to do, but she would never have to know. This was the best way to save her a mountain of heartache. In a couple of months, JT would be legally hers. She would have everything she wanted.

Chase wished he could say the same for himself.

Standing, he extended his hand. "You've got a deal."

Warren smiled and stood as he shook Chase's hand. "I'm proud you're my son. I wish I had told you before."

Warren's statement, words Chase had wanted to hear since he was twelve years old, caused a monumental ache to settle around his heart. Could he take this declaration at face value? He didn't want to doubt his father's sincerity. "Why didn't you?"

Warren sighed and dropped his gaze. "I've never been very good at personal relationships. Business relationships, yes, but personal, no."

Chase wondered whether he was following the same

pattern. Here he was married to the woman he loved, and he couldn't even tell her. "So why now?

"I want to do right by the one son I have left. When you told me off a few weeks ago, I began to realize I was pushing you away the same as I did Tyler. I couldn't let that happen again."

"So if you feel that way, why did you use the custody issue as leverage to get Tyler's company?"

"Because I didn't know any other way to get it." Warren placed a hand on Chase's shoulder. "Will you help me? I'm still working on this relationship stuff. I hope this can be a new beginning for you and me."

Chase nodded, gratitude filling his heart. "You and me both."

Laughter, music and gregarious talking filled the brightly lit room. Glowing chandeliers hung from the ceiling of the hotel ballroom. Dozens of tables were arranged around the room with a long buffet table on one side and a disc jockey on the other. Dori greeted and hugged everyone as they came through the door. Sitting nearby in his carrier, JT gurgled and cooed from all the attention. Standing by her side, Chase occasionally put his arm around her waist and drew her close. Acting like a happy couple. If only it were true.

She smiled even though inside she was crying. They had signed the adoption papers, and JT was theirs. Somehow Chase had gotten his father to drop the custody battle, and all had been smooth sailing in the adoption. She should be fabulously happy, but she wasn't. Chase seemed strangely distant when they were alone.

Chase leaned over and whispered in her ear. "I don't know about you, but I'm getting tired of standing here. Can we eat? The smell of that food is making my stomach growl." He made a growling sound in her ear that sent shivers down every nerve in her spine.

"That sounds bad. Go get some food," she said, hoping that when he left, her heart would stop beating faster than the mariachi music. "Bring something for me, too. I'll meet you over at the table where my parents are sitting."

"Good. I'm headed for the food line."

Dori watched Chase maneuver his way across the crowded room. He stopped to talk to several people along the way. Everyone loved him. She most of all. She wanted to tell him how much she loved him, but if he didn't feel the same, telling him would do no good. Their marriage was a bargain, and the bargain had to be kept.

When Dori sat down at the table with her parents, her mother turned to her. "Now aren't you glad I decided to do this? Everyone is having such a good time."

"Yes, Mother," Dori said, knowing any other answer would fall on deaf ears.

Teresa cooed at JT. "And my little grandson is the life of the party." She looked up at Dori. "Where's Chase?"

"Right here with food for my lovely wife." He put a plate in front of her, then leaned over and kissed her cheek.

She let the shivers subside before she spoke. "Thank you."

"You know this party isn't just for JT. We have to introduce the happy new couple," Luis boomed.

"Dad, let us eat first, please," Dori pleaded.

"All right, but as soon as you're done, I'll have the disc jockey announce you." Luis clapped Chase on the back.

While they ate, the disc jockey played a variety of songs to please everyone in the four generations of Moraleses and

Juarezes gathered at this celebration. Dori ate slowly because she didn't want to be the center of attention. She was afraid people would notice something amiss when her father introduced Chase and her. Everyone would see they weren't the deliriously happy couple they were supposed to be.

After Dori finished eating, she noticed her father going to talk to the disc jockey. She leaned over to Chase and whispered, "We're up next. Make it good."

He whispered back. "You can count on me. I'm always good."

"Chase, don't kid. This is important."

"Who's kidding?" Grinning, he took her hand and pulled her to her feet.

They walked hand in hand across the ballroom to where her father stood waiting with a broad smile. Luis addressed the gathering while Chase put his arm around her waist and held her close. As he held her like this, she wanted the night to last forever. If only he treated her like this when they were alone. Luis finished his announcement, and the crowd applauded. Then he indicated that Chase should say something.

Taking the microphone, he stepped away from her and looked over the crowd. Smiling, he looked back at her and nodded for her to join him. When she stood beside him, he again took her hand. Her heart filled with pride. He leaned over and gave her a little kiss on the cheek, then spoke into the microphone. "I'd first like to let my beautiful wife say a few words."

She looked at him. Was this his way of making it good? Wishing he really meant those words, she tore her gaze from his and looked around the room. Her heart hammering, she hoped she made sense. "We're so happy to be here tonight. Thanks for all your support and love. We're grateful to have a fantastic family to share this wonderful moment with us."

Family and friends applauded. Trying to keep her composure, she handed the microphone back to Chase.

Putting his arm around her, he took the microphone and turned his attention to the audience. "Dori has said it well. I also want to thank y'all for coming here tonight and celebrating our joy in becoming JT's parents. Now enjoy the food and the music."

Chase handed the microphone back to Luis. The disc jockey put on another disc, and soon the sound of Van Morrison's "Tupelo Honey" filled the room. Then Chase looked down at her, and for a moment, she felt as though they were the only two people in the room. She couldn't mistake the look in his eyes. Like their wedding night. What would it take to see love in those eyes? What would it take for him to truly think of her in terms of this song? But how could he think of her as sweet as honey when she had given him little reason? Could she ever break through the armor around his heart? Why did he have to look at her that way now?

Chase dropped his gaze from hers and stepped away. "Let's go back to the table," he said, guiding her in that direction.

Dori's heart did a little dance when he smiled and took her hand again. Maybe there was a little crack in his armor. Emotions of every sort flooded her mind. She needed to get away for a moment and collect herself. "Tell Mom and Dad I'll be there in a minute. I'm going to the restroom."

"Okay." Chase headed toward their table as Dori made her way through the crowd of well-wishers.

As Dori came out of the restroom, she heard someone

call her name. Glancing around, she saw Natalia walking quickly toward her.

"You two looked really good together. He just has to be in love with you. No guy looks at a woman that way without being in love." Natalia stopped Dori's exit.

Shaking her head, Dori leaned back against the wall. "It's not real."

"He looked pretty smitten to me."

"Yeah, for a moment I almost believed I had made a crack in that wall he's erected around himself. JT's the only one who gets through to him. Sometimes, I feel like the invisible woman."

"That way you could sneak up on him," Natalia said with a laugh. "Well, you'd better get back in there and be the attentive wife."

When Dori returned, she searched the room for Chase. When she saw him, her heart skipped a beat. Then it jumped into her throat when she saw Warren standing beside Chase. What was Warren doing here? Had Chase invited him?

Holding JT, Warren was laughing and smiling. He was talking with Chase and her parents as if he did this every day. How could he come here and ruin her evening? Why had Chase let him? Anger boiled up inside her as she marched across the room.

As she drew close, Chase spied her. He came to her side and put his arm around her waist. She felt the pressure as if he was trying to keep her under control. Normally, his touch would send her pulse racing. Now it only raised her blood pressure, not from passion, but from fury.

"Hi, sweetheart. Look who's here." Chase's eyes pleaded for peace.

"I see," she replied, realizing Chase was as uncomfortable as she was. Maybe Warren had invited himself. She wasn't going to let the man upset her. "Hello, Mr. Davis. I'm so glad you're finally getting a chance to meet your grandson."

"Hello, Dori. Congratulations on your marriage and your new son." Smiling, he shifted JT to one arm and extended his hand.

"Thank you." Dori smiled in return, but inside she was burning with rage. How dare this man come in here and act like he had never done anything to hurt her family?

"Dori." Chase grabbed her arm. "Let's get a little fresh air."

She didn't protest. When they reached the doorway leading to the balcony off the ballroom, he stood aside and let her go out first. As they stood in the dim light, she glared at him. "Why is he here?"

"Your mother said he called and wanted to come. She didn't want to say no. He's a very persuasive man."

"He doesn't belong here."

"Dori, you're going to have to get used to it. He's JT's grandfather, too."

"I can't believe you're on his side."

"I'm on nobody's side. I make my own choices," Chase said as the muscle worked in his jaw.

"I don't understand your choices."

He narrowed his gaze and lightly gripped her upper arm. "Let me explain. He's my father, and believe it or not, he's not all bad. You told me once how well Tyler treated his employees. Where do you suppose he learned that? Warren Davis may be lousy at personal relationships, but he's a great boss. And the way I see it, he's working on that personal thing. Sometime, Dori, you're going to have to get over your hatred."

A sinking sensation hit her square in the stomach. "I never said I hated your father."

"But you act like it." Releasing his hold on her, Chase smiled, but his words didn't match the expression on his face. "He's done some bad things, but God expects us to forgive, doesn't He?"

Feeling sick inside, all she wanted to do was run away where she didn't have to look at the disapproval in his eyes. She could only nod as he continued to stare at her.

"Well, at least we agree on that much." He crossed his arms. "If you find having Warren Davis for a father-in-law so difficult to contend with, we can still get that annulment."

Dori felt the color drain from her face. "Is that what you want?"

"We did say after the adoption we would reassess this marriage. Looks like that time has come." He turned and walked back into the ballroom.

Dori's heart broke as she watched him walk away. Was he walking away from their marriage? She couldn't let that happen, but how could she stop him? All the progress she had made with him over the past weeks lay in ruins like the confetti that littered the floor. She wanted to blame Warren, but that would only prove that Chase was right. She wanted God's forgiveness as well as Chase's, but she had to forgive Warren first.

Chapter Fourteen

Sunday morning following the celebration, Dori sat next to Chase in church and rued her temper. He seemed to be engrossed in the sermon, but she couldn't keep her mind on any of it. Despite Chase's declaration that they should reassess their marriage, he hadn't said another word about it. Why had she accused Chase of siding with Warren? She had done the same thing Tyler had done. She had made Chase choose between her and his father. She closed her eyes. *Heavenly Father, please give me the strength to forget and forgive the past where Warren Davis is concerned because I can't do it on my own.*

When church finally ended, Dori's mother greeted them and immediately took JT from Dori's arms. "Oh, he's getting so big."

"Tell me about it." Dori held up her arm and flexed it. "See that muscle. That's from lugging him around. I think he's going to be tall like Dad."

"Do you have JT's things in the car?" Teresa asked. "I can get them right now so you can be on your way to the baseball game. I'm looking forward to baby-sitting. I haven't had much chance since you and Chase got married."

Nodding, Dori glanced at Chase who was talking with Luis. Seeing them together served to remind her that somehow she had to learn to get along with her father-in-law if she wanted any chance to have a real marriage with Chase. Today would be a test of her resolve while she sat with Warren in the W.T.D. Enterprises luxury box at the Rangers game. "You don't get to baby-sit because Chase works so much he wants to spend time with JT. I'm surprised he's not taking JT to the game."

Teresa chuckled. "I bet Chase can't wait until JT's old enough to go to a baseball game."

"Yeah, Chase might have withdrawal symptoms because this is the last game of the season," Dori replied with a halfhearted laugh. "Let's get that stuff."

"Since Chase likes to take care of JT, do you want to go to a movie with me this Friday?" Tesesa asked as they made their way to the car. "That new movie starring all those different actresses starts Friday, and your father won't go because he considers it a 'chick flick.'"

"That sounds like Dad." Laughing, Dori handed her mother JT's things. "I'd love to go. I want to see that movie, too, and I'm sure Chase has the same opinion as Dad."

"Good. We'll talk about it when you get back from the game."

"Okay," Dori replied as Chase and Luis joined them.

"Ready?" Chase's expression told her he was asking about more than going to the game.

"Sure." Dori forced a smile, but dread filled her heart. She felt like Daniel on his way to the lions' den.

* * *

"Too bad the show was sold out. Guess we should've left earlier," Teresa said as they drove away from the theater. "Did you enjoy the baseball game Sunday?"

Dori knew her mother didn't care about the game. She wanted to know how things went with Warren Davis. "Everyone was civil."

"How about you and Chase?"

"What do you mean?"

"Is everything all right with you two?"

Dori stared straight ahead. She didn't dare look at her mother. She couldn't lie to her.

"Does your silence mean you're having problems?" While they waited at the traffic light, Teresa touched Dori's arm. "I'm not meaning to pry, but I just sense there's something wrong."

Turning to look at Teresa, Dori nodded. "It's a mess."

"Your marriage?"

Dori nodded again.

"Would you like to explain?"

"I don't know."

"If you want to talk, I'll listen without making any judgments." The light changed and Teresa drove ahead.

Dori didn't know what to do. She wanted to tell her mother everything. But if Dori told her mother, would she betray Chase's confidence? She didn't need to do anything else to make him angry. Now he avoided her in the evenings when he came home. He often took JT upstairs with him while he watched some sporting event on TV. He was politely distant. They were strangers occupying the same house. Even her attempts to be civil to Warren didn't seem to please Chase. Maybe he still expected more, but she couldn't bring herself to be friends with Warren Davis. That would take more time. "I'm not sure I can talk about it."

"Well, why don't we go to that little dessert place we like and have some comfort food? And if you feel like talking, we can do it over something delicious and not fattening at all." Teresa laughed. "Okay?"

"Okay," Dori said, knowing that she was blessed to have a wonderful mother.

When they were settled at a table for two near a window that looked out on the street, Dori studied the menu even though she knew she would order her favorite chocolate cake. Looking at the menu gave her an excuse not to talk or at least gather her thoughts before she did. After the waitress took their order, Teresa mentioned how quiet the house was now that Natalia was back at college and talked about how much she looked forward to the forecast for cooler weather. Dori recognized her mother's small talk as a way to ease into the discussion she hoped to have about Chase. But Dori wasn't brave enough to start that conversation on her own.

Finally, their order arrived. Teresa reached across the table and took Dori's hand. "Let's ask the Lord to bless this food and the conversation."

Dori bowed her head. As her mother asked a blessing, Dori prayed silently that God would help her make things right with her family and Chase.

After Teresa finished praying, Dori took a bite of her cake and let the sweet, rich chocolate melt in her mouth. Comfort food was the right word for this confection, but it couldn't bring comfort for things she planned to tell her mother before the night was over. Dori placed her fork on her plate and picked up the mug of coffee and wrapped her hands around it as she took a sip. The heat of the mug warmed her hands but not the cold places in her heart. She looked over at her mother. Would she understand?

Teresa set her mug on the table and returned Dori's gaze. "I know I'm not supposed to give unsolicited advice, but let me just say a few things. The first months of marriage can be rough as a couple tries to get used to one another. Both you and Chase have been on your own for a good while. It can take some adjustment living with another person. And adding a baby into the mix can make it even more difficult. Give it some time, Dori. Things will be better. Believe me."

Shaking her head, Dori swallowed hard. This was it. Time to tell her mother the reason for their marriage. "It's not what you think, Mom."

"Then what is it?"

Dori wanted to cry, but she squared her shoulders and looked her mother in the eye. "We're not really married."

Teresa's frowned. "How is that possible? I saw the wedding pictures."

"Oh, the wedding was real, and we have a paper that says we're married. But the marriage is in name only. It was a business arrangement to keep Warren Davis from having any chance to get custody of JT." Holding her breath, Dori waited for her mother to digest the information.

"Whose idea was this?"

"Chase's, and I thought it was the only way to protect JT. Warren threatened to fight for custody by bringing up my past." Hanging her head, Dori sighed heavily.

Teresa took Dori's hand and squeezed it. "It's okay, Dori. I understand."

Dori looked up. "You do?"

"I know how much you love JT," Teresa said with a nod. "And how much you loved Marisa and Tyler. That explains everything."

"It's a relief for you to know, but I don't know what Chase will say about my telling you."

"Tell me what the plans are for the marriage now that the adoption is final."

"I don't know."

"And what does that mean?"

"Chase's original proposal involved getting an annulment after the adoption was final." Dori sighed again. "We were supposed to reassess our feelings after the adoption, but we've done nothing."

"Why not?"

"Basically, Chase has been ignoring me. Now I'm just waiting for him to say it's over."

"Do you want it to be over?"

Dori swallowed hard. What could she tell her mother? "I don't know."

"Are you in love with Chase?" Teresa raised her eyebrows in a question, then took a bite of her cake.

"Why did I ever think I'd be able to fool you?" Dori asked, shaking her head. "I'm better at fooling myself."

"How's that?"

"Because of what Warren Davis did to Tyler and Marisa, I was trying so hard to not like Chase I didn't realize I had fallen in love him until we were on our way to Lake Tahoe. The realization nearly undid me because he doesn't love me."

"Are you sure?"

Dori nodded. "The other night at the celebration he

reminded me that an annulment was still an option. That conversation erupted over Warren again. But Chase hasn't mentioned it again."

"Dori, you need to get past Warren Davis."

"I know," she cried softly. "But it rips my heart out every time I see him acting like he's never done anything to hurt our family. It's a huge source of contention between me and Chase."

Teresa took another bite of her cake and chewed it slowly. Finally, she placed her fork on her plate and looked directly at Dori. "Eat your cake, and listen to me."

"Okay." Her appetite nearly gone, Dori barely nibbled at her cake.

"I know Warren Davis has done some things that hurt all of us, but I truly believe he's trying to make up for those misdeeds. I thought you ought to know your father and Mr. Davis are going to be doing business together. They've signed an agreement for your dad's company to handle all of W.T.D. Enterprises' outside printing needs. This is a big contract for your dad's printing business."

Dori took in the information with a sinking sensation in the pit of her stomach. She smiled halfheartedly. "So Warren Davis is winning over everyone except me. Seems I have no choice but to join the crowd."

"It won't hurt you. Warren wants to have a part in JT's life." Teresa slowly nodded. "You know I always considered JT our special gift from God, and I think he's produced a special gift in bridging the gap between Warren Davis and our family. God approves."

The jovial buzz of nearby conversation and the clink of silverware and dishes filled the air while Dori considered some response to her mother's assessment.

Finally, Dori asked, "Are you sure Warren isn't trying to fool us?"

"Yes. He said Chase made him see he'd been wrong. That's why I invited him to the reception when he called."

Dori shook her head. "Why didn't you tell me?"

"There was never an opportunity, but I'm telling you now. So I hope you can make things right with your husband."

"How can things be right when I love him and he doesn't love me?" Dori asked with a shrug.

"Tell him how you feel."

"So he can reject me, or just stand there and stare at me when he can't return the feelings?" Dori released a long shaky breath. "I don't want to see the pity in his eyes. It could make the situation that much more uncomfortable."

"Well, suit yourself, but you've told me what's in your heart, and you feel a lot better for it. Maybe telling Chase will do the same thing. Take a chance."

While Dori drove home, she rehearsed what she planned to say to Chase. Her stomach churned. Her heart raced. *Lord, give me the strength to tell Chase how I feel.* When she walked through the door from the garage, the family room was empty. With a determined step she went in search of Chase. He was probably in his office.

As she walked through the bedroom to the office, the sound of male voices filled the air. Her heart plummeted when she saw Chase talking with Warren while he held JT. She stepped into the office. Chase and Warren turned to look. Her resolve to tell Chase that she loved him died when she looked at Warren.

"Hi, Dori." Chase walked over to her. "You're home early. I thought you and your mom were going to a movie."

"It was sold out, and we didn't feel like going to the ten o'clock show." She smiled, vowing not to let her irritation show. She didn't like Warren in this house, but she had to get over her anger or she would only drive Chase further away. "How are you, Warren? I'm surprised to see you here."

"Just stopped by to see my grandson. He's getting bigger every day. He looks so much like his daddy." Warren put his hand on Chase's shoulder. "Well, I'm going to head home, son. I'll see you in the morning. Good night, Dori."

"Good night," she said, watching him stick out a finger for JT to grab before he kissed the top of the baby's head. Warren shouldn't be allowed. She shook away the disparaging thought.

"I'm going to see Dad out." Chase handed JT to Dori, then continued talking with his father as they left.

So it was "Dad" now. Dori turned away, feeling exhausted from suppressing her anger. As she held JT in her arms, she noticed a paper lying on the desk. The bold print said something about Davis Import and Export Company. Leaning over, she picked it up and began to read. Her brow knit as she took in the words.

The letter, from one of the company's biggest accounts, mentioned the recent acquisition of Davis Import and Export by W.T.D. Enterprises.

Nausea rose in her stomach. She didn't want to believe what she was reading. Chase had sold Tyler's company to Warren Davis. The specter of Scott rose in her mind as she continued reading. Another betrayal. And to think she had almost laid her heart out for Chase to trample on.

"Dori, give that to me."

She turned at the sound of Chase's voice. "It's too late. I've already read it." She handed it to him. "So this is why you and Warren are so chummy all of a sudden. I should've known. You did this to win his approval."

"You're wrong. It's not like that at all. I did this for you."

Dori laughed derisively. "For me. How could this possibly be for me?"

Chase released a harsh breath. "He said he'd drop the custody battle if I sold him the company. I did it to keep him from dragging your past through the courts."

Part of her wanted to believe him, but Scott had stood before her in the same way. He had told her he had done everything for her. Chase was just like him. "You didn't do it for me. You did it for yourself so you could adopt JT and please your father. You used me to get what you wanted."

"Please, Dori, listen to reason. You're just upset right now." Chase reached out to her.

Holding JT close, Dori pulled back. "Don't touch me. I think this is the right time for that annulment you mentioned the other night. You can move out. I'll start whatever it is we need to do to annul this marriage. It's obviously served its purpose for both of us. It no longer needs to exist."

"I didn't mean it that way, Dori. What about JT? Doesn't he deserve a real family?"

Dori glared at Chase. "You call this marriage a real family? I think it'll be easier to end this now while JT's a baby. I told my mother everything tonight."

"Oh, I see." Chase hung his head. "Okay, if that's the way you want it. I'll pack some things tonight and leave. I'll be back later to collect the rest of my stuff."

"That sounds reasonable to me." Dori turned away. She didn't want to look at him or think about what she had almost done. She could thank Warren for one thing. He had saved her from making a grave mistake.

Chapter Fifteen

The following morning while Dori finished putting a load of clothes in the wash, the doorbell rang. She hurried to the door. When she saw the image of a male figure on the other side of the leaded glass, her heart jumped into her throat. Was Chase coming to get the rest of his things? She didn't know whether she could face him. Cautiously opening the door about a foot, she saw Warren holding a shopping bag in one hand as he stood on the front porch. Her defenses rose immediately. What did he want?

"Hello, Warren. Chase isn't here."

"That's okay. I didn't come to see him. I came to talk with you." Warren stepped closer.

"About what?" Dori eyed him through the narrow space. Was he here to make sure she didn't try to gain the family fortune from Chase? "I'm not sure we have anything to talk about."

He put his hand on the door. "I have something for you. Just hear me out. Then I'll leave. May I come in?"

At least he had asked and hadn't barged in demanding to talk with her. Stepping aside, she let him in. "We can talk in the living room."

Warren glanced around the room as he took a seat on the couch. "Where's that grandson of mine?"

"Taking his morning nap," Dori replied, sitting at the far end of the couch.

"I've forgotten that babies do that," he said with a smile.

"What did you want to say?" Dori folded her arms across her midsection. What cruel thoughts lay behind that smile? "If you're worried that I'm after Chase's money, you don't have to be. We signed a prenuptial agreement."

"I know. I'm not here about money."

"Then why are you here?" Dori unfolded her arms and twisted her hands in her lap.

Warren reached into the bag he had set on the floor at his feet. He pulled out what appeared to be several photo albums. "I thought you might like these." He held them out to her. "Pictures of Tyler while he was growing up. When JT is older, you can show them to him."

"Thank you." Dori took the albums and set them in her lap without opening them. Staring at Warren, she couldn't get over his hesitant demeanor. This wasn't the arrogant, pompous man she had come to know. He seemed almost contrite. Why? Not knowing what to expect from him, she carefully opened the top album. A smiling baby stared back at her. "These look just like JT," she said, lifting her gaze to meet Warren's.

"That's one of the reasons I brought them over." Warren nodded and slid closer to her on the couch.

Dori resisted the urge to move away. Instead, she let Warren help her thumb through the album. He explained the pictorial biography of his firstborn son as a baby, pre-schooler and elementary school student. When Warren finished going through the first album, Dori picked up the second one, her heart aching over the terrible tragedy that had claimed her sister and brother-in-law. The second album contained pictures of Tyler in junior high and high school. As Warren slowly turned the pages, she let out a little gasp when she recognized a picture of Chase. He and Tyler stood together in front of an outdoor basketball hoop.

"That's Chase, isn't it?" She looked at Warren for confirmation.

He nodded. "Yes, that's another reason why I brought these over. I wanted to talk with you about Chase."

"What about him?" Dori swallowed a lump in her throat. She had let her anger over the selling of Tyler's company dictate her action, but she had done the wrong thing. She hadn't been able to get Chase out of her mind or her heart.

"First of all, I want to apologize for the way I treated you and your sister. I was wrong about her, and I was wrong about you. I want you to know I'm pleased to have you as my daughter-in-law." Warren smiled and set the album aside. "I know it's a lot to ask you to forgive me, but I hope you can for Chase and JT's sake."

Staring at Warren, Dori didn't know what to say. He didn't know about the annulment or that she had asked Chase to leave last night. Chase had tried to tell her Warren was working on that personal thing. She should do the same. Yet, even now the urge to strike out at him reared its ugly head. He had been so cruel, but she had to find it in her heart to forgive him. Why was it so hard? Her prayers didn't seem to help.

"I've made a lot of mistakes in my life," Warren said, interrupting her thoughts. He jumped up from the couch and started pacing the room. "I want a fresh start with my grandson. Please give me that chance."

"Is this about JT, or is this about you and what you want?"

His shoulders slumped, and he stopped pacing as he turned to face her. His brilliant blue eyes that usually made her cold swam with sorrow. "I want to make up for my mistakes with Tyler and Chase. Chase is a fine man. I'm proud he's my son."

"You have a strange way of showing it. You didn't even acknowledge him by giving him your name." Dori laughed halfheartedly.

Warren clenched his fists at his side. "That's only one of the many mistakes I've made. When my father died, I left Boston and moved to Texas to make my fortune. I did well, but I thought marrying a young woman from a prominent family would enhance my standing. That was my first mistake. By the time Tyler was two years old, Sally and I led separate lives except for the necessary social engagements. I was immersed in my business dealings, and she spent her time in social and charitable activities. About that time I met Chase's mother, Loretta."

Stunned, Dori continued to sit on the couch as Warren started pacing the room again while he poured out his life's story. Shifting in her seat, she wished somehow, he would stop. She didn't want to hear this confession. He was oblivious to her discomfort. "Mr. Davis, why are you telling me all this?"

He stopped and looked at her as if he suddenly realized he was talking to someone he barely knew. "I want you to understand why I treated you and your sister the way I did. I want you to know what Chase had to deal with when he was young." He didn't wait for her approval as he launched into the remainder of his story. "Loretta worked as a waitress at the hotel in New York City where I stayed on business trips. She let me know she was interested in me in no uncertain terms. I resisted in the beginning, but eventually, I gave in. My next mistake. We had an affair that lasted nearly five years."

"If you knew it was a mistake, why did you continue with it?" Dori asked, furrowing her brow.

Warren released a heavy sigh. "She blackmailed me, threatening to tell Sally everything if I didn't help her get acting and modeling jobs. She moved to California and did some acting, but when her career began to wane, she started demanding more money. I paid because I wanted to keep an eye on Chase, and despite my troubled marriage, I still didn't want Sally to know. When I went to visit him on his eleventh birthday, I found out Loretta was into drugs and drinking heavily."

"How could you have left your son in a situation like that?" Dori asked, interrupting Warren's speech.

He gazed at her as if he was weighing his answer. "I wanted to get Chase away from Loretta, but I couldn't upset Sally, who was recovering from breast cancer. Strangely enough, her illness had brought us together. I realized how much I loved her. The thought of losing her terrified me. Do you know what I mean?"

Nodding, Dori thought about how her heart ached for Chase. She had been such a fool for telling him to leave. "Yes."

"Then you can understand how I struggled with the

decision to get Chase. But the final straw came when I went to visit a few months later and found he'd been left alone for a week. I stayed with him until Loretta finally showed up. I told her I intended to take Chase away from her no matter what she said to my wife. I set out to get custody, but a few weeks later Loretta showed up in Dallas. She said I could have Chase for a price. I figured no price was too much to pay to get my son away from her. I gave her a large six-figure sum, and she signed away her parental rights. I never saw or heard from her again."

Dori stared at Warren who looked out the front window. His figure, silhouetted against the sun glinting off the glass, reminded her of Chase as he had stood in that same room months before and told her that his father had never given him the Davis name. "Chase doesn't know this story, does he?"

Warren turned to face her. "Oh, he realizes some of it, but he never knew about the money I paid."

"Why not?"

Sitting on the couch again. "Maybe I've made another mistake not telling Chase the whole story, but I couldn't tell him then or now what his mother had done. It was hard enough for him to know how much Sally detested his presence in our home."

Dori nodded. "He did mention to me that Sally was never a mother to him."

"Chase was a constant reminder of my infidelity. I could never undo the hurt I caused Sally. But I tried to please her. That's why I never gave Chase the Davis name."

"Don't you think he should know?"

"He's never asked about it, and I didn't want to dredge up the past and all its pain. If he asks, I'll tell him. The personal lines of communication between us have opened up in the past few weeks. We've talked, not about the past, but our future relationship. He's forgiven me." Warren looked up. "I'm hoping you can do the same."

God expected her to forgive, but she couldn't say the words.

Warren sighed again. "I know I don't deserve your forgiveness, but I had hoped you'd understand. After Sally died from a recurrence of the breast cancer, I was looking forward to Chase's return after he finished graduate school and Tyler's engagement to the daughter of a longtime friend and business associate. Then out of the blue, Tyler showed up with your sister. I'll admit I didn't handle that situation well. My big concern was that, like Loretta, your sister was after money."

"That wasn't true."

"I know that now, but at the time I was basing things on my own experience with women. I alienated one son and didn't know how to talk with the other. I didn't know how to tell either one of them I loved them. I've learned one important lesson. When you love someone, you have to tell them."

"That's true." Blinking, she fought back the tears stinging her eyes. Pressure built in her chest. Her heart ached for the young boy whose mother had abandoned him to a father who didn't know how to love him. And now she had turned Chase away, too. She had been no better than Warren. She had judged Chase on her past experiences with other men. He didn't deserve that. She had to forgive Warren and find some way to gain Chase's forgiveness. She had to tell Chase she loved him.

"Do you forgive me?" he asked as he gazed at her.

"Yes, I do." Her voice sounded shaky even to her own ears.

"Thank you, Dori. I'll try my best to be a good father-in-law. Let me know if I get out of line," he said with a wry smile. "Could I see JT before I go? I won't wake him."

Dori nodded. "We can peek in on him."

While Dori stood next to Warren as they watched JT sleep, she thought of all the times she had done this with Chase. She prayed that she would have a thousand chances to share this experience with him again.

After they finished looking in on JT, Dori walked to the door with Warren. "Why did you buy Tyler's company?"

Warren placed his hand on the door handle. "I wanted to make sure that company was in good hands until JT is old enough to see what his father built. Maybe, someday, if he wants, he can run his father's company. But only if he wants to. I've learned you can't tell your children what to do. It's a lesson I learned too late for Tyler, but not for JT." Suddenly, Warren reached over and gave Dori a hug. "Thanks."

Realizing she shared the same hopes for Tyler's company with Warren, Dori could only nod as she hugged him back.

After Chase arrived at his office to catch up on some work after his Saturday morning workout, he was surprised when Warren walked in. Chase had to tell his father about the annulment. There was no point in prolonging the pretense of his marriage. Would his father be happy? Chase wasn't looking forward to telling Warren no matter what his reaction.

"Hello, Chase," Warren said, laying a folder on top of Chase's desk. "I have a company here I want you to look at. Tell me if their numbers look good."

"Sure. I'll take a look and get back to you as soon as I can." Chase took the folder and opened it. When he glanced up, Warren was still standing there. "Is there something else?"

"Yeah." Warren stepped closer to the desk. "I went to visit that pretty little wife of yours, and we've come to an understanding. I know that little gal didn't like me much, and she had good cause. But I thought I'd try to make some amends this morning by taking her some photo albums. We had a good talk. So I thought I could take you and Dori out to dinner. How about seven-thirty out at the club on Friday night?"

Chase gazed warily at his father. "Dori didn't mention anything about asking me to move out of the house last night?"

Warren stared at Chase. "No."

Sighing, Chase stepped from behind his desk. "I can't believe she didn't tell you we're having the marriage annulled."

"You have some explaining to do." Warren motioned for Chase to take a seat as he sat down in the chair next to the desk. "I want to know what's going on."

Chase rubbed the back of his neck. What would his father think when he learned the whole story? "All right. I'll tell you."

With an aching heart, Chase told his father how the marriage had come to be. When he finished, he stood and stared out his office window.

Coming around the desk, Warren put a hand on Chase's shoulder. "You haven't told me the whole reason for this marriage."

Puzzled, Chase looked at his father. "What do you mean?"

"You didn't tell me that you love her."

"What makes you think so?"

"The way you stood up for her. Just the way Tyler did

with Marisa." Warren raised his eyebrows in a question. "Admit it."

"You're right."

"Why didn't you explain to her why you sold me the company?"

"I did."

"Obviously, not in the right way. You know the mess I made of my relationships. Don't follow in my footsteps."

"What makes you think I'm following in your footsteps?" Chase asked, not wanting to admit his father was right. "I haven't purposely set out to hurt the people I love."

"And you think I did?"

"It appeared that way."

"Let me explain a few things."

"Yeah, like why you never gave me your name."

Warren released a long, slow sigh. "When you came to live with us, Sally was devastated to learn about my affair even though it had been over for years. She insisted I not recognize you as my son, and I agreed because I knew how much I had hurt her. I don't know that it made any difference because most people guessed anyway, but it pleased her. When Tyler went away to college, she demanded that I send you away to boarding school. So I did."

Chase stood and walked over to the window and looked out. "You sent me away to get rid of me."

"Not to get rid of you. To give you a good education at a very good school."

"I hated being sent away."

"And I hated sending you away, but you would've been unhappy living with us. To Sally, you were a reminder of my affair." Warren joined Chase near the window. "I couldn't please both of you, so I had to choose. I thought the choice I made was for the best. I loved you both."

Not looking at his father, Chase leaned back against the windowsill. His heart ached. All this talk revived all the hurtful feelings from the past. He turned back to Warren. "Why did you sabotage my reconciliation with Tyler?"

Warren rubbed a hand down his face, then shook his head. "One of my many mistakes. I thought if you and Tyler got back together, I'd lose you, too. Instead of telling you how I felt, I tried to keep you apart. That's why I said you're following in my footsteps. You haven't told Dori you love her. Don't give up without a fight."

"But how can I change her mind? What should I do?"

"You'll figure it out."

Chase parked his car in front of Tyler's house. Dori's house now. Gripping the steering wheel, he stared straight ahead. He was here under the pretense of getting the rest of his things. Otherwise, Dori probably wouldn't let him in. What could he say to change her mind? Could he convince her to reconsider the annulment? Could he open himself up for rejection again? Would her rejection make him feel any worse than he already did? All these questions cluttering his mind gave him a headache.

Warren had told Chase he should figure it out for himself, and he had been thinking about it all afternoon. He had to tell Dori he loved her. That's what his father meant. Look what had happened when he had told Warren how he felt.

As he rang the bell, his heart pounded. His mouth was drier than West Texas. How was he going to start? When the door opened, the sight of Dori took his breath away. "Hi. Please let me come in. I need to talk to you."

"I can't talk now. I—"

"Dori, let me talk with you," Chase interrupted. "Hear me out. Then I'll leave."

"If you'd let me finish, I was trying to tell you I have company. Natalia's here. I can't talk now. Do you understand?"

"I thought Natalia was back at college."

"She's home for the weekend because Manny's gone with the football team. A&M plays at Kansas this week."

"Sorry, I should've let you explain. Is it all right if I see JT?"

"Yeah, he's with Natalia." She turned and walked toward the family room.

Chase followed. When he entered the room, Natalia looked up. "Hi, Chase. Forget your key?"

Shaking his head, Chase wrinkled his brow. Had Dori not told Natalia their marriage was over? She was acting as though nothing was different. "Didn't Dori tell you—"

"Natalia and I have been busy," Dori interrupted as she slipped her arm through his.

"And you can help," Natalia said, seemingly oblivious to the tension between Dori and Chase.

"Help with what?" Chase asked.

"Which one do you like better?" She poked a catalog under his nose and pointed at two different dresses. "Dori's helping me pick out some dresses."

"You're asking the wrong person. I don't know anything about women's dresses."

"You did okay with Dori's dress. Just tell me which one you like," Natalia said.

"This one," he said, just pointing at one. He wished he hadn't come in here. He couldn't talk with Dori now. Not with Natalia there. Maybe if he went upstairs with JT and took enough time, she would finally leave.

"Thanks, I like that one, too."

Chase stared at Dori. "I'm going upstairs with JT."

Dori shrugged. "Whatever you want to do."

Chase plucked JT out of his playpen and went up to Tyler's den. In so many ways, this was still Tyler's house. Chase wanted more than ever to share it with Dori and make it theirs. But what was God's will in all this? As he climbed the stairs to the den, Chase realized he had forgotten to pray. *Lord, I don't know what You want for Dori and me. Forgive me for leaving You out of the equation. I love Dori and JT. I want us to be a family. Please give me the courage to tell her. Help Dori to forgive me, too.*

Feeling a little better, he settled on the couch with JT and turned on the TV. He flipped through the stations. Then it hit him. Something seemed very odd. Dori hadn't told Natalia or his father about the annulment, but she had told her mother. Why? What was going through his wife's head? He continued to flip through the stations. Finally, he came to a college football game, but he couldn't concentrate on it. Instead, he wondered whether Dori would give him another chance. At least she was willing to talk.

With the football game serving as background noise, Chase bounced JT on his knee. JT laughed, and Chase's heart broke at the thought of being separated from this little boy.

After Chase left the room, Natalia laid the catalog on the couch, and gazed at Dori. "What's going on between you two?"

"What do you mean?" Dori asked, swallowing a lump in her throat as her heart pounded.

"Something's not right." Natalia wrinkled her brow. "You could cut the tension in this room with a knife."

"I didn't think you noticed."

"I noticed. I just didn't want to make a big deal out of it while he was here. I wanted to talk with you alone."

Dori closed her eyes and choked back a sob. Immediately, she felt Natalia's hand on her arm. Dori opened her eyes as the misery welled up inside her. "Last night I told him I wanted the annulment and asked him to move out."

"Why?" Natalia's frown deepened.

"Because I'm stupid."

"That's an understatement, but that doesn't explain anything." The twinkle in Natalia's eyes softened her words.

Dori released a harsh breath. "I found out he sold Tyler's company to Warren, and in a fit of anger, I told Chase to move out. I was so wrong. He took a few things when he left last night, and now he's here to get the rest of his stuff."

"It's not too late to tell him how you really feel."

"I wish I could believe that."

Shaking her head, Natalia put a hand on her hip. "Believe it. That man is waiting upstairs to talk to you. I'm outta here, and tomorrow I expect to hear that you've patched things up."

"I wish I had your confidence."

"Get going. I'll talk to you tomorrow." Natalia gave Dori a little shove toward the stairway.

"I'm going, I'm going." Dori grabbed Natalia's arm before she left. "Say a prayer."

"I will. Now quit stalling." Natalia motioned for her to move.

Waving to Natalia, Dori started up the back stairs. When she neared the top, sounds of a sporting event floated down the stairs. Then, above the noise coming from the TV, she heard Chase's voice. He seemed to be talking with someone. Thinking he might be on the phone, she stopped and waited.

"I wish you could talk so you could tell your mom not to kick me out. Tell her I was only trying to help. She should understand that. Don't you think, JT?"

Dori leaned back against the wall. He wanted to stay, but she wanted him to stay because he loved her, not just for JT. She took the last two stairs in one step. As she entered the room, Chase stood holding JT. The sight of them together tore at her heart. She had to let Chase stay no matter how he felt about her because he loved that little boy. *Lord, give me the courage to face Chase. Help me say the right thing to him.*

She fought the fear that gripped her. This was her opening. Warren's words echoed in her brain. "When you love someone, you have to tell them." Telling Chase was the right thing to do, but what would he think when only yesterday she had asked him to leave? He would surely think she didn't know how she felt. "Chase, Natalia and I are done. Let me put JT to bed, then we can talk."

"Can't we talk now?" His gaze narrowed as he spoke.

Dori shook her head. She was putting off the inevitable, but she didn't want any distractions when she bared her soul to Chase. She wanted a little more time to formulate what she planned to say. "No, I need to put JT to bed so he doesn't start crying in the middle of our conversation because he wants his nighttime bottle. I don't want any interruptions."

"Okay, I see your point," Chase said, surrendering JT to Dori's open arms.

* * *

Chase shut off the TV. He couldn't concentrate on the game, not when his whole future depended on what transpired in the next few minutes. Making his way down the front staircase, he surveyed the living room and dining room and remembered the first time he came to visit Dori here. He never dreamed he'd fall in love with the little spitfire who had despised the sight of him. She didn't feel that way anymore, but had her opinion changed enough to accept his love? Gazing out the large window above the front door, he stopped for a moment and gripped the wrought-iron railing and prayed again. *God, please give me the right words to say to Dori. And if it's Your will, let us be a family.*

Chase reached the bottom step and glanced in the direction of the nursery. Dori appeared in the doorway. She stopped when she saw him. Their gazes held. She tucked her hair behind her ear as she closed the door behind her.

The gesture made Chase's heart sink. She wasn't looking forward to this conversation. He steeled himself for rejection, but he wasn't going to chicken out this time. He was finished running away from his feelings.

"Are you ready to talk?" he asked as they met in the walkway alongside the sunken living room.

"Yes, we might as well sit in the living room since we're here." She went to the couch without waiting for his response.

Chase followed and stood in the center of the room. "I have some things to say—"

"Chase, I was wrong. I don't want the annulment," Dori interrupted. "You don't have to leave."

Relief washed over him, and for a moment he was tempted to not tell her how he felt. He could stay without ever revealing his love for her, but he couldn't live that way any longer. She had to know and accept or reject him on that knowledge. "If I stay, there's something you should know. After I tell you, then make your decision."

"There's nothing you can say that will make me change my mind because—"

"Just hear me out," Chase interrupted as he shifted his weight from foot to foot. He weighed his words carefully. "I should've said this in the beginning instead of using JT as an excuse." Chase glanced toward the nursery, then back at Dori. "If I stay, you've got to know I want this to be a real marriage because I love you. I realized that I loved you when we were going over those wedding vows. I should've told you then. If you can't live with that, Dori, I'll pack my things tonight and go."

Covering her mouth with one hand, she lowered her head. He wanted to slink away somewhere. He should have expected his pronouncement to garner that kind of reaction. Oh well, now it was out in the open. He didn't have anything to hide any longer. He waited for her to lift her head and meet his gaze. When she did, tears trickled down her cheeks.

"Do those tears mean I should go?"

"No, no, don't leave." She jumped up from the couch and threw her arms around his neck. "I want to be married for real. I love you, too."

Chase took her arms from around his neck and held her at arms' length. "You do?"

Nodding, she put her arms around his waist and hugged

him again. "That's why I cried. I thought of all the time we've wasted not telling each other how we feel." She gazed up at him. "Let's promise each other we won't ever do that again."

"Promise." He felt a silly grin cover his face.

"The only problem I can see is when my mother finds out she'll expect us to have that church wedding."

"I'm ready. I don't mind marrying you twice." Chase pulled her close, bringing her feet off the floor. He captured her mouth in a kiss. He had dreamed of this for months. Dori kissing him for real. Three little words had made all the difference. They were worth repeating every day for the rest of his life. Setting her back on the floor, he gazed into her eyes. "I love you more than you'll ever know."

"Why don't you show me how much?" Dori rubbed her index finger across her thoroughly kissed lips.

"Right now?"

"Right now." Dori placed her hand in his.

Chase led Dori back to the master bedroom. "I think Tyler and Marisa would approve."

"And JT."

"Yeah, JT," Chase replied as he stopped at the bedroom door. "'Our special baby,' as your mom calls him. Without him we'd never have met and fallen in love."

"Yes, a truly special gift from God. He used JT to mend a lot of lives."

"Mine most of all," Chase said, pulling Dori into his arms. "Having your love and JT in my life is more happiness than I could ever have imagined."

"I love you, Chase. I wish I'd told you before." She leaned back and gazed into his eyes.

"Me, too. And I should've done the same." He picked her up and carried her over the threshold. "It's time we made this room—this house—our own. We can't change the past, but we can do better in the future."

"Our future together."

* * * * *

Dear Reader,

Thank you for choosing to read *An Unexpected Blessing*. I hope you enjoyed this story and found a blessing through reading it. As in Dori and Chase's lives, God can take even the bad things and give us an unexpected blessing. Chase and Dori discover how God works in their lives as they learn how to forgive and find the blessing of love.

Sometimes, even Christians find it difficult to forgive someone who has hurt them deeply. But God knows how healing comes through forgiveness. That's why His forgiveness reaches us only as we forgive others. This story, involving family relationships and how they shape us, shows how God's forgiveness and our forgiveness can repair even the most broken relationships and lives.

I enjoy hearing from readers. You can write to me at mwhren@bellsouth.net or P.O. Box 16461, Fernandina Beach, Florida 32035. Please visit my Web site at www.merrilleewhren.com.

May God bless you,

Merrillee Whren

QUESTIONS FOR DISCUSSION

1. When Dori first meets Chase, she makes assumptions about him based on the actions of Chase's father and the estrangement Chase had with his half brother. Why is she so quick to judge? Why does it take her so long to realize that she was wrong? Have you ever misjudged someone? How did you deal with the situation?

2. Chase doesn't like to talk about his past because it opens up old wounds. Do you have things in your past that are hurtful to think about? Have you learned to deal with them? If so, how?

3. Dori questions why God allows bad people to prosper while good people may suffer. In light of Matthew 5:45, how could you answer Dori's question?

4. When questioned about his faith, Chase says his brother's death has caused him to examine his relationship with God. Has there ever been a time in your life when something happened to make you look at your relationship with God? Has this helped you have a closer walk with Him?

5. Chase regrets being estranged from his half brother for many years. How does Chase plan to make up for this? Have you ever had regrets about a decision you have made? How did you deal with the regrets? Do you think you can make up for wrong choices? How can God help you deal with wrong choices?

6. Dori has a problem with trust because people she loved betrayed her. Have you ever had to deal with betrayal? How did you deal with it? What does Matthew 5:38–44 say about the way you should treat those who may hurt you?

7. Chase and Dori decide to get married to protect their nephew. In doing so, they believe they are sacrificing the opportunity to find real love for themselves. In the end, their sacrifice brings them love. Can you name examples of people who have made sacrifices that have brought them an unexpected blessing? Has this happened in your own life?

8. Dori has a large, loving family. Chase has never known that kind of family life. He longs to be a part of her family. How can families help each other? Why is that important? How does your family help you?

9. Dori and Chase want to adopt their nephew. How does the adoption show their love for this child? How is having a relationship with God like being part of a family? What do Galatians 3:26, Galatians 4:6 and Ephesians 1:4–5 say about being in the family of God?

10. Dori has difficulty forgiving Chase's father for the way he treated her sister. What prompts Dori to finally find it in her heart to forgive him? What can you learn from Dori's struggle with forgiveness? Why does God expect us to forgive others? How does Matthew 18:21–22 help you understand what it means to forgive?

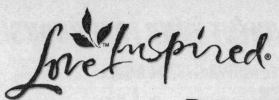

BUTTERFLY SUMMER

BY
ARLENE
JAMES

Introducing a brand-new 6-book
saga from Love Inspired...

Davis Landing

**Nothing is stronger than
a family's love**

Becoming the makeover
candidate in her family's
magazine wasn't something
Heather Hamilton had
planned to do, but she
refused to miss a deadline.
So the shy auburn editor
found herself transformed
into a beauty that no one,
especially photographer
Ethan Danes, could keep
their eyes off of....

Steeple
Hill®

www.SteepleHill.com

Available July 2006

wherever you buy books.

LIBS

REQUEST YOUR FREE BOOKS!

2 FREE INSPIRATIONAL NOVELS
PLUS A
FREE
MYSTERY GIFT

Love Inspired

YES! Please send me 2 FREE Love Inspired® novels and my FREE mystery gift. After receiving them, if I don't wish to receive any more books, I can return the shipping statement marked "cancel." If I don't cancel, I will receive 4 brand-new novels every month and be billed just $3.99 per book in the U.S., or $4.74 per book in Canada, plus 25¢ shipping and handling per book and applicable taxes, if any*. That's a savings of over 20% off the cover price! I understand that accepting the 2 free books and gift places me under no obligation to buy anything. I can always return a shipment and cancel at any time. Even if I never buy another book from Steeple Hill, the two free books and gift are mine to keep forever.

113 IDN D74R   313 IDN D743

Name	(PLEASE PRINT)
Address	Apt.
City	State/Prov.	Zip/Postal Code

Signature (if under 18, a parent or guardian must sign)

Order online at www.LoveInspiredBooks.com

Or mail to Steeple Hill Reader Service™:

IN U.S.A.	IN CANADA
3010 Walden Ave.	P.O. Box 609
P.O. Box 1867	Fort Erie, Ontario
Buffalo, NY 14240-1867	L2A 5X3

Not valid to current Love Inspired subscribers.

Want to try two free books from another series?
Call 1-800-873-8635 or visit www.morefreebooks.com

* Terms and prices subject to change without notice. NY residents add applicable sales tax. Canadian residents will be charged applicable provincial taxes and GST. This offer is limited to one order per household. All orders subject to approval. Credit or debit balances in a customer's account(s) may be offset by any other outstanding balance owed by or to the customer.

LIREG05

ALL OUR TOMORROWS

BY

IRENE HANNON

Hoping to heal her shattered life, Caroline James threw herself into work at the local newspaper in her hometown. But then David Sloan walked back into her life. Had the Lord reunited David and Caroline so they could help each other learn to live and love again?

Available July 2006
wherever you buy books

Steeple Hill®

www.SteepleHill.com

LIAOT

Love Inspired®

TITLES AVAILABLE NEXT MONTH

Don't miss these four stories in July

ANY MAN OF MINE by Carolyne Aarsen
A special Steeple Hill Café novel in Love Inspired

Sick and tired of her small town—and the rough-and-tumble guys who inhabited it—Danielle Hemstead had big plans to move to the city and find true love. But when a new man came to town, she questioned her agenda. Had love found her or were looks deceiving?

BUTTERFLY SUMMER by Arlene James
Davis Landing

When magazine editor Heather Hamilton underwent an outer transformation, photographer Ethan Danes took notice. Could her new look bring this shy woman out of her self-imposed cocoon and into Ethan's waiting arms?

ALL OUR TOMORROWS by Irene Hannon
After losing her fiancé in an act of violence overseas, reporter Caroline James threw herself into work at a local newspaper. David Sloan was her fiancé's brother, though he had secretly cared for Caroline for years. Perhaps the Lord brought them together for a reason—to learn to live, laugh…and love again.

THE HEART OF A MAN by Deb Kastner
Dustin Fairfax's inheritance was on the line, and to get it he had to…*get a makeover*. He dreaded going through with it—that is until he saw his personal image consultant, Isobel Buckley. Maybe a little wardrobe change would be just what he needed to win the fetching stylist's heart.